A Day In The Life

A Novel

Tom Walker

Fomite
Burlington, VT

ISBN-13: 978-1-942515-47-0
Library of Congress Control Number: 2016933656

Fomite
58 Peru Street
Burlington, VT 05401
www.fomitepress.com

IN MEMORIAM

GARY MICHAEL HOLLIS

(1940 − 2014)

Tom Walker

They tell us that suicide is the greatest piece of cowardice...
that suicide is wrong; when it is quite obvious that there is
nothing in the world to which every man has a more unas-
sailable title than to his own life and person.

> — Arthur Schopenhauer

He blew his mind out in a car
He didn't notice that the lights had changed...

> — John Lennon and Paul McCartney, "A Day in the Life"

Chapter One: 10:01 p. m.

DEAD MAN DRIVING

It had been dark for three hours. Time to leave the house. Time to die.

George Noel Gordon Bombazine, professor emeritus of English at Mount Olympus College in the Sonoran desert of southwest Arizona, hated driving after dark. His night vision was poor. But by now traffic would have thinned, almost disappeared. He felt braver and calmer than he had all day, fully up to the task ahead. Bring 'em on, he thought. Now he was quoting George W. Bush? Laughter bubbled in his throat and he tried to smile. *It is a far, far better thing that I do, than I have ever done.* Dickens, right? Sidney Carton. *Death be not proud though some have called thee mighty and dreadful.* John Donne. But where? One of his Holy Sonnets, circa 1618...

Before locking up to leave, he'd checked on Argos's dog bowl in the kitchen. Argos was his Alaskan malamute rescue who looked like a wolf or a Siberian husky — grey and white, with oversize paws, a bushy white tail that curved like a showgirl's plume, and cerulean marbles for eyes. The historical Argos had been the first to recognize Odysseus on his return from Troy; exiled from Odysseus's house, the dog had refused to die until his master returned. He'd waited twenty years. When Odysseus reappeared, Argos had just enough strength left to drop his ears and wag his tail. "Dogs are true friends, often better than other men," Nicolai Berdyaev (a Russian ethicist Bombazine admired) had written, and gone on to call the man-dog relationship "metaphysical." Dogs were psychic and clairvoyant, Bombazine believed, and he wondered if Argos smelled death on him already. He shivered at the thought as if he'd swallowed an ice cube. Dogs smelled everything. Even cancer, if a Science Channel special Bombazine had watched could be believed.

A hunk of English Stilton—Argos's favorite—had remained untouched in the bowl. Argos had fasted all day. A hunger strike? The dog had rejected half a T-bone steak, some dry Alpo, and now two dollars worth of expensive cheese. Exasperated, Bombazine had spent ten more minutes, which threw him off schedule, composing a last-minute e-mail asking his ex-wife Pru to come by tomorrow morning and feed Argos. When she came, she would find his suicide note on the kitchen island. He hoped she would feed Argos before she found the note and then take him home with her.

Eventually Pru would recover from her shock and grief, but he feared that Argos was grieving already. Dogs were known to starve themselves when their masters died, or were about to die. Having finished his e-mail to Pru, Bombazine had whistled for Argos and hunted him down. He'd found him sitting on his haunches, sulking and listless, in the studio wing of the house where Pru used to compose and play her cello. Maybe Argos was missing her and that's why he was depressed. But Pru had come by earlier today. So that wasn't it.

Bombazine had squatted for a man-to-man talk in a tone gentle but firm: "Argos, I know you understand what I'm saying. You should eat. Don't look at me like that. Didn't I let you watch me make love to that blonde? Okay, try to. I didn't do so well. But you did get to watch, so the least you could do is eat something. It's not often I ask anything of you, and normally you eat like a fucking horse. What's wrong, guy?"

Argos's marble-blue eyes widened with puzzlement. Guy! Why had he called Argos that? He never called Argos guy. It was what his father had called him instead of using his name, which he hated. Bombazine wondered if men ultimately turned into their fathers the way women ultimately turned into their mothers. The thought was alarming. But no one could say he'd turned out like his father. He had turned out even worse. A complete failure. A suicide.

"Later, dude," he said. "Old Odysseus is splitting. I love you, you fucking wolf." He held the dog's head in both his hands and kissed the top of his head and tried, without success, not to cry as his eyes commenced to water.

Nonplussed, Argos had stared at him, and then his eyes widened with alarm, as if he'd had a sudden realization. He began to pant and his breath was an ill wind. Bombazine had risen to head out. Argos trailed close behind. The dog whined as the front door closed in his face. He wanted to come along—he didn't know about the cold, deep lake water in which his master meant to drown himself. Could Argos swim? And how would he get home? He had to stay.

As Bombazine started up the Mercedes E-Class hybrid his ex-wife had given him, Bombazine could hear Argos clawing at the inside of the front door, barking in vociferous protest. Argos knew. He didn't know the details, but somehow knew his master did not intend to return. Through eyes blurred with tears, Bombazine took a last look at the split-level ranch-style eyesore in which he had lived for years; it resembled something Salvador Dali might have designed—a flawed, lopsided house that appeared to be melting but which, for all its creepiness and spooky emptiness, Bombazine had grown to love, or at least like, because it was home. Before he and Pru moved in, locals had warned them that the house was haunted. After tonight there would be no doubt.

With a screaming squeal of tires, spraying pebbles, he sped away from it for the last time.

—⁓⁓— —⁓⁓—

His Mercedes—quiet, stealthy, powerful—seemed to glide through the cool September night. The air was sweetly redolent of honeysuckle and wisteria, and that was strange, since neither was indigenous to this area. He'd brought along a CD of the Mahler 2nd Symphony, the "Resurrection," which he planned to blast out sforzando on his state-of-the-art stereo system with its throbbing bass subwoofer as he gunned the Mercedes up the steep cliff at Mount

Makeout that led to a breach in a dark stone wall through which he would fly the car, like a Kamikazi pilot, into the deep, black water below. No music, not even Mozart's Requiem, could be more fitting than the Mahler as he zoomed through the air and nosedived to his death below. "Death by Water" T. S. Eliot had named a section of his poem "The Waste Land." Bombazine loved Eliot's poetry even though the dour pedant was a bank clerk from St. Louis, an expatriate who'd become more British than the Brits. Bombazine admired "The Waste Land" more than Eliot's "The Love Song of J. Alfred Prufrock," a poem with which he too painfully identified.

He had to drive past the campus and through The Village to get onto the interregional highway that led to Mount Makeout. That short drive would call not for a symphony but a prelude, perhaps an overture. Or some Country Western. Yes, a little Country in the plaintive mode. A "somebody done somebody wrong" song. He switched on the radio and touched the screen icon for the all-night Country classic station.

Absently (he'd never cared much for either classic) he listened to Jim Reeves' "He'll Have to Go" and Faron Young's "Hello Walls," but the next classic fit so well that he sang along in a voice choked with tears. "Yesterday, When I Was Young," a late sixties hit by "Hee-Haw's" Roy Clark, was the confession of an aging, perhaps dying man defeated by life and humbled by regret. "Yesterday, when I was young, so many happy songs were waiting to be sung..." But he "played the game of love with arrogance and pride" and "ran so fast that time and youth ran out." He'd "never stopped to ask what life was all about," and only now, too late, does he see the error of his ways.

It was a tearjerker and Bombazine began to sob; he couldn't stop himself; this was an appropriate night for tears and he was a crybaby anyway. How was it, he wondered, that a "Hee-Haw" TV singer told us more about living, and perhaps dying, than Plato and Kant and Hegel could? More than Irving Berlin and Cole Porter had, too. And certainly more than the writers and singers of today's pop and rock and rap and grunge and hip-hop. But why was he asking such questions now, with minutes to live? He had to wonder. Why wasn't he asking about the final things, eschatological matters like heaven, hell, purgatory, judgment, reward, punishment, oblivion, reincarnation? And what about suicides? What happened to their souls in the hereafter? Or was there a hereafter? He hoped not.

Was he really going to suicide? He fucking was! The fact that he was so calm assured him that he could. For weeks he had wondered what this moment would feel like, and now he knew. With his life expectancy down to a few minutes, he felt celestially calm, as if he'd just popped a Thorazine or a Valium. In death he would find peace, Poe's surcease of sorrow, the relief from pain so many television commercials promised.

He cruised past the campus, where lights continued to burn in the ersatz cathedral-like edifices and along the boulevard that connected them. What infinite wisdom had been imparted in those buildings today? What lessons learned, eternal truths revealed, what Keatsian odes scanned for meter? Those buildings had been his workplace and he would never see them again. That wrenched his heart and he cried even more. It wasn't much of a campus, really — it looked like a studio set for some black-and-white thirties movie — and he no longer worked there. Yet he'd loved it. And still did.

When he reached the Village and eased up Main Street, he hoped for activity, a little night music, sounds of youthful mirth. But the street had rolled up its carpets and locked its doors. The Village was like a ghost town. He had never seen it so dead. Or was he dead? Not yet. He'd just never been here this late on a Wednesday night. The party animals were partying in private. Main Street wasn't Bourbon Street. Main Street in the Village was Primrose Lane, where life was a holiday; its merchants and residents turned in at a reasonable hour.

He would never see the Village again, never see its pastel hues melt together in the rosy morning light the way he had this morning, driving in for breakfast. With a sigh of regret he cruised on, pressing north, passing the dark closed-up shack of the restaurant Caramba! where he had breakfasted. Like Jesus's last supper, his last meal had been marred by dread, frissons of doom, a lack of appetite. He wished the radio station would play that Roy Clark song again. Another line went "The taste of life was sweet as rain upon my tongue." Nice. That might be a better epitaph for his tombstone than I TOLD YOU I WAS SICK, which he'd requested. Edgar Lee Masters, a humorless man, would have preferred the poetic Roy Clark epitaph.

7

Main Street receded until it vanished in his rearview mirror, and then he was on the highway to Big Town. There was no traffic. Good. He didn't want anything to slow him down. He had planned his suicide with the precision and exactitude with which nocturnal executions were planned in state prisons. Everything had to be done a certain way. He drove faster, exceeding the speed limit of sixty on this stretch at night, and soon he was doing seventy. In the glare of his brights, the highway took on a strange color, a shiny brown sepia tinged with red, as if the pavement had been washed with blood.

The landscape, what little of it he could make out in the dark, was a parched sandy flatland of mesquite and juniper and strange-looking gnarled trees festooned with Spanish moss, like trees in the Gulf states of the Deep South. Further on, the country, with its fields of bluebonnets, was beautiful by day but weird at night. Now he tasted fear, a metallic taste, as if a coin were in his mouth. But fear was called for. He should be afraid. Fear and trembling were in order. His fear contended with desire. Who wrote that? A. E. Houseman? How often in his own life had fear contended with desire and won?

It would not win tonight.

What a day this had been. A day of realizations, admissions of guilt, painful revelations. New mirror images appearing too late to make a difference. Abruptly he found himself in the mountainous area; its rushing river, the Xanthus, or "River X," had been dammed into lakes to prevent flooding while it provided the area with hydroelectric power. In minutes he and the Mercedes would be sinking to the bottom of the deepest lake.

It was Mahler time.

—⁓— —⁓—

He still had two or three miles to drive and needed the inspirational music to keep him from turning back like the coward he'd always been. His empty stomach churned and rumbled in protest. Something craven in him wanted to live. But there was no turning back. Fumbling with his right hand, he slipped the compact disc into the player, found the last movement of the symphony, and maxed the volume, all without reducing speed. He was going close to eighty.

The Finale was long and he'd have to skip around to hear the part he wanted. He lowered the windows for the world to hear Gustav Mahler's majestic music. Soon it filled the surrounding countryside. In the "March of the Dead" section he recognized the Dies Irae motif from the Catholic Mass. He heard drum rolls, ringing gongs, the clarion calls of hunter's horns played offstage. The trumpets of the Apocalypse rang out. A mezzo-soprano was intoning a sorrowful solo (about death) in German. The Last Judgment was at hand, the demons of the Day of Wrath unleashed. Graves were splitting open and rotted corpses, moaning and trembling, were rising from their coffins to march in procession.

Abruptly he found himself behind two cars maddeningly creeping along, and two others, one a jeep, were cruising alongside him in the right lane. Horns honking. He swore to himself. What was going on? There was also a vehicle, a pickup truck, right behind him, tailgating. For a moment, he came to a full stop, turned his head, and looked around.

He could not believe what he saw. Traffic everywhere. He was caught in a traffic jam.

Traffic? At this hour? Where had it come from? What shit luck! God DAMN it! He pounded the steering wheel with the palms of his hands as hard as he could. From the opposite direction, heading back toward the Village and campus, came a string of SUVs. It was worse than the five o'clock rush hour. There was a farm community nearby named Welfare, and apparently Welfare's hayseeds were either on their way home from Big Town or on their way there, the late hour notwithstanding. Coming and going, the vehicles crept along single-file, like hearses in a funeral procession. His funeral? Was this a time warp? A flash forward? Had he died already?

He cursed again, louder. He couldn't wait any longer. Ignoring a sign that prohibited passing, he veered between two pickups and passed a jeep and an SUV. The SUV gave a long angry honk. He honked back. Like the World War I poet Alan Seeger, he had a rendezvous with death. He'd published a monograph on Seeger in *Partisan Review* and won an award for it.

In the Mahler Finale the whole chorus was singing now, its male half reaching the lowest vocal note in the classical repertoire, then rejoicing rapturously, joyously, victoriously with tolling church bells. *"Triumphieren! Wem in Leidenstagen! Herr ich habe miBehandelt"*! In the throes of musical ecstasy, Bombazine almost lost control of the wheel. He swerved in front of another pickup. Where were these stupid farmers going? Where had they been? Couldn't they hear the transfigurative music? Fifty meters ahead, the badly engineered multi-pronged fork in the highway, with it traffic lights dangling from overhead wires, was visible at last.

His turnoff point was just past it. He'd been here often enough to find it blindfolded. His heart was in his mouth, yet he was singing in fluent German along with Mahler's chorus, never missing a note, remembering every syllable from having heard the Finale so often. "*Hor auf zu beben!*" he sang at the top of his voice. "*Bereite dich zu leben!*" [Cease trembling! Prepare yourself to live!]

The light, his light, was red. He braked to a jarring halt and waited for it to change. Seconds dawdled and dragged by like hours. What the hell was taking so long? Was the mechanism faulty? If the light was stuck you could proceed with caution and go. You didn't have to wait all night. Didn't these stupid farmers know that?

There was more honking. And male shouting, a palpable fury in the air. He had to go right now. Heedlessly, recklessly, he ran the light and almost hit a black-leather-clad motorcyclist who'd come roaring through the intersection from the blind side. It was the first red light he'd ever run in his whole life. There was a cacophany of honking. A man behind him was yelling, cursing at him. Fearlessly he honked back, uncaring. Fuck you, he thought, I am seconds from eternity.

Mahler's celestial trumpets and moose hunter's French horns blared. Tympani boomed like thunder. The symphony was cracking the speakers. The resurrection was at hand, his timing perfect. Crying out joyously, he steered the Mercedes off the highway, onto the road that led to the crest of Mount Makeout. He sighted the breach in the dark-red granite wall on the left. Galvanized with adrenaline, laughing like a loon, he had never felt so brave. Or so free. Now everything was happening the way he'd planned and hoped and dreamed it would. Ahead in his bright lights the road had a blood-red sheen.

Chapter Two: 5:48 a. m. (earlier the same day)

Daybreak

He would either do it today — his seventieth birthday — or on the night before Thanksgiving. Two months hence.

Today could be the most important day of his life — the day he ended it — and what he should be feeling was fear. And he was afraid. But more than afraid, angry. And more than angry, furious. Just before dawn, George Noel Gordon Bombazine, a huge hairy hulk of a man big of belly, woke up and kicked the covers off the king-sized bed in which he now slept naked and alone. He was angry because he'd been dreaming that he wouldn't kill himself until Thanksgiving.

And why had he postponed it? Because of a movie in the works.

A movie!

There really was a movie in the works: it wasn't just a dream. The plot was cobbled from a book of poems, written as monologue epitaphs, on which he was the nation's foremost expert. That book was Edgar Lee Masters' *Spoon River Anthology*. Set for pre-production work, the filmmakers were said to need his input for their screenplay. How much input was uncertain. Reportedly the screenwriters and the director were fighting with the producers and the studio head. He might be asked to rewrite the script; more probably, though, if the film got made, a small option or consulting fee would be his compensation.

But that was fine. Seeing his name in the credits was enticement enough: privately, though he would not admit it, since Tinseltown deserved its sobriquet, Bombazine had dreamed of seeing his name writ large, or even small, as the credits rolled on the wide screen at the end of an Oscar-winning film. Yesterday he'd heard about all this from his publicist, Meridel Baxter, who'd heard it from his New York agent Barbara ("Babs") Katz, who'd heard it from Bombazine's longtime editor at Grove/Atlantic Lionel Motherwell, a close friend of Lionsgate Films studio head Israel Tannenbaum. Lionsgate wasn't Hollywood in the manner of, say MGM, but with offices in Santa Monica it would do. And another studio, as yet unidentified, was said to be interested as well.

The question was, how much of this was hearsay and rumor? Bombazine was skeptical. The film was budgeted at $80 million and its investors were anxious enough to make coffee nervous. Five co-producers had opened the studio's wallets to six bankable stars (George Clooney, Brad Pitt, Naomi Watts, Julianne Moore, Keira Knightley, Matt Damon) cast as Spoon River Cemetery corpses, resurrected in flashback to their youths and interacting with each other in a turbid small-town drama. Ang Lee, winner of two Academy Awards, would direct. Those seven big names had already prompted talk of Golden Globes and Oscars.

The studios knew about Bombazine's additions to the anthology he'd compiled, ten years earlier, of Masters' free verse epitaphs on gravestones in the cemetery of a fictional Midwestern dogpatch called Spoon River. Bombazine's forthcoming edition, *Return to Spoon River*, premiered a dozen poems heretofore suppressed and unpublished; they were signed "Dexter Wallace," the pseudonym Masters used when hiding out from enemies real or imagined, and Bombazine had discovered them in the basement of an abandoned farmhouse in Petersburg, Illinois, where Masters spent his youth. Some of the new interrelated poems were racy enough to have been shocking and scandalous for their time, and the screenwriters could not wait to use them in their script.

Enter George Noel Gordon Bombazine? Maybe. Bankable stars didn't come cheap — they could break a studio's bank — and neither did Oscar-winning directors. The project needed all the help it could get. Bombazine's new edition would hit the bookstores and be available on Kindle and Nook and Amazon and iTunes in November. But the studio had gotten a peek at Grove/Atlantic's galley proofs of *Return to Spoon River* and contacted Bombazine's editor, who had e-mailed them.

Why was Bombazine skeptical? The coincidence of his book's coming out as the film went into preproduction could be no more than coincidence. Chance, not fate. And if he shone a searchlight on his subconscious, he might see the project as an excuse to put off until Thanksgiving what he'd planned to do tonight. Kill himself.

Too many ifs were involved. Movies based on literary classics often bombed if not produced by Ismail Merchant and directed by James Ivory, and Merchant and Ivory hadn't made too many movies since Merchant died in 2005. Trashy plots based on graphic novels or Young Adult bestsellers were safer bets. Sure things. They rang the cash registers. Who needed literature?

Yet some courageous studio (Lionsgate?) was willing to open its pockets to gain prestige—and hope for reviews from the *New York Times* and *The New Yorker* and *Rolling Stone* and TV critics that would guarantee a return on investment. *Spoon River*, Bombazine fantasized, could be a classic art film, a cinematic masterpiece worthy of his collaboration. Much of his career had been spent analyzing the characters in the poems on which the film was based, and now he had new characters to introduce. Hadn't he an obligation to help the movie succeed? Might it not create a fresh readership for Masters' poetry and his own oeuvre as well? Was there cause here to live just a little longer?

What do do?

The day before Thanksgiving was his backup date, his Plan B, if he didn't suicide tonight. He dreaded Thanksgiving more than he did killing himself. He could not endure another Thanksgiving—he hated the holiday. He knew it was a phobia, a compulsion, but he wanted to ruin this Thanksgiving—or at least disrupt it—for as many people as he could.

So he might wait until Thanksgiving Eve to kill himself. But he hated postponements; they bespoke wishy-washiness, infirmity of purpose, and senior-citizen memory lapses. For a perfectionist born under the sun sign Virgo, though he pooh-poohed astrology, such human frailty was inexcusable. As a compulsive spoiled brat growing up in an affluent Houston enclave (River Oaks), he'd thrown tantrums when something he'd been promised and looked forward to was canceled or postponed. As a compulsive adult, he had to do things a certain way, his way, according to schedule. And today, not Thanksgiving Eve, would be when he'd kill himself unless something unforeseen happened.

But something unforeseen had happened, damn it, and that's why he was angry. His publicist had called last night from the East Coast, giddy about the movie and screenplay.

"Aren't you excited, Georgie?" Meridel Baxter asked.

"Confused," he told her. "Tell me again where I come in."

She sighed. "Jeez, babe. You're the world's foremost expert on *Spoon River Anthology*. It's, like, the most anthologized poetry high schoolers get crammed down their throats, except maybe Poe and Frost and that fucking Ancient Mariner."

"Meridel, I know what *Spoon River Anthology* is."

"You said you were confused, so let's take it slow. One: they're constructing a story from the poems and making a big-budget period film and calling it *Spoon River*. Two: they want everything to be authentic and may ask you to rewrite the script and hire you as a consultant. Three: they'd like to meet with you. I'm your publicist, not your agent, which I should be, so there's no moolah in it for me. And maybe not

17

much for you. But think what it might do for the sales of *Return to Spoon River*."

"I should tell readers to buy my book because some movie's getting made? That's whoring for Hollywood."

"So what? Didn't Faulkner whore for Hollywood and write *noir* screenplays? Or was that Hemingway?"

"Faulkner. *The Big Sleep*. He was broke."

"Besides, it may not be Hollywood. Think Lionsgate."

"I don't want to whore for Lionsgate, either."

"Criminy, babe! What's wrong with you today?"

"It seems disingenuous. I don't want people buying my book thinking they're buying a novelization of the movie."

"They won't be. Here's how it will work. The rough cuts and test screenings knock 'em dead and get the ball rolling. Readers gobble up everything they can about *Spoon River Anthology*. They'll either buy *Return to Spoon River* or some anthology that doesn't have the sexy new poems. But your new book has them. You'll be pitching the movie and your book at the same time."

"I don't know," Bombazine said. "It sounds too good to be true."

"Babs think you should do this. Have you talked to her? That fat sow is your agent, remember? It'll need marketing. I'll get you media—you're a sexy distinguished-looking old guy. Mature. Telegenic. I'll get you on Oprah, Charlie Rose, the Book Channel, PBS, NPR, and maybe an interview in *People*."

"Great," Bombazine grumbled. "*People* magazine. My ultimate fantasy."

"Don't be a snob. People who read *People* are the happiest people in the world. Do this for me if not yourself. I've never had a movie gig. Babs has but I haven't."

"Vicarious thrills for you and a trip to movieland. That's why I should do it?"

"Yes. Be generous for once."

That hurt. He did not think of himself as ungenerous. He pressed it: "I'm usually selfish?"

"Do you want the truth?

"I guess not."

"You're a pretty selfish old dude. But I can live with that. I haven't known a man who wasn't in love with himself. It's the testosterone. Just don't be a killjoy. This could be fun for all three of us. By the way, I've booked a signing and reading for *Return to Spoon River* in November at Barnes and Noble Fifth Avenue."

Meridel waited, but Bombazine gave no response. He was thinking: Will I still be alive in November?

"Tell you what," she said. "I'll fly out and see you tomorrow. I have to be in L. A. day after tomorrow. I'll pay you a visit and crash with my old friend Karla. You need me to hold your hand while we get this party started. We'll conference call Babs and your editor at Grove/Atlantic. What's his name? I always forget. Linus Motherfuck?"

"Lionel Motherwell. He edited my novel back in 'sixty-eight.'"

"Nineteen-sixty-eight? Jesus, I wasn't even born yet. Don't worry, I'll run the video call. We'll Skype Manhattan together. We're going to the show, baby. The big screen in THX."

"Meridel, don't come out here."

"I worry about you. You're a hermit, a recluse. You need some company."

"I don't," he said. Actually, he could use a little company in his final hours. Did suicides merit hospice care? But he couldn't let her distract him from his suicide mission.

Meridel was pushy. "We'll celebrate your birthday together."

"I don't want to celebrate my birthday."

"Look for me mid-afternoonish. Don't collect me at the airport. I'll cab it. Or rent a Prius or Aston Martin."

"I may not be around tomorrow."

"Why not? Where are you going?"

"I don't know."

"Don't you dare go anywhere. I'm heading west tomorrow and stopping off to see you." She hung up.

Bombazine shook his head and wondered why his publicist took such a personal interest in him. She was more of an agent than his agent was. And why did she call him "babe" and "baby" so much? Did she really find him sexy and distinguished looking? Was she flirting? Cruel enough to prick-tease a septuagenarian whose rope might not rise without Viagra? It was probably how media Valkyrie at Madison Avenue or Thirty Rockefeller talked. Or she was talking down to him? Condescending, patronizing, the way young women talked to old men, as if to baby them.

He should not flatter himself. What would a foxy little blonde in her forties who looked thirty want with a senior citizen on Medicare with one foot in the grave? Could she, after years of working with him, have developed a crush the way secretaries did on their bosses? No, he thought. You're dreaming. She flirts with everyone.

Remembering that conversation now, he lay back with an exasperated sigh. This was to be his big day, a day of reckoning, his *dies irae*. A day crying out for Kierkegaardian fear and trembling. Or apocalyptic jubilation. A day for a hero's death by his own hand, like the heroes in Greco-Roman tragedy. He wanted to go out in a blaze of glory. Yet here he was, waffling and vacillating. Having second thoughts. Playing the wuss.

Bombazine cursed softly. Christ, he thought, I hate being old.

Chapter Three: 6:13 a. m.

BOMBAZINE DEFINED

George Noel Gordon Bombazine */n./ s./ middle French/*: 1. a suicidal overweight professor emeritus, retired critic, anthologist, novelist of small renown, and reclusive curmudgeon at loose ends with nowhere to go, nothing to do, no one to do it with. 2. A writer whom words fail now. 3. A vintage car without an engine. 4. A jockey without a horse. 5. A used to be. *Cf.* has been.

His best years were behind him and so were those that qualified as mediocre. Ahead were a few hideous years of loneliness, indignities, irascibility, arthritis, immobility, boredom, depression, dentures, canes, crutches, wheelchairs, diapers, catheters, nursing homes and uncontrollable bowel movements—years one could easily avoid, the actor Dennis Leary suggested, by smoking cigarettes and dying ten years earlier. But Bombazine hated cigarette smoke. He recalled a Colonel at the Officer's Club in the Pentagon confiding, "Lieutenant Bombo, when I get to the point where I can't wipe my ass, I'm going to blow my brains out." The Colonel never got to that point—a Viet Cong mortar shell blew his brains out three months later one rainy day in the lower Mekong Delta—but

Bombazine remembered the Colonel's vow.

Browning had called old age "the best of life for which the first was made," but he should've written "the worst of life" instead, rhyming first with worst and telling the truth. "Life is too strong for you. It takes life to love life." Who said that? Lucinda Matlock, Edgar Lee Masters' hardy frontierwoman in *Spoon River Anthology*. Aging Lucinda bragged about how strong she had been. But she also said "At ninety-six I had lived enough, that is all." Well, old girl, thought Bombazine, at seventy I have lived enough, that is all. Sorry I haven't enough life left to love life anymore. But I don't.

And how could he? Unhappiness had supped at his table far too long. Sure, he had toughed it out for seventy years, but to what end? This? An earthworm survived too. So did a cockroach. Middle age had been bad enough. Time had not been kind to him. Three decades ago, soon after he'd divorced her, his first wife "Tencha" (short for Hortensia) had been killed in a grisly auto wreck on a freeway over-pass just outside Mexico City. Had she cursed him with her final breath? Their little son blamed him for her death. His second marriage, though better than his first, would ulti-mately prove an exercise in stultifying boredom. His career had earned him acclaim, though not all he deserved. An ac-ademic journeyman, he had taught at five colleges, drifting from one to the next, never happy at any; at the fifth college (Mount Olympus), conspired against by a tenure committee hostile to liberals, he'd unwisely stopped publishing. The Mount Olympus mossbacks concluded that not having pub-lished, he should perish, and made him professor emeritus after bumping him into premature retirement. He'd felt like Julius Caesar on the Ides of March. Now he was divorced from his second wife (Pru had left him for another professor in the department) and estranged from his older sister Catherine and thirty-five-year-old son Miguel, and his best friend was his dog, Argos.

As for human friends, he had alienated or outlived or lost track of all but one. There had never been many. Owing to his intimidating size and gruff demeanor, people tended to be afraid of him, unaware that he was afraid of them. His students liked him anyway, his peers did not. His one remaining friend was his former campus colleague Professor John Jacob Auchincloss, "J. J." —a priss, a gossip, and a poseur, not to mention a windbag, a misogynist, an anti-Semite, a name dropper, and a Republican. J. J. was probably the best read person Bombazine knew: proof positive that books do not always dispense wisdom. Also the ugliest person Bombazine had known as a civilian, J. J. was repellant and buffoonish in so many ways that Bombazine found him lovable, like the fools in Shakespeare. J. J. was his drinking companion, baseball pal, Scrabble nemesis, political sparring partner, and confidante. In those alleys of campus politics dark with internecine treachery, J. J. had tried to protect him. Bombazine trusted the man.

They had met years earlier at a campus cocktail party for new professors. Both had built reputations in somewhat more attractive venues—J. J. in Boulder, Colorado and Chapel Hill, North Carolina and Whittier, California; Bombazine in Amherst, Massachusetts and Austin, Texas and Ann Arbor, Michigan. On their downhill slide, fate had thrown them together. Martini in hand, J. J. had swaggered up to him at that party and said, "So you're the George Gordon Bombazine. I hear you're a liberal. I won't hold it against you. I'm glad our institution of higher learning hires the neurologically challenged."

"And you are—? Dr. Alfred E. Neuman, I presume?"

"I'm *the* John Jacob Auchincloss. You've read my history books and biographies and columns and articles."

"I have? I thought you were George F. Will. You both wear a bow tie."

"George wears the kind you clip on, old sport. I know George. We talk baseball. And you're a George too. But what the deuce kind of name is Bombazine? I thought bombazine was a twilled fabric."

"It is. Few people know that. Few men, that is."

J. J. whinnied like a horse. "Old chap, I think I like you. Let's get another drink. I detest faculty parties, don't you?"

J. J. turned out to be his friend, but his best friend Argos was even more loyal. If you were a dog's master, the animal was loyal to you whatever your politics, and Bombazine feared that sooner or later political differences like J. J.'s racism and anti-Semitism would rend the fabric of their friendship like a strip of thin satin. But Argos was old and running out of time. That gave Bombazine another reason to commit suicide: When Argos died, J. J. would be his one and only friend.

"Why do I like you?" he'd once asked J. J. "You're a racist right-wing crypto-Nazi woman-hating war-mongering climate change-denying greedhead."

25

"So? You're a pinko faggot peacenik socialist towelhead-loving tree-hugging America hater. Nobody's perfect."

"I'll deny the faggot. Though it shouldn't matter. Some of my best friends are gay."

"Old chap, you have no friends, gay or otherwise. Just me. And that bloody dog."

"Yes. And that terrifies me."

"If I could find a real friend, I would. I just like you for your hot tub."

It was a ritual not unlike rowdy fraternity brothers punching each other on the shoulder. But Bombazine knew that J. J. knew how alone he was in the world; J. J. was that alone himself. That's why for Bombazine suicide had acquired the allure of a forbidden fruit. The trouble with suicide, Bombazine's late pen pal Gore Vidal had written him, is that there's no future in it. But apart from the screenplay — a tempting opportunity if genuine — and the publication of *Return to Spoon River*, Bombazine's future was worse than none. His present was nothing to brag about either:

He lived alone with an old dog in a spooky echoing ranch-style house containing seven bedrooms and four bathrooms: a prison from which he did not wish to escape. He had no place else to go and needed to be accessible to his ex-wife Pru, who owned the house, if she came back. He missed her. The six bedrooms that were sheeted up, one formerly Miguel's, had a spectral air, and at night strange noises could be heard from them.

His health was failing. His weight was a problem, his drinking another, but food and alcohol were his comforts and he was too old for miracle diets and too proud to join Alcoholics Anonymous. He was also too vain to use a walking stick even though he needed one. His high blood pressure and cholesterol levels were held in check by beta blockers that were surely destroying his liver. His short-term memory was so short that some days he couldn't remember what he'd had for breakfast. Words were failing him, so were names, and for an author and scholar the inability to come up with the mot juste was cause for alarm if not suicide.

He feared that he was impotent; having not been to bed with a woman in years, he wasn't sure of it, but he no longer woke up with erections, and even with his erotica library and girlie magazine collection, it took him forever to whack off. Had his balls dried up? He rejected boner pills: Viagra, Cialis, Levitra, Yohimbe. No man should have to pop a pill to make love. Not even to his wife. Not that he had a wife anymore.

He ached. No joint in his body was free from pain. His left knee ached from a high school football injury sustained fifty-five years ago, and he hadn't even liked football, having played it to please his father. His back and behind ached from sitting at his computer all day, and over a thirty-year span his chiropractor had failed to ease his pain for more than three days at a time

He had outlived his teeth, which now demanded crowns, bridges, root canals, and implants and could not handle corn on the cob, popcorn, nuts, or hard candy. He would not consider dentures—he would rather gum it.

Twice he'd gone into atrial fibrillation, a fluttering erratic heartbeat that called for electric cardioversion zaps, frequent blood tests, and daily blood thinners. Strokes terrified him, hospitals more, and he mistrusted the cardiovascular industry and its lobby the AMA.

His bathroom cabinet was a pharmacy of multivitamins, fish oils, stool softeners, painkillers, sleeping pills, bladder relaxants, antacids, antioxidants, and chalky liquid remedies for constipation and diarrhea. On most of them the expiration date had expired.

He feared he was going crazy. The country he loved had already gone. America got crazier every day and no one seemed to care. But he'd read enough about abnormal psychology (a term now politically incorrect) to know that when one is convinced everyone is crazy but him, he's the crazy one.

He knew that none of these woes was reason enough to end his life; all of them put together weren't. It was when cancer, the Big C, got tossed into the witch's brew that suicide became an attractive alternative. George Noel Gordon Bombazine was in an intermediate stage of prostate cancer.

Chapter Four: 6:24 a. m.

DR. FALLOPIUS

Prostate cancer!

Bombazine groaned. This morning those words inspired such nausea that he didn't want to get out of bed even if it was his birthday. Nausea was a symptom of cancer and cancer was Kierkegaard's sickness unto death, and he'd rather die at home than in a hospital if he didn't commit suicide. So he continued to lie, supine and corpse-like, on his king-sized bed in his master bedroom and think about his future, if he had one, and he probably didn't.

When had he decided to kill himself on his seventieth birthday? It was after his last appointment with his Houston oncologist Dr. William Robert "Billy Bob" Fallopius. Bombazine's malignancy, a biopsy revealed, was then in a Gleason 7 stage (which wasn't so bad) with a PSA of 6 (which wasn't so good), and Dr. Fallopius diagnosed it as "lethal and usually fatal though not alway totally fatal." Which meant it could be treated if he underwent Intensity Modulated Radiation Therapy (IMRT) five days a week for the next two months and things went "real well." However, cautioned the doctor, things did not always go real well and sometimes the radiated patient died. And even if things went real well, it could mean pain, nausea, depression, suicidal thoughts, mood swings, death, and a loss of bladder control.

"Let me radiate you anyway," urged the doctor. "The alternative is even worse."

Bombazine had asked himself: Am I afraid to die? No. Well, yes. It depended. "Why should I let you radiate me?" he asked Dr. Fallopius.

"Because you are in an intramediate level of prostate cancer."

"Don't you mean intermediate level?"

"That's what I said. An intramediate level. Either we treat it or we don't. If we don't, the cancer will spread and lead to pain, nausea, incontinence, urinary difficulty, urethral burning, impotency, metastasis to the bone, and fatal death. You've probably underwent some of those discomforts already."

The doctor's grammar and syntax bothered and offended Bombazine, who had read up on him. New Hampshire-born, the man had attended Exeter and Yale; he chose to play dumb. Bombazine suspected he had dumbed himself down to feel at home in Houston-area country clubs membered with good ole Texas boys whose cinematic idols were Chuck Norris, Dwane "The Rock" Johnson, and Jean-Claude Van Damme. Bombazine also wondered how long the doctor had been "Billy Bob" if he'd been born in New Hampshire. His Texas accent seemed to come and go the way the accents of certain politicians did, depending on where and to whom they were speaking.

Bombazine had asked: "And IMRT treatments will cure my discomforts?"

"No, it will intensify 'em. IMRT treatments will result in even more impotence and incontinence and sterility."

"Then why should I be radiated?"

"Your symptoms may disappear after a year. Incontinence means you'll wet your pants and wear adult diapers. Sterile means you won't manufacture no more procreational fluid."

"Pro what?"

"Semen. I don't like that word. Sounds nasty. I prefer 'procreational fluid.' You will stop having sex. Since you don't have sex, that shouldn't be a problem. You will also experience skin irritation like a bad sunburn. But there's good news, too."

"What is it?"

"Hold your horses. We ain't through with the bad news. Your prostate is located smack dab below your bladder. The radiation will shrink it and cause urine leakage. Plumbing problems, we call 'em." The doctor gave a laugh. "All sexual activity including onanism will be difficult if not impossible."

"Did you say onanism?"

"Self-pollution. Masturbation."

"I can't jerk off?"

"I don't like that expression either. Forget about sex, Professor. You're an elderly old man and single who don't have carnal relationships and don't want any more children. Masturbation don't clean out your pipes. It's an unnatural perversion. Read what happened to Onan in Genesis thirty-eight after he spilled his seed on the ground."

"What happened to him?"

"They named a perversion after him. Onanism."

My God, Bombazine thought, this man is my doctor? My life is in his hands? Bombazine had read that the doctor was a born-again end-of-days Pentecostal evangelical Nazarene deacon. Would he feel obligated on religious grounds to keep his terminal cancer patients alive with IMRT radiation and cardiopulmonary resuscitation machines and mechanical respirators and sinister ventilators while they howled in pain and begged to die? Bombazine had filed an advanced directive, a living will, with his five primary care physicians (none knew about the others) and Houston attorney stipulating that no extraordinary means be employed to prolong his life if ordinary means failed to.

Rumor had it that Dr. Fallopius was descended from the sixteenth century anatomist for whom the Fallopian Tube was named. The doctor confirmed the rumor and claimed he had DNA evidence to substantiate it. Bombazine hoped it was true. Maybe he had intelligent genes swimming in his pool with the others. But the man was probably right: at seventy he didn't need sex, though he thought about it even more now than when he was young and virile. Goethe had bedded nubile nymphs well into his seventies and Leopold Stokowski had married Gloria Vanderbilt when he was six-ty-three and she was twenty-one and Hugh Hefner, older than Melchizedek, was still banging his *Playboy* Playmates like a tambourine and marrying them; when Hefner died they'd have to beat his dick to death before they could close the casket. But Bombazine was not Goethe or Stokowski or

Hugh Hefner, and certainly didn't want any more children. His bisexual bipolar thirty-five-year-old son Miguel refused to speak to him except to curse him in Spanish and ask for money in English.

Bombazine could not believe this "highly regarded oncologist" was for real. Like an actor miscast, he didn't even look the part. In his late forties, a foot shorter than Bombazine (who stood six-five), built like a fire hydrant, Dr. Fallopius was one of those vertically challenged men who walk on tiptoe or wear cowboy boots to look taller. Today he wore his cowboy boots—expensive ones, ostrich perhaps. His yellow hair, combed forward to hide his baldness, was dyed; his biceps and forearms bulged, like Popeye's, with a weight-lifter's muscles; his face seemed frozen in the smile of a quiz show host; his teeth gleamed too brightly, as if whitened with chemical agents. He was reputedly a model husband and father, a pillar of the community active in the Shriners and Elks, who went to church twice on Sundays, dutifully tithed, generously contributed to Baptist missions in Zimbabwe and Tanzania, and Bombazine couldn't stand him.

That made Bombazine feel guilty—it bespoke snobbery, stereotyping, a superior attitude. He saw himself as tolerant and open-minded. A liberal humanist. But love the man or hate him, he was stuck with this man. In Houston Dr. Billy Bob Fallopius was to oncology what Dr. Michael DeBakey had been to heart surgery. He had graduated from Johns Hopkins Medical School in Baltimore, completed a residency at M. D. Anderson Cancer Center in Houston, and never left the Bayou City. *The New England Journal of Medicine* praised his radiation methodologies. Fellow oncologists in Canada, Mexico, Australia, and the United Kingdom called him courageous because he was brave enough to tell cancer patients point blank that they might die soon, very soon, unless they did exactly what he told them to. Often they died anyway, but that was not his fault. They had come to him too late.

"You say you lost your mama to cancer?" he'd asked Bombazine. "I'm sorry to hear it."

"That happened twenty-five years ago. I got over it."

"I'm sorry because experts—of which I happen to be one of—think cancer runs in families."

"My cancer might be inherited from my mother?"

The doctor smiled as if the question came from a child. "You couldn't inherit prostate cancer from your mother, Professor. Women don't have prostates. I'd say cancer is hereditary in five to ten percent of all cases."

"Which five to ten percent?"

"How should I know? I'm not a statistician."

Bombazine closed his eyes and gritted his teeth.

"I do know breast cancer has a genetic factor," Dr. Fallopius allowed, "but I don't think you have to worry about breast cancer. You're a man. Here's some true facts about what you have to worry about. First, every man past seventy, which you are, is gonna have prostate cancer at some point in time in his lifetime."

"I'm sixty-nine," Bombazine corrected.

"You're gonna have prostate cancer 'cause you already have it. Prostate cancer grows real slow, but it don't just go away. Irregardless of what you've heard, you maybe won't need treatments. You're old enough to just wait it out. We call that 'watchful waiting' and 'active surveillance.' Aggressive therapy will not extend the life expectancy of a real old man like you fixing to die anyway."

"I'm not 'real old' and I'm not fixing to die."

"We're all fixing to die, Professor. That's a true fact. It's part of the humanist condition. In your case we can ignore the cancer till it's metastasized and threatens your life. A normal, active, healthy man like myself has a PSA of below one. If yours gets up to twenty, you're dead. You're at six, so watchful waiting and active surveillance is one option."

"What's another?"

"It would help if you had some condition that might kill you first. Then you wouldn't need IMRT or chemo or any other aggressive therapy."

"What condition could kill me first?"

The doctor shrugged. "A fatalistic condition. Do you have a brain tumor?"

"No. I would've mentioned that."

"You coulda forgotten to. Ever been treated for Alzheimer's?"

"Never had it."

"Huntington's Disease?"

"No."

"Parkinson's? Naw, your hands don't shake. How about Guillain-Barre Syndrome?"

"Wasn't that what Joseph Heller had?"

"Who is Joseph Heller?"

"Never mind. I don't have it."

"Are you clinically depressed?"

"I should be. I have cancer. But the answer is no."

"Some doctors think depression can kill you. I don't. That's why I don't prescribe antidepressants. A man should man it up. Ever been treated for Hodgkin's Disease? Leukemia? Lymphoma?"

"None of the above."

"No strokes or aneurisms?"

"No."

The doctor sighed with exasperation and shook his head, as if Bombazine were a recalcitrant patient reluctant to cooperate. "Look, Professor. Atrial fib ain't gonna kill you and neither is your sore knee or the fact that your back hurts. Heck, my back hurts. You could stand to lose a hundred pounds, but your weight ain't gonna kill you, 'cause you're so tall you can carry it. Heck, you don't even smoke. The average life expectancy of the American male is seventy-six, but you could live to be a hundred. With prostate cancer you'd be facing years of a horrible slow death instead of the kind of death we're hoping for."

"Doctor," Bombazine said, "you've got quite a bedside manner. Do you know that?"

"You ain't sick in bed yet. If I were you, I'd let me radiate you. IMRT is the mildest most unobtrusive treatment I prescribe. I can radiate your whole prostate. Or I can radiate just the malignant quadrants, which is all four of 'em. I use a needle to implant little-bitty metal rods like gold pins called markers through your heinie hole. A narrow tool I insert will blast the markers into the prostate. Then we study the markers with a CAT scan to tell us which quadrants to radiate first.

"The good news," he added, "is that the markers eventually dissolve. Poof! Those little suckers are gone."

"That was the good news?"

"Yessir."

"Could we kill me now and get it over with?"

The doctor smiled even though he'd been smiling and shook his head. "Do I look like Dr. Kevorkian? I took a hypocritical oath to do no harm. Which option do you want?"

"Let me think about the IMRT."

"Don't think too long. I'm real busy and we'd need to set up a treatment schedule. IMRT can be fun. Once you're radiated you can glow in the dark and scare trick-or-treaters at Halloween." The doctor burst into laughter, then abruptly stopped laughing. "Take all the time you want to think about it, Professor, and call me in the morning with your decision."

Chapter Five: 6:37 a. m.

"No Tengo Nada Por Lo Que Vivir"

His decision was No. Bombazine had called Dr. Fallopius the following morning and told him IMRT was out. He would go the "watchful waiting and active surveillance" route and take it from there.

"Don't misunderestimate the efficacy of radiation," Dr. Fallopius warned.

"Yesterday you said 'watchful waiting' was an acceptable alternative."

"I tried to sell you on radiation."

"You didn't close the sale."

"I'm not a salesman. I'm a healer. Call me if you change your mind."

"Physician, heal thyself," Bombazine had wanted to add but lacked the nerve. It wasn't fair to blame the doctor, who was only doing his job, for his misfortune. But with all his other ailments, Bombazine didn't see battling cancer as worth the effort. Why not end things now? *"No tengo nada por lo que vivir,"* the Spanish painter / sculptor Oscar Dominguez had said before slitting his wrists. *"I have nothing left to live for."* Many painters and sculptors killed themselves. Many warriors, even. The fearless warrior T. E. Lawrence of Arabia wrote, "O Lord, I am so tired. I want to lie down to sleep, to die. To die is best because there is no reveille." He had killed himself riding a motorcycle. Bombazine was tired of standing reveille (getting out of bed) every morning. Besides, who wanted to go on living in a world where everyone said "at this point in time" instead of "at this point" or "at this time" and said "crispy" instead of "crisp" and condoned the use of torture so long as the government called it "enhanced interrogation?" His country was not getting smarter or saner. His countrymen religiously defended capital punishment, torture, and creationism, denied evolution and climate change, and rejected gun control and gun safety measures and affordable health care for themselves and their families. Like Dr. Fallopius, they had dumbed themselves down. Many had been dumb to begin with and hadn't far to go.

Now death was Bombazine's only escape hatch. H. L. Mencken wrote that of all escape mechanisms, death is the most efficient. The FDA, it was said, was about to approve a miracle drug that would enable people to live for over a hundred years—a dubious scientific advance, Bombazine suspected, unless accompanied by Ron Howard's alien cocoons or Ponce de Leon's fountain of youth. Who'd really want to live to be a hundred? Even one's Whole Life insurance policy would expire first.

Having read article after article, essay after essay, book after book about suicide, Bombazine knew that many old people yearned to kill themselves but lacked the gumption because religion told them they would slow-roast in hell, like rotisserie chickens, if they did. The very old would wel-

39

come a death that was quick, sudden, and painless. It was a slow death they feared — the untreatable diseases, the shitting and pissing the bed, the sleepless nights, the weeping, the strokes that rendered them immobile and mute as they lay in some hospital room agonizingly conscious, staring up at a crack in the ceiling, struggling to breathe through tubes and parched lips. Nobody, not even they, could pull the plug, because they were a financial investment, with money to be made by keeping them alive.

Assisted suicide, thank goodness, was coming; three states had already legalized it. But it was advancing too slowly, and its opponents ("It's a slippery slope!") were as fierce as Darwin's or Galileo's had been. No law, Bombazine held, should have dominion over a man or woman's death. Let people call him a coward. It took courage to kill yourself; that's why so few did it. There was no shame involved. The late novelist William Styron, with whom Bombazine briefly had corresponded, had written that there should be no more reproof or accusation of cowardice attached to victims of suicide from clinical depression than to victims of terminal cancer. Cowardice was not a factor in either case. I was clinically depressed, thought Bombazine, before I knew I had terminal cancer. I should be twice as depressed by now.

He had great minds on his side. "Every man has a property in his own person," the father of liberalism John Locke wrote, "and this nobody has a right to but himself." The psychoanalyst Bruno Bettelheim said, "The decision to remain alive or to die is the supreme example of self-determination." To prove he meant it, Bettelheim killed himself. He was eighty-six and had lived long enough. And in *The Myth of Sisyphus*, Albert Camus wrote, "There is but one truly serious philosophical problem, and that is suicide. Judging whether life is or is not worth living amounts to answering the fundamental question of philosophy."

What a statement! Bombazine thought. He revered Camus. He also revered the British suicide expert A. Alvarez and the French suicide expert Emile Durkheim and the Jewish American suicide expert Howard I. Kushner. He revered the suicide experts of Sweden, Denmark, Norway, Finland, France, Belgium, Switzerland, Ireland, and even Russia, the former Soviet Union, home of Russian Roulette and suicidally depressed poets and novelists and composers: a breeding ground for suicide even more fertile than Scandinavia. All those experts, most of them suicides themselves, had agreed that each suicide "victim" gives his or her act a personal stamp expressing his/her temperament and mental state. The means by which Bombazine would end his life — death by drowning from driving his Mercedes E-class hybrid into a deep lake below a cliff — was his personal stamp, his way of going out in style with pizzaz. For him the crucial *how* was determined. The only question was *when*.

Paradoxically, Bombazine's suicide experts found, more men killed themselves than women did, but more women tried to kill themselves or threatened to than men did. More single people killed themselves than married people. More white males killed themselves than nonwhite males did. More older males killed themselves than younger males did; that was surprising, though it did not include men past the age of sixty.

Most of the findings did not surprise. More childless people killed themselves than parents did. More married women who'd remained childless killed themselves than married mothers did. Islamic terrorist suicide bombers had the highest rate of any sampled group. (No huge surprise there.) More soldiers on active duty than civilians living at home killed themselves, and more veterans killed themselves than civilians who'd never served in the military. American soldiers back from Iraq and Afghanistan killed themselves at a per diem rate of twenty-two, a much higher figure than Vietnam War veterans. Atheists and agnostics were more apt to kill themselves than devout churchgoers were. People living in snowy Nordic climes with long, dark winters and freezing temperatures were more apt to kill themselves than those living in sunny climes with beaches and swimming pools and volleyball nets and barbecue grills and girls in bikinis.

It saddened Bombazine to learn that artistic types like poets and painters and novelists and actors and composers killed themselves at ten times the rate of people who could in no sense be called creative. But his most baffling discovery was that such a small percentage of people, even old people, diagnosed with terminal illnesses killed themselves or tried to. Another disturbing discovery was that highly educated types like himself, with postgraduate degrees, were more likely to kill themselves than high school dropouts, flunkouts, nitwits, illiterates, simpletons, imbeciles, dyslexics, and extremely slow learners who used to be called retards before the term became politically incorrect. Bombazine, in fact, fit a baker's dozen categories of high suicide probability, being white, angry, male, agnostic, depressed, reclusive, idle, unemployed, alienated, embittered, divorced, possibly impotent, and saddled with a masters degree, a PhD, and the title professor emeritus.

Why haven't I already killed myself? he wondered. I've had every reason to.

But what if *Return to Spoon River* was a best seller and the movie won Oscars? Would that be a reason to live? No, it would be all the more reason not to. Nothing failed like success—ask F. Scott Fitzgerald or Richard Corey. Even Jim (the Door) Morrison and Elvis (the King) Presley could be diagnosed as chronic suicides. There was something romantic about going out on top in a blaze of glory and the prime of life. Tragic but romantic. Hadn't the Japanese author Yukio Mishima killed himself in a ritual suicide on the heels of his literary triumph? Suicide was a celebration. Age was a factor too. There was nothing tragic about the death of an old man or woman. The deaths of young persons were tragic because they'd been cheated out of their destinies, not allowed to leave their mark on the world. But by seventy a coot or a crone or a codger was unlikely to produce much more of value. If one's best work was not done by then, it never would be. Since Bombazine was seventy, who would care?

He tried again to push himself out of bed but only sank back and stared at the ceiling fan. Sunlight rimmed the room. If this was to be his last day, he needed to haul his big butt up and get on with it. Tonight was the night he'd take the most exciting trip of a life which had lacked for much excitement. He understood why celebrities killed themselves:

they were impatient and couldn't wait to get *on* with it. Like The Doors, they wanted to "break on through to the other side." Bombazine could break on through tonight. Only a glorious, historic, fantastic day could postpone it. He was dying to die.

It was just past dawn. By dusk he'd be ready for Mount Makeout.

Chapter Six: 6:54 a. m.

MOUNT MAKEOUT

Tonight's plan was fail-safe. At the witching hour (not midnight but ten—he couldn't stay up till midnight), after the traffic thinned and the streets were hushed, he would climb into his car and drive past the campus, through the Village, and north on the Interstate that led to the Arizona city locals called Big Town. But he wasn't going to Big Town. His would be a shorter trip, one way. He was headed for Mount Makeout.

On that drive, the desert flatland, with its sparse yellow grass, soon would morph into mountains studded with junipers and saplings and fields of bluebonnets that swayed like cerulean seas; you couldn't see that at night, but he'd gazed on such beauty in the daytime and marveled at it. High in those mountains were treacherous cliffs. En route, past a confusing four-traffic-light fork in the highway, was a cutoff that led up a winding mountain road (Frontage Road 1409) to the steepest cliff. Stratified with limestone layers from the Cretaceous epoch 45 million years ago, the cliff, with its spectacular view, had been called Mount Makeout until an icy night, thirty years ago, when a college foursome drunk on beer and tequila skidded off the road at a high speed, plowing through a guardrail of woodposts and plastic blockouts and crashing in flames on the rocks below. Since then nobody drove up to Mount Makeout to make out, and few people still called it Mount Makeout. Students now rented rooms by the hour at the Motel 6 near the campus.

Even in daytime, the frontage road was unsafe. And now there was a gap in the dark-red granite wall, along the steep ascent, that Bombazine knew well; each of the past three days, he'd driven up there and gotten out of his Mercedes to inspect it. The breach remained unrepaired, as if a slab had been removed and its replacement postponed or forgotten. The opening was just wide enough to drive a car through; Bombazine had measured it. A hundred feet below, straight down the gorge, was a deep lake formed by the damming of a rushing river, the Xanthus, nicknamed the "X." From where he'd stood, Bombazine could stare down into the deep black water below. He'd felt its pull; the moment was a flash-forward—for an instant his soul yearned to leap out of his body. This was the ideal place to do himself in. It was a portal to eternity.

By God, it had to happen here. He was sure of that.

Yesterday he'd returned to the site to find the section of wall still missing, the black hole gaping, nothing having been done to repair the breach in three days. That was less remarkable than it sounded. Road repair in Mount Olympus County progressed at a speed like that in the mountainous villages of nearby northern Mexico. A mañana pace. Nobody used the perilous frontage road anyway—it should have been blocked off and closed. Tonight he would drive—propel—

his Mercedes up the canyon road, through the opening in the wall, off the cliff, and into the lake, the X. Like Percy Bysshe Shelley, Bombazine had never learned to swim. Shelley had drowned and so would he.

But Bombazine's role model was not Shelley but a character in T. S. Eliot's "The Waste Land." Like Eliot's Phlebas the Phoenician, he would "rise and fall and pass the stages of his age and youth, entering the whirlpool." In seconds his life would pass before his eyes as Phlebas the Phoenician's had. What a glorious way to go! Flying through the air, whooping with terror and jubilation; taking a nosedive and making a gigantic splash; sinking to a cold watery grave as your life passed before your eyes. "Fear death by water," Eliot warned, but Bombazine would not. He feared death by every life-threatening agent except water. He certainly did not want to immolate himself in a fiery explosion — the idea of burning to death terrified him. "Old age should burn and rave at close of day," Dylan Thomas had admonished. Bombazine was willing to rave but not to burn. Nor did he want to bleed to death, howling in pain, helplessly trapped and mangled in a wreckage nobody might discover for hours or even days.

He needed that hole in the wall to drive his Mercedes through. The thing had to be done a certain way. That would make it fail-safe.

Like the Thane of Cawdor in Macbeth, nothing in his life would become him like the leaving it. I have not lived bravely, Bombazine told himself, but I will die bravely. He looked forward to seeing his life pass before his eyes as he

47

drowned. Recently, in dreams at night, he'd seen something like it: a rapid-fire black-and-white montage of forgotten faces, like a sped-up newsreel, from the eight decades in which he'd lived. Faces! A male newsreel voice identified Paul Wolfowitz and Jody Powell, Oliver North and Xavier Cugat... Buckminster Fuller, Bennett Cerf, Henry Wallace, Bobby Baker, Sander Vanocur and John L. Lewis. Next came Mandy Rice-Davies, Boy George, George Gobel, Fulton J. Sheen, U Thant, Faye Emerson, Edwin Meese. In another black-and-white newsreel dream a few nights later, Anthony Eden appeared, followed by Niels Bohr, Cory Aquino, Alexander Dubcek... Adam Clayton Powell, Christine Jorgensen, Syngman Rhee, Francis Gary Powers... John Ehrlichman... Sonja Henie and Dagmar... Jocelyn Elders... Joseph Kasavubu... Eldridge Cleaver... David Ben Gurion... Eamon de Valera... George Shultz... Kid Gavilan... Earl Butz... Gennifer Flowers. Even Gene Vincent, he of the rockabilly classic "Be-Bop-A-Lula," young again and flashing perfect white teeth, made an appearance. Most of the faces wore artificial, mask-like smiles, macabre and chilling. Death masks, though not all the celebrities were dead.

The dreams had been unsettling. Even creepy. Why had those people appeared, or reappeared, to him in his sleep? Did the dead wait for him on the other side?

On other nights, he dreamed of authors few Americans would recognize if not English teachers themselves — faces of poets he'd written essays, reviews, exegeses, and critical articles about. He recognized John Hall Wheelock and Allen Tate and William Carlos Williams and Horace Gregory and

Muriel Rukeyser and Elizabeth Madox Roberts and Hilaire Belloc. Edgar Lee Masters appeared in one dream, a round-faced balding little fellow, in wire-rimmed glasses, who'd been Clarence Darrow's law partner but looked more like a bank teller than a counselor or poet.

"Are you George Gordon Bombazine?" Masters had demanded in that dream. His eyes were wild, his face baleful; he seemed angry.

"I am, sir. A champion of your poetry. What an honor to meet you."

"Forget my poetry, you sycophantic parasite. Write about my plays and biographies."

"But Edgar Lee, I keep your poetry alive."

"You barely keep yourself alive, you hack. You will die soon and learn what it's like down here. It's worse than the Spoon River graveyard. Stay out of my coffin, ghoul." Then, for emphasis, Masters grabbed him by the throat with one hand and commenced to choke him with inhuman strength. His fingers were icy as he pulled Bombzine's head toward his own, as if to kiss him.

Terrified, Bombazine had come awake in a cold sweat. What had that dream meant? That he soon would join Masters in the hereafter? Fine! He was ready to. Unbeknownst to Pru, Miguel, Catherine, or anyone else but his attorney in Houston, he'd recently rewritten, amended, photocopied, and refiled his will. Pru would be generously remembered; Miguel and Catherine, who misused and abused him, would receive more than they deserved. Ancillary notes to Pru would specify what to do with Argos, with his Mercedes after it was dredged out of the lake, with his library and journals and research papers, computer hard drive, erotica collection, letters from Richard Wilbur and Yvor Winters and Anatole Broyard and Gore Vidal and William Styron, and the ashes of his cremated carcass. Also his clothes, which didn't amount to much, since he'd never been a dresser. (Pru said he dressed like a priest on vacation.) His clothes could go to Haven for Hope or the St. Vincent de Paul Society or the Salvation Army if anyone there really wanted to wear the clothes of a man who'd killed himself. His will expressly forbade a service in a funeral parlor or a church or anyplace else. He did not want an obituary in the newspaper, especially not the *Mount Olympus College Mountaineer*. He wanted no eulogies recited, orations delivered, sermons preached, dirges sung, spirituals wailed, or tears shed. He was not, however, averse to tributes from peers and colleagues.

His forthcoming Edgar Lee Masters book, heavy with new annotations and footnotes, would not be a best seller, but he did hope it would sell. Tencha, the femme fatale he'd married in the seventies, had ridiculed his published work, even his novel, as abstruse and recondite, though she hadn't used those words but bilingual invectives harsher and profane. Last week he'd found an angry letter Tencha had mailed him from a vacation resort in Seville in 1977, demanding to know why he wrote about writers no one had ever heard of. It went: La Bamba, sometimes I express myself better in Spanish, my native tongue. *Entonces, ¿por qué me casé contigo Jorge? ¿Por qué me casé con un hombre con tan poco dinero — un 'estudioso' al que tendría que mantener? ¡Eres un ridículo!* You are a joke! *Si, escribes libros, pero son libros sobr personas que nadie conoce. Libros para bibliotecas. ¿Por qué no escribes sobre grandes escritores como Octavio Paz, Ortega y Gasset, Pablo Neruda y Gabriel Garcia-Márquez? ¡Sí, los he leído!. Es por que en el fondo eres muy poco hombre, Jorge te identificas con otros poco hombres. Hombres con pocas ambiciones y sin agallas. Hombres sin sentimientos ni cojones. Hombres como tú.* Are you even a man? *Mi familia dice que me debería deshacer de ti. Mis hermanos te matarían si yo se los pidiera!* You have embarrassed me before my family. As a husband you are an embarrassment. I do not know what I want, but I know that you do not have it. *Adios,* La Bamba! — Tencha.

Actually, she had a point. Other people asked those questions tactfully and delicately. Why was he so taken with obscure dead authors of best-forgotten masterpieces? Why didn't he write about the giants, the colossi, the immortals? His two biographies chronicled the lives of Edward Arlington Robinson and Robinson Jeffers. Mid-level poets, good but not great. He'd applauded Jeffers as an early icon of the American environmentalist movement and praised Robinson for having created the handsome rich suicide Richard Cory and the born-too-late alcoholic Miniver Cheevy. Bombazine had also penned definitive critical studies of Sidney Lanier and William Vaughn Moody and Stephen Vincent Benet. Also Randall Jarrell, a so-so poet he revered for having committed suicide. And he'd sung the praises of Adelaide Crapsey and Witter Bynner and Thomas Bailey Aldrich and Arthur Davidson Ficke, poets

who weren't even household names in their own house-
holds.

Edgar Lee Masters, of course, had been a major exception:
the literary star to which Bombazine had hitched his wagon.
Widely read even in European countries though he was
quintessentially Midwestern, Masters, famed for his collo-
quial free verse, deserved more acclaim than he received.
Bombazine saw him as the Grant Wood of American poetry.
With his monologue gravestone epitaphs of over two hundred dead and buried Spoon River villagers, Masters demy-
stified rural small-town American life and showed it to be
as fierce and colorful and exciting beneath its placid surface
as life in a big city. He had his favorite charcters, of course.
There was Spoon River's venal bank president Thomas
Rhodes, who believed the wealthy deserved rights denied
the poor... its alcoholic attorney Benjamin Pantier, who lived
in the dingy back room of his office with his dog... its village prostitute Daisy Frasier, who donated her profits to the
local school fund... its forlorn brokenhearted Ann Rutledge,
Abraham Lincoln's first sweetheart... Bombazine treasured
these and admired the others, many of them based on actual
persons whose embarrassed families were so enraged by
Masters' recognizable portraits that they physically threatened the poet.

Subjects of Bombazine's scholarly articles published in
The Paris Review and *Partisan Review* and *Kenyon Review*
numbered Countee Cullen, John Crowe Ransom, Louis
Untermeyer, William Empson, Conrad Aiken, Elinore
Wylie, Joseph Langland, Trumbull Stickney, Vachel Lind-

say, and Hilda Doolittle, who signed her poems "H. D." and was openly a lesbian when coming out of the closet wasn't safe. All had been fine writers, uniquely gifted, worthy of rediscovery, and Bombazine deemed it his mission to bring their work to light. Thanks to him, obscure voices like John Hay's and Bliss Carman's and George Sterling's and Guy Wetmore Carry's could be heard also, even if nobody was dying to listen.

But had he overdone it? Settled for being a big frog in a small pond? Played it safe? One could not lose a competition with no competitors. Mostly he'd contented himself with championing a team of bench warmers. One poem in *Spoon River Anthology*, "Petit, the Poet," was disturbing because Tencha, having read it, said the epitaph was about him.

PETIT, THE POET

Seeds in a dry pod, tick, tick, tick,
Tick, tick, tick, like mites in a quarrel —
Faint iambics that the full breeze wakens —
But the pine tree makes a symphony thereof.
Triolets, villanelles, rondels, rondeaus,
Ballades by the score with the same old thought.
The snows and the roses of yestyerday are vanished;
And what is love but a rose that fades?
Life all around me here in the village:
Tragedy, comedy, valor and truth,
Courage, constancy, heroism, failure —

All in the loom, and oh what patterns!
Woodlands, meadows, streams and rivers —
Blind to all of it all my life long.
Triolets, villanelles, rondels, rondeaus,
Seeds in a dry pod, tick, tick, tick,
Tick, tick, tick, what little iambics,
While Homer and Whitman roared in the pines?

Tencha was schizoid, a fractured personality, the kind-
est and cruelest woman he had ever known; but schizoids,
blessed with two pairs of eyes rather than just one, can be
blessed with extraordinary insight. Weren't the obscure
poets he championed rather like Petit the Poet? Wasn't he
like Petit the Poet? Tick, tick, ticking away on his word pro-
cessor, playing it safe while other scholars took risks with
daring, scathing, iconoclastic criticism of the High and
Mighty? What if he was Petit the Poet? He certainly wasn't
Homer or Whitman.

Maybe he should've written another novel. "Why haven't
you?" his corpulent New York agent Barbara "Babs" Katz
had demanded to know back in the seventies.

"Easy old girl," Bombazine had responded. "Don't bust
your bodice. My first novel didn't sell."

"Of course it didn't. A satire about the military industrial
complex! Who wants to read that? Write a dirty-book pot-
boiler and make us rich, Georgie."

"You're already rich. You have other writers. My anthologies do well."

"Not as well as they used to. Write another novel. The fiction market wants sexy stories for bored housewives. First-person romance novels with virginal repressed heroines ready for a hero with a large endowment. Think Erica Jong's *Fear of Flying*. Think Gael Greene's *Blue Skies No Candy*."

"Babs, those are female writers."

"So? We'll give you a pseudonym. Penelope Pursewarden. You wouldn't want to sully your rep by using your real name anyway. Write a best seller. Let's make some money. I want to winter in Nice and gamble in Monte Carlo. I'm not getting any younger. Just fatter.

"I used to be beautiful," she wistfully added.

"You're still beautiful."

"I'm not. I weigh two hundred pounds."

"So what? I weigh two-sixty."

"You're not beautiful either. Make us rich, Georgie."

"You got it."

But he had never written that bawdy best seller Babs wanted. Later she'd suggested vampire romances and Young Adult thrillers and other commercial crap he would never write. He was not really a novelist but a scholar, a critic, an anthologist who happened to have written a novel, a best-forgotten masterpiece about Pentagon waste and corruption. But all his work was sacred to him—his work had been his life.

"Your life? You know nothing of life, La Bamba," Tencha had told him. "Nor do the worthless writers you write about and the ones who review your *mierda*. You *pendejos* carry the bones of the dead from one graveyard to another! Academics! You should work for a cemetery!"

"Why did you marry me, Tencha? You knew what I did for a living."

"*Quien sabe?* I have made many mistakes and you were the worst. I was pregnant and Catholic. I loved you out of pity like you were a stray dog. You were what gringos call a mercy fuck. Yes, we used to have sex a lot, but what else was there to do? You are not a good fuck. You are not a good anything, *pobrecito*. Not even a good man."

Tencha knew all about men, good and bad. As an International Relations major she'd had relations with men of three different nationalities on three continents and wanted to go to Africa and make it four. She'd requested that Bombazine take her with him to Cape Town or Johannesburg the next time he went there to write about some South African poet nobody cared about (except the poet's friends and relatives, *la familia*) so that she could fuck him. She was serious. Tencha had the soul of a camp follower, a groupie, a star fucker.

Why did I marry such a woman? Bombazine asked himself now. I should not be glad she's dead, but I am glad. But how much of what she said about me was true?

Chapter Seven: 7:07 a. m.

THE POWER OF THANKSGIVING

The clock continued to tick. Tick-tock, tick-tock. We all have to die, but how many of us would want to know the day and the hour beforehand? Not many, Bombazine told himself.

A better question: Why was the day before Thanksgiving his backup date, his Plan B, should something unexpected happen? Answer: Thanksgiving was the holiday he hated worse than any other, and to kill himself then might ruin it for Dr. Trevor T. Merriman, the English professor and literary deconstructionist who'd married Bombazine's second wife Prudence ("Pru") after a clandestine affair about which Bombazine had been the last to know and a divorce free of the acrimony he had every right to feel. Now Bombazine sought revenge. Trevor loved Thanksgiving the way children love Christmas (another holiday Bombazine wasn't wild about) and probably more than he loved Pru. Trevor loved every national holiday, state holiday, local holiday, and campus holiday. As his last act, Bombazine might disrupt and perhaps even ruin Trevor's Thanksgiving this year with his suicide.

But should he postpone things until Thanksgiving eve

just to stick it to Trevor? Sartre would have said No. Sartre would recommend that he kill himself tonight and be done with it. Take the plunge, the existential risk, and to hell with Trevor and Thanksgiving. "There is only one day left," Sartre wrote, "always starting over: It is given to us at dawn and taken away from us at dusk." Elsewhere Sartre wrote, "Suicide is an opportunity to stake out our understanding of our essence as individuals in a godless world." Sartre himself had not committed suicide, but why should he have? The French were not forced to celebrate Thanksgiving.

Thanksgiving! An annual farce, a hoax, a fiction, a bogus four-day weekend that replayed painful tapes from Bombazine's boyhood. Conservatives whined that liberals waged war on Christmas, but Bombazine waged war on Thanksgiving. Americans mistakenly thought the holiday started in 1621 with some Pilgrims and friendly Wampanoag Indians schmoozing elbow to elbow and smoking peace pipes at picnic tables in the woods near Plymouth Colony, having feasted on roast turkey and corn on the cob to give thanks for a bountiful harvest. Actually the annual holiday had begun in England sixteen years earlier, to give thanks that Catholic terrorists hadn't succeeded in blowing up Parliament and assassinating the Protestant King James I. The Pilgrims then brought the holiday to the New World from England along with syphilis and other sexually transmitted diseases.

During Bombazine's childhood in Houston's affluent River Oaks, adults from both sides of his family would congregate at his parents' house during the Macy's Parade and start drinking as soon as they arrived. Some had begun at dawn. Congenial at first, they'd be quarreling before the overcooked turkey was served. Scabs of family feuds and grudges were reopened. Thanksgiving meant watching endless football games on TV (Bombazine disliked the sport and hated the halftime festivities) and stuffing his face with stuffing and mashed potatoes and other bacon-greased starches. If the nauseous foodfest was so delicious, why did Americans just eat it once a year?

As married couples, he and Tencha and later he and Pru got invited to multiple Thanksgiving dinners that resulted in his getting drunk and overeating at not just one but several. Now, with Tencha dead and Pru gone, the only thing worse than being invited to multiple Thanksgiving dinners was not being invited to any and spending Thanksgiving all alone, with Argos, in the gloom of his empty house. This year, if he wasn't dead, the Thanksgiving holiday would find him alone once more. But he would be dead. By his own hand.

There were more conventional ways to suicide than the Mount Makeout method. A gun was out—politically incorrect, since he donated to the Brady Campaign Against Gun Violence. Nor would he wrap his lips around some filthy rusty exhaust pipe and inhale carbon monoxide. Butcher knives were too messy, and he had no bathtub in which to drowsily soak and bleed to death in warm water after opening his veins with a razor blade. Nor did he have a barn in which to hang himself from the rafters with a strong rope. But there was a kitchen oven in which to stick his head; sleeping pills and tranquilizers to overdose; sedatives to inject; lethal poisons to ingest. And he could have someone help him; assisted suicide was legal in Oregon, Washington State, and Montana. He had always wanted to see Montana anyway.

But he had to do it his way and do it alone. He wanted an exit to rival Tencha's, whose death had been a matinee solo performance in broad daylight. Tencha had gone out in spectacular style, bleeding and blinded and screaming in rush hour Mexico City traffic. Bombazine wanted to make a huge splash even if no one heard or saw. Besides, there were things a man should do for himself. Killing himself was one. He would not have someone hold his sword, as Brutus did, while he fell on it.

He wondered why he was so calm. The prospect of drowning himself in a few hours ought to shrink his testicles, shrivel his penis, loosen his bowels. He had never seen himself as brave. Maybe subconsciously he didn't think he'd go through with it. He would, though. The savage god Suicide beckoned. He had to follow and obey.

Chapter Eight: 7:16 a. m.

FIFTEEN HOURS TO LIVE

With fifteen hours to live, he continued to lie abed, staring up at the ornate faux Victorian ceiling fan. His eyes roamed the master bedroom. Spacious enough for a movie star, it contained just three items of furniture: a night table, a chest of drawers, a vintage caned rocker. On the wall was a grandfather clock that chimed the hours. His second wife had furnished the bedroom with family heirlooms and estate sale antiques—a mahogany breakfront bookcase, a French vanity dressing table, an armoire wardrobe, a Chinese Chippendale desk—but now they were gone, gone with the wind, gone with Pru. Her spirit haunted not just the master bedroom but the other rooms. The house still belonged to her (she'd bought it with cash) and there were nights when he thought he heard the thin eerie sound of her cello from the opposite wing. He'd been dreaming.

Nee Prudence Cartier-Vandiver, Pru came from a patrician WASP family in Vermont. An only child and a musical child prodigy, or close to one, she's been educated at Barnard and Julliard before teaching cello, composition, and music appreciation at a couple of Sister Schools and then heading west, to Mount Olympus College, where she'd been active in women's causes and postfeminist organizations. He'd approached her after a concert the day after landing his teaching post; she had played Elgar's cello concerto. He had taken her to dinner at a vegan restaurant she'd heard about. What he liked best about her was that she was less like his demonic first wife than any woman he could've found. The earth did not move under his feet as it had with Tencha, but something clicked — a recognition neither physical nor spiritual yet palpable. Compatibility. He and Pru knew they could live together.

Pru was not beautiful or ugly or pretty or plain. Bombazine's sister Catherine called her nondescript, but she wasn't. Pru defied description. Hers was an intelligent face, too long and thin, a Modigliani painted when the master was drunk or hung over. She was four feet ten inches tall — no taller than her cello — and sensitive about her height, though she refused to wear high heels. (She found them oppressive and uncomfortable and put them in the same category as "falsies.") She weighed a hundred pounds and worried about getting fat.

After one too many glasses of wine at the vegan restaurant, he'd suddenly blurted, "I think we should get married."

Thus far he hadn't touched her. She'd laughed. "We hardly know each other."

"I know you. Today you played the Elgar concerto better than Gregor Piatagorsky. But not as well as Yo-Yo Ma. You should use less bow pressure in that slow passage toward the end. Place your bow a little further from the bridge."

He was winging it, but he could tell she was impressed. Tongue in cheek, she said, "Oh, really? I should marry you because you know something about the cello?"

He took another chance. "I know you're in your late thirties. You biological clock is ticking. You may not get a better offer."

She glared at him—had he gone too far? "Look, Mr. Retro," she said tightly. "I don't need marriage and children to define or fulfill me."

"Good. Because I couldn't do either."

"You're a tad old-fashioned, aren't you."

"I'm a postfeminist, like you. Before that I was a feminist. And a pre-feminist."

"Which is what," she said, pretending to be bored. "There's no such thing as a pre-feminist."

"I was one. In high school I made my dates pay their own way to the movies."

"You're ridiculous. Such a silly man." But he could tell she was curious. "And when do you think I should marry you?"

"When? You already want me to set a date? If you're going to rush things, forget it."

She laughed affectionately. "George, that has to be the worst marriage proposal I've ever heard. And I thought I'd heard them all. Don't take it personally, but I wouldn't marry you if you were the last man on earth."

That was when he knew he had her—it was the way she'd said it. He knew she found him attractive and had not received many proposals. He took her home (she lived alone), asked to come in for a drink, made passably successful love

63

to her, and married her the following month. It was as if fate had penned a script. Everything was easy and effortless. After being battered and bullied by Tencha, it felt good to be the Alpha Male in a relationship again. Her family took it well—he didn't have their kind of money, but he did have a name as an author and critic they'd heard of, and they'd come to fear their little princess might end up a spinster. They hadn't known that marrying him would entail her becoming the stepmother of a monster. Nor had she. But that's what happened.

She'd acquitted herself admirably, beyond the call of duty. Miguel was a handful, but he had loved and accepted Pru, and he was often away at boarding schools. Bombazine was in her debt. For years, after Miguel had left for college in upper New York State, they had driven to the Mount Olympus campus together every morning, taking turns behind the wheel. Remembering this made him want to cry. He wanted her back.

Now the phone rang. He groped for it on the night table. "What," he growled.

"You sound just awful," laughed Meridel Baxter, his publicist. "Did I wake you?"

"Not really. I was lying here thinking about killing myself."

"Well, don't. I have news, babe. Good and bad.'

"What's the bad?"

"MGM bailed. Babs says they found the project too artsy."

Despite himself, he groaned. "What's the good?"

"Lionsgate is still interested. The studio with the screenwriters that know about you. Miramax may partner in the financing."

"And how should I feel about this?"

"Are you serious? Lionsgate did *The Hunger Games* and the *Twilight Saga* and the Tyler Perry movies. *Crash* won the Best Picture Oscar."

"I missed those movies. I watch Woody Allen movies. Are you still coming today? You don't need to."

"First class on Delta. I'll be at you house around two with lunch."

"Don't bring lunch. I'm not hungry."

"I'll also bring your birthday present. How old are you now?"

"Too old for you. Unfortunately."

"But my mom's available. Ha-ha, just kidding. See you around two, babe." She rang off.

Bombazine had shaken his head. Now he'd have to shave today. But Meridel always made him feel better. Were he twenty years younger, with lead in his pencil, he would move on her. She had a frantic brightness and what looked to be a hard, firm, cheerleader's ass that made him not want to die yet. But he wasn't twenty years younger.

———— ————

He pushed himself out of bed and stumbled toward the bathroom. Argos, who slept at the foot, stirred and roused himself with a groan. Bombazine massaged his tummy with his toes and said good morning. As if annoyed, Argos sneezed and farted.

The master bathroom was a study in wretched excess: Pru loved high camp décor. It tickled her. She could be whimsical, like the spoiled rich girl she was, and the master bathroom reflected it. From its high ceiling hung a crystal chandelier. The gold fixtures on the black sinks reminded him of men's rooms in Vegas casinos. The gleaming ivory commode sported a heavy gold flush handle. There were scalloped sterling silver soap dishes with angel faces. There were heavy black Turkish bath towels, a mirror on every wall, a shower large enough for six people after an orgy. There were three powder-blue French towel cabinets and a powder-blue Italian Renaissance vanity. The bathroom was Pru's quirky museum — it bespoke her sense of humor and the absurd, a side of herself she rarely revealed. Bombazine hated the bathroom — the whole house, actually — but dared not change anything, and he was afraid to leave.

In their divorce settlement, out of guilt perhaps, Pru had offered to let him live in the house until he died, assuming she never returned to it. The feathers of his manhood ruffled, he'd declined the offer before reconsidering and accepting it the next day. Free rent for life sounded nice. More importantly, he hoped she would come back, and living in this house he'd be immediately available to her. She had not strayed far. After honeymooning with her new husband, Trevor T. Merriman, in Uplands, Swansea, Wales (the home of Dylan Thomas), Pru had moved into Trevor's russet-colored three-storied faux-Victorian mansion near the campus. Straight out of some forties Hollywood period movie, it had turrets and gables and a tower with a conical roof.

Bombazine had tried to take losing her with aplomb, but he'd been devastated. Adultery he could forgive. Hadn't

John Updike's philandering husbands defended it as necessary to survive the fatal anaesthesia of marriage? A Philip Roth protagonist dismissed marital fidelity as a retrograde goal, unattainable in the 21st century. *Greater love hath no man than that he lay down the wife of his friend* read some graffiti Bombazine had seen scrawled on a men's room wall. Though never unfaithful himself, he could forgive Pru's infidelity. She was twelve years his junior and Trevor even younger — a lanky, strapping Welshman with a thick shock of red hair, huge hands, and the vigor of a lumberjack. He probably had a big cock, too. Time was on his side. What Bombazine couldn't forgive was that Pru had left him for a literary deconstructionist.

Still trying to urinate but unable to get it started, which was often the case, he wondered if Pru might come back when she realized what a mistake she'd made by marrying such an empty-headed self-important oaf. The chance that she might was reason for him to stick around a little longer. It bothered him that Pru would be devastated by his suicide whether he committed it tonight or at Thanksgiving. But he couldn't let conscience deter him. He had already written a first draft of the thoughtful, considerate suicide note he would leave her in the kitchen. Rereading it now brought hot tears to his eyes, and that was a sign that the letter was maudlin and needed to be rethought:

My dear Prudence: My darling, I did myself
in not because I had to but because I should.
I refused to live without you any longer. But

please don't feel guilty. I'm sorry to have done it without telling you, my love, but it was time. I have prostate cancer that would have killed me unless I underwent radiation treatments that sounded messy and unpleasant and a bother. What seventy-year-old scholar wants to wear Depends? Woody Allen said he wasn't afraid of death but didn't want to be there when it happened. I didn't want to be there when I died of cancer. Or become so depressed I HAD to suicide. I hear that the pain of clinical depression is intolerable, and I'm pretty depressed already. I chose to cross the River Styx right now. Call me pro-active. Tell Trevor I said good-bye—for a deconstructionist he really isn't such a bad sort. Tell him thanks for the Scotch again. I didn't waste it, I drank it all. I'm sorry I didn't make you happy and I hope he does.

Ciao, mi amor. Sei l'amore della mia vita. You were the love of my life. Finish that cello concerto you're writing for me.

—Love, Georgie

His first wife, dead for thirty years now, had been wealthy too. How curious that both his wives had been heiresses with hyphenated surnames when money, ancestry, and pedigree mattered so little to him. Hortensia Villa-Lobos, "Tencha," had been a cyclonic force of nature for whom a

cyclone should be named. She'd looked like a movie star—
voluptuous, long-legged, slim-waisted and buxom, with the
high cheekbones of an Aztec princess. Her grey-green eyes
blazed. Her lightly accented English was sexy, her skin fair,
lips full and plump. When people stopped her to ask if she
was Sophia Loren, they would get a piece of her mind. One
gloriously sunny day, as they walked along the Avenida
Javier Mina in Guadalajara, an elderly tourist couple with
a Midwestern accent had made that mistake. They'd asked
for her autograph.

Tencha had flung the pencil and the notepad onto the
sidewalk. "*Esta ciego?*" she had snarled at the couple, who
edged away, having turned pale. "You are blind? Sophia Loren's mouth is too big and I'm younger! Go back to your
nursing home in the States! *Vete! Dejame sola!*"

The doddering old couple hobbled away as quickly as
they could. "You needn't have been so rude to them," Bombazine admonished Tencha. "You frightened them."

"They insulted me, La Bamba. This happens to me all the
time. What if someone stopped you and mistook you for
Jackie Gleason? "

Bombazine had shut his eyes and shaken his head. He had
married the only woman in the world who felt being mis-
taken for Sophia Loren was an insult.

Tencha's allegedly aristocratic family had moved to
Mexico City from Madrid in the thirties after a falling out
with Franco, then moved to San Antonio in the forties when
Miguel Aleman Valdes, a politician they had supported,
became president of Mexico and announced that his admin-

69

istration was nationalizing lands the Villa-Lobos family had confiscated from mestizo peasants. "*Los muy pobre campesinos*," Tencha called them. "Maybe my family did help itself to the peasants' land. The government had no right to interfere. Other families in Mexico City stole *campesino* land too and no one came after them. Valdes betrayed us. He did not care about poor people. To his face my father called him a lapdog of Mexican *capitalistas* in bed with with American *imperialistas* and Russian *communistas* who'd followed Trotsky to Mexico. *Si*, my family confiscated land, but they never missed Mass on Sunday and they prayed to La Virgen de Guadalupe and stuffed the collection baskets with pesos earned by putting the lands to good use."

Her family lived in a palatial villa in Polanco, a posh area in a wealthy borough of Mexico City, but woe betide anyone who called her a Mexican or a Mexican American. She was pure Madrid *Castilliano*, with no mestizo Indian blood in her veins. Tencha was a racist, an ethnicist, a bigot. She ostracized everyone, even herself: secretly, Bombazine suspected, she hated being Hispanic. When he'd met her, Tencha's *bandido* brothers Raoul and Ramon were getting rich from land fraud in South Texas, smuggling undocumented workers from Nuevo Leon and San Luis Potosi across the border to work the citrus farms of Valencia oranges and lemons in the broiling sun and paying them a dollar a day. They got by with it by making Texas border patrolmen shareholders in their corporation. For all their lofty Castillian ancestry, they quickly had adjusted to the role of corrupt *Mexicano* gangsters.

Bombazine had met the woman with whom he would wreck his life at a multicultural (largely Hispanic) book festival at Houston's Shamrock Hotel in the early eighties. On that fateful day he, like Carole King, would feel the earth move under his feet. He did not know that the person who makes the earth move under your feet can be the worst person in the world for you. Seismic oedipal and astrological oppositions might be at work. Tencha had felt the earth move too, but Tencha often felt it move; a literary camp follower, she would jump into bed with any man she found sexy if he was artistic or intellectual and with any artist or intellectual if he was sexy. Having found Bombazine intellectual and sexy, she had sidled up to him on a Friday afternoon after he'd read his prizewinning essay extolling Gilberto Owen Estrada, a Mexican poet who had died, tragically, at the age of forty-eight. The reading had so stirred the audience that he'd received a standing ovation. At the moment Bombazine was full of himself. It was the zenith of his life to date. What could go wrong today?

"*Hola*, Professor Bombazine," she said, extending her hand. "Bravo! You were *magnifico*! I am Hortensia Villa-Lobos from Mexico City. My family knows Octavio Paz and Gabriel Garcia-Marquez very well and hosts them often at the Casa Villa-Lobos. Do you speak Spanish?"

"I do. I speak, read, and write it."

"*Quieres dormir conmigo*? Would you like to sleep with me?'

The earth moved. Bombazine said, "I beg your pardon? Did I hear you correctly?"

71

He had heard her correctly. She was the most beautiful woman who'd ever propositioned him in Spanish, English, or any other language, and he fantasized about Latin women, whom he found powerfully earthy and ultrafeminine. "I'd love to," he cavalierly tossed, flattered by the bawdy flirting. "But I'm busy at the moment."

She seemed insulted — maybe she wasn't flirting? "It has to be now," she snapped. "*Andale, hombre. Vamanos!* Take me to your room, please. Do not waste time with formalities."

"*Lo siento, señorita.* I am sorry, but usually I demand flowers or candy first."

"*Ten cuidado,* señor. Do not make light of me. Do you think I joke? Do not waste an opportunity you will not have again. I am the most beautiful woman in Texas."

Bombazine glanced around uneasily. No one had overheard. He was excited if she was serious and curious as to why she'd be flirting so outrageously if she wasn't. It didn't occur to him that either way, she might be off her rocker. Against his better judgment, acting out of character but still sky high from that standing ovation, he escorted her up to his room. It was the boldest thing he'd ever done, the wildest risk he'd ever taken, and he would regret it till his dying day.

She had not been joking — ascending by themselves in the elevator, he'd believed it when she fumbled with his fly and unzipped it. She may indeed have been the hottest woman in Texas. Tencha was insatiable. They hadn't left his room until Monday morning, having hung the DO NOT DISTURB sign on the doorknob. By then the room smelled as

72

carnal as a zoo. It also smelled of spicy food: they had taken breaks from lovemaking and sleeping to consume six gourmet meals cooked by the Shamrock's Madrid-born *chef de cuisine* (Tencha knew him) and delivered by Room Service, and to drink several bottles of 1800 Coleccion Jose Cuervo tequila that accompanied the meals. Tencha could put away tequila like a man.

It was as if Bombazine were acting out some lurid porno fantasy. It was unreal. He'd fallen madly in love that weekend. When Plato called love a "serious mental disease" he had not meant Platonic love. Only a man with a serious mental disease would have been crazy enough to pursue a woman so patently crazy herself, on the strength of a sordid, seamy one-night stand that lasted three nights. An orgy for two. Yet he couldn't help himself. At forty he was old and experienced enough to know better, but not only was he bewitched, bothered, and bewildered, as the Rodgers and Hart song would have it, he was beguiled, smitten, and spellbound. The danger of going to bed with strangers is that no matter how wrong for you they may be, you can fall in love with them. Bombazine learned that the hard way.

Tencha was on the pill even though birth control was against her religion, but she turned up pregnant anyway. Having missed a pill or two, she was furious at herself, but abortion was impossible for a devout Catholic girl like herself. "Contraception *si*, abortion no," she said. "I am very religious but not *fanatico*." She was positive the child was his, for there had been no other man, and he did not doubt it. The child had to be his. "I had not been with a man for a

73

whole year when I met you," she assured him. "I had been like a nun. I had sworn off men. If there had been someone else, I would tell you." Bombazine was willing to marry her not just because he'd fallen in love with her but because he'd been paid a visit by Raul and Ramon, *los dos hermanos*, each brandishing a pearl-handled Mexican dueling pistol from the era of Emiliano Zapata and Pancho Villa. They had come to protect her honor, such as it was, so Bombazine assured his future brothers-in-law that he would do the honorable thing by their sister. He and his pregnant bride honeymooned in Guadalajara, Xochimilko, and Frenchman's Cove, Jamaica—Errol Flynn's old hideout, the loveliest paradise on earth. Their lovemaking was epic; he could not get enough of her; she had unleashed every ounce of carnality in him, and sexually she was insatiable.

After the honeymoon, things went downhill like an avalanche. Only the sex, always passionate if lacking in tenderness, was good. Within a month they had fallen out of love. Or infatuation. Within six months she was derisively calling him "La Bamba" and complaining that the role of a college professor's wife bored her. She hated the other faculty wives, who looked askance at her and probably thought she was mestizo. With her movie star looks, she argued, she deserved an underworld czar, an international trafficker in diamonds, or a shipping magnate like Ari Onassis, some dashing dynamo with a yacht and a fleet of Bentleys or Rolls-Royces. She deserved a billionaire, and Bombazine was not even rich. She had more money than he did. For the rest of her life, she feared, she'd be stuck in podunks like Ann Arbor, Michigan and Austin,

Texas where nothing happened but football games. She had only married him, she added, because he'd impregnated her and her religion forbade abortion. She was the prisoner in a shotgun marriage. *Una boda de penalti.* Divorce was not an option—the Church forbade divorce too. She felt imprisoned and Bombazine was her jailor.

A few days after the marriage, he had taken her to Houston to meet his parents. They were polite and cordial enough, as was Tencha, but Bombazine knew his father was unhappy about his having married a Mexican woman, especially a pregnant one. At one point, when they were alone, Mirabeau had told him, "Your mother was hurt that you didn't invite us to the wedding."

"Dad, it was a small ceremony. I barely made it to the church myself."

"Are you sure that baby's yours?"

"Of course I'm sure."

"There's something about this woman I don't like. But at least we know you aren't queer."

That was vintage Mirabeau. Bombazine asked, "Is that your blessing?"

"Guy, you know I don't like Mexicans. Not even the ones that work for me. Are you going to name the kid after me?"

"What if it's a girl? Tencha's in charge of that."

Tencha had borne him a son, Miguel, whom she named after Cervantes. They were not exactly model parents. They never visited her family in Mexico City and were never invited to. A *niñera* tended to the baby while he and Tencha ate

75

and drank and fucked and fought and shopped and traveled. Now he principally recalled the fucking and the fighting. Sex bonded them, but their quarreling "o'erflowed the measure," as Shakespeare's Philo said of Antony's passion for Cleopatra, and sometimes prompted neighbors to call the police. Tencha could not control her temper—screaming curses in Spanish, she would charge him with a frying pan, a butcher knife, a wine bottle. More than once he had to hit her in self-defense. He had never struck a woman, and it flooded him with shame and remorse, as if she'd been a child. What had the arguments been about? He could not remember. It didn't take much to push Tencha into a rage: drunk, she'd be spoiling for a fight like a bully in a bar. She was a loosely corked bottle of anger. Alcohol made her aggressive and pugnacious. The issue at hand, the bone of contention, was just a variable. Afterward, she'd always want to make up by making love.

And they always would. That's when they would have their best sex. Violence could arouse Tencha. Theodor Reik would have diagnosed her as a sexual sadomasochist. Bombazine the amateur shrink told her she indulged in counterproductive passive-aggressive behavior to demonstrate her emotional fortitude, induce guilt in him, and achieve a sense of vindication even in defeat. She scoffed and called him a *joto*.

She disclosed that as a child, her impudence had gotten her whippings by her father, Don Miguel Villa-Lobos, a punitive old-school *padron* ("*un padre de la escuela antigua*") who sounded like the bearded autocratic villain of the Zorro movies. A mean man with a leather belt. Tencha learned to enjoy the beatings—they were the closest she ever got to Don Miguel. There were also spankings with hairbrushes by her grandmother, a witchy *vieja* of the even older school, who liked to beat her granddaughters' bare behinds a fiery red after inspecting the crotches of their panties (*las pantaletas*) for crusty evidence.

Tencha was seriously disturbed, borderline psycho, and she knew it. In her more lucid moments he would beg her to get help, counseling, psychotherapy, a Catholic exorcism. But no. "*Me temo*, I am afraid," she responded. "I think psychiatrists are witch doctors. *Curanderos*."

"Darling, that's silly and superstitious and you know it," Bombazine told her.

"I know, I know. Be patient with me, La Bamba. You married me for better or worse. I know I am crazy sometimes. I am two women and sometimes the first woman watches the second woman from higher up and begins to cry. But she cannot stop her. I hate myself. I will get well, I promise. I love you. Give me time. Do not believe me when I say I hate you. You are my only hope, *mio caro*. Do not leave me."

He left her the next day. After another ugly fight, this one in Puerto Vallarta at dawn, he learned that she'd bought a 9 mm. Smith & Wesson 952 semiautomatic. She asked if he wanted to see it and he said no. He'd caught the next flight to Houston and filed for divorce there. He did not ask for custody of Miguel and couldn't have gotten it if he had: never violent with the child, thank goodness, she'd be indifferent to him one day and smother him with affection the next. Miguel's *niñeras* worked around the clock. No court would have awarded Bombazine custody. And what did he know about raising a child by himself? His parents were old and infirm. The boy was better off with her even if she was emotionally confused and immature. He was emotionally confused and immature too. After the bicultural divorce, which took forever, his visitations were sporadic. Bombazine loved Miguel like a son — that was easy, Miguel was his son — but found it impossible to like him. Miguel was too much like his mother.

Five years later, alone and drunk on tequila and driving ninety on an expressway out of Mexico City, Tencha was killed in a bloodsplattered accident in a red Alfa Romeo Spider convertible identical to the one Dustin Hoffman drove in *The Graduate*. Her destination was anyone's guess. Driving without a seat belt, she'd opted too late to turn onto an exit ramp, changed her mind at the last split-second, been sideswiped by a truck, and rammed into a concrete abutment. Dazed, blinded by blood, she'd struggled out of the Spider and staggered directly into oncoming traffic. A Volkswagen van hit her, catapulting her through the air over a four-feet-high guardrail. She fell to the serpentine level thirty feet below, landed on a tour bus, and bounced off it as though it were a trampoline. But she still wasn't dead. It took a lot to kill Tencha. She would not die until forty-five minutes later, when the ambulance arrived.

Como uno vive se muere. As we live, so we die. Learning of Tencha's death, Bombazine shed tears of grief and remorse. But not many. Tencha had galvanized his life with the passion of grand opera but warped his life, too. Her death was his escape from her. Miguel blamed him for the ghastly accident even though Bombazine had been 2,000 miles away at the time, guest-lecturing on the unjustly neglected poet Anna Hempstead Branch (the creator of The Poet's Guild) at Brown University in Rhode Island. Brown was one of his favorite colleges for a reading and a conference.

"Mama killed herself," the boy was to accuse him, "because of you."

"Miguel, no. It was an accident."

"She was drunk because you weren't there."

"Your mother was a sick woman, Miguel. I know you loved her. As did I. But she was a little crazy."

"She was sick, yes. But you don't abandon a sick person, *cobarde*. She missed you. She never got over you leaving us.

"Your leaving us," Bombazine said gently. "Watch your grammar."

"*¡Hijo de la grande puta! Zonzo!* Who cares about grammar? Mama was a kindhearted person. She had a loving side and you know it, *cabron*."

That hurt because it was true. Tencha indeed had a warm, kind, compassionate side that caused almost as much trouble as her cruel, dark, violent persona. She'd leave their car at a stoplight to help a blind man cross the street. She'd pick up hungry feral cats and bring them home, a practice that literally drove Bombazine, who hated cats, to drink. She'd weep to see a sign-bearing bum (I WILL WORK FOR FOOD) on a corner and couldn't pass a panhandler without emptying her change purse for him. She could be as kind as she was cruel. But she was always something extreme.

79

One day, he had dropped her off to shop at Neiman Marcus's in Dallas; they planned to meet for lunch in the Zodiac Room in one hour. Instead of his credit card he'd given her four fifty-dollar bills. When they reconnected, he asked what she'd bought.

"Nothing. I had to give away the money."

"You what?"

"Don't be angry, La Bamba. There was an old chicana hunchback crying in the ladies room. She wore a grey uniform and she was mopping up. *Pobrecita!* She looked so pitiful. She told me she'd just learned that her ninety-year-old father had died in Piedras Negras. She couldn't stop crying. I gave her the money."

"Why didn't you give her your money?"

"I had none on me. I will pay you back. I have more money than you do anyway."

"Since when do you care about the poor? Your family stole land from Mexican peasants."

"*Es possible que why I care, stupido!*"

At Tencha's funeral in Mexico City, no Villa-Lobos family member would speak to him, though Raoul and Ramon fixed him with murderous glares. When Bombazine married Pru the following year, little Miguel was sent to live with them, and did until he left for college at Rensselaer Polytechnic in Troy, New York in the eighties. He wanted to be an engineer like his late paternal grandfather Mirabeau Lamar Bombazine; had he inherited Mirabeau's engineering genes? Pru had been an ideal New Age stepmother, nurturing and caring, gentle and understanding, and Bombazine not much of a father when he was home and even less of one when he wasn't. Not a father at all. Painfully, every time he looked at Miguel he saw Tencha. Too beautiful for a boy, Miguel looked and walked and sounded like her. Had her soul taken over his? For some reason the boy hated him. What Miguel didn't know was that hating his father hurt his father less than it hurt him.

He hoped that Miguel would not be crazy like his mother. The hope was partially fulfilled, because Miguel was crazy in his own way. Rearing him had been an Herculean task, a challenge, an ordeal. Miguel missed Tencha, missed Mexico, and loathed America, especially Arizona and its conservative *gringo* politicians and aged retirees, whom he called *"los barbarianos."* The boy was angry, hostile, impudent, rebellious, defiant, and no fun. He managed to get expelled from three boarding schools—one of them military, another Catholic, the third military and Catholic. His favorite movie was *The Omen*, his favorite role models John Hinckley Jr. (who'd tried to assassinate President Ronald Reagan) and Squeaky Fromme (the Manson family member who'd tried to assassinate President Gerald Ford). He challenged older schoolmates, bullied younger ones, and fought with his teachers in the Castillian Spanish Tencha had taught him rather than English; even his Spanish teachers weren't sure what he was saying. He would curse them bilingually in the same sentence.

Once, he punched a male physical education coach in the nose, breaking it, later claiming that the man had groped him ("He was a *maricon*! What was I supposed to do when he grabbed my basket?"), and had gotten away with it when the coach refused to press charges. Miguel smoked unfiltered cigarettes at ten and marijuana at eleven. He had no interest in sports or girls and refused to attend football games or pep rallies or recite the Pledge of Allegiance or sing the school song. He excelled at math even though he never studied, frustrating his instructors, and in history class argued that America had stolen the Southwest and California from Mexico and ought to give them back. He flunked history and civics while making a perfect score on his SATs.

Bombazine was, of course, appalled and embarrassed by his son's conduct even as he privately admired such antics and occasionally took fatherly pride in them. He would never admit that pride to anyone, not even to Miguel or himself. And why not? He wondered now. He didn't know.

One private military school expelled Miguel for bringing three grass snakes to class in his pants pocket and turning them loose in the aisle. That night, Bombazine sat him down for a serious talk. "Why did you do that?" he asked.

"Why did I do what," Miguel (then thirteen) asked. The question seemed to annoy him.

"Bring those snakes to class in your pants pocket."

"Because I could not fit them all in my shirt pocket."

Bombazine closed his eyes and ground his teeth. "I love you, Miguel," he said. "You're my son. But you cause your mother and me a lot of trouble."

"My mother is dead."

"Your stepmother, then. We have to make a change."

"Good. What?"

"We have to find you a new school."

Miguel looked disappointed. "I was hoping you meant a new father."

Though hurt, Bombazine had to laugh. "Am I so bad? Why don't you like me?"

"Who says I don't?"

"Do you?"

"No."

"What can I do to make you like me?"

"Kill yourself."

The boy was incorrigible. By his twentieth birthday, having somehow made it through Rensselaer Polytechnic without flunking out or getting expelled, Miguel had spent four years in psychoanalysis. Bombazine had footed the bills, which were exorbitant. He and Pru saw little of Miguel after his graduation and leaving home and never heard from him unless he was broke. The wandering Miguel was peripatetic; as he searched for himself, his life became a series of forwarding addresses: Mexico City, San Francisco, Houston, New Orleans, Toronto, Boston, Provincetown. To his shame Bombazine didn't miss him. With Miguel conveniently out of sight and out of mind, the years flew by without much trouble. Miguel was always trouble when he was around

But of late, he had resought psychiatric help. "Professor, I think your son may be homosexual," one of his therapists given to stating the obvious reported as Bombazine was signing another check. "In fact, I think he is homosexual."

"What makes you think so?"

"He told me."

"He used the word homosexual?"

"He prefers queer. He's quite homophobic, considering, but that's not unusual in homoerotic subjects. He said he dreams about 'huge mouth-watering dicks' and wakes up wanting to suck one and then he wants to kill himself."

"What else did he say?"

"That he's manic depressive. Bipolar."

"I suspected that. What else?"

"That he's a girl trapped in a man's body. He has no urgent desire to transition, but he's thought about it. For now he just wants a masculine gay man for a partner and can't find one. And how could he? Gay men are never masculine or they wouldn't be gay."

"Come on. You're serious? How long have you been a therapist?"

"This is not about me, Professor. It's about your son. He's passive-aggressive and socially maladjusted. He may have what we call a dysthymic disorder. He suffers from clinical arrested development. He regresses and sometimes speaks in nursery rhymes."

"You've heard him do that?"

"With me he broke into a nursery rhyme — 'Itsy Bitsy Spider,' I believe. You should talk to him sometime."

"He won't talk to me. What else did he tell you?"

"That he hates you."

Chapter Nine: 7:54 a. m

DECONSTRUCTING TREVOR

Money had never mattered to Bombazine because he'd never had to worry about it. His father had left him and his sister reasonably secure with a pile of IT&T stock, a small soybean farm on the White River in Arkansas, and three gourmet restaurants in Montrose, a fashionable Houston suburb. He and Catherine had sold the farm and the restaurants right away. He'd made good money compiling American literature anthologies many college English departments adopted. No English professor in America knew more about obscure or totally neglected American poets. His teaching salaries had been decent. With St. Martin's Press, in 1968, he'd published a well-reviewed satirical novel — *In the Belly of the Pentagon* — based on his Army experience; there had been no film options, but he'd received small royalties until the hardback was remaindered and the paperback out of print. Now the book only existed in libraries and rare-book sites online.

Pru had called him tightfisted, but he preferred the word thrifty. (She was, after all, rich and he wasn't.) How he missed Pru! It was still hard to believe she'd left him. If only she'd told him she was unhappy. How was he supposed to know? She had never complained. A warning might've helped, but he hadn't gotten one. As husband and wife they'd lived together so effortlessly, for so long, that at some point he'd dozed off, and when he woke she was tearfully confessing that she was in love with a professor in his department and wanted a divorce.

He could not believe it. He tried to laugh it off. "Just tell me it's not Trevor T. Merriman," was his cavalier response.

"It is, darling. I'm sorry."

He'd felt the blood drain from his face. "Is our pistol handy? Where is it?"

"We don't own a pistol, George. Please don't treat this as a joke."

"Don't go," he said later as she was leaving. He remembered Tencha's having said that to him. *On récote ce que l'on seme.* What goes around comes around.

"Don't leave me," he pleaded.

Pru had felt guilty and ashamed and burst into tears and hugged him and left that evening. Her affair with Trevor had gone on under his nose. That he hadn't suspected said much about him, for Pru was transparent and Trevor's office across the hall from his. Bombazine did not put up a fight; if any man deserved to be cuckolded, he was that man. As a husband he had failed not just once but twice. Too often he'd been away at conferences — guest lecturing, promoting his books, reading his critical articles, accepting awards — and Pru had not asked to accompany him. He'd never invited her, of course — it had never occurred to him. Still, she might've asked.

He had not meant to be any more negligent or distant or thoughtless than other hubands seemed to be. Didn't time create a little distance, a progressive drifting apart, in even the best marriages? It was inevitable. Even when he and Pru were in the house together, each would be alone in his or her wing. Theirs was a mature and efficient arrangement, respecting each other's privacy and career and need for alone time. Pru used her wing as a studio for her piano, cello, and recording. Bombazine worked in the library, in the other wing. On a typical evening, he and Pru would stop working, fix and eat supper together, watch PBS or the History Channel, then go to bed, read, and fall asleep. Often they would fall asleep watching PBS or the History Channel. Sex happened rarely. After all that XXX-rated porn movie sex with Tencha, making love to Pru was G-rated. Pru was politically conflicted about sex anyway. She could enjoy it, yes, but to her, vaginal or anal penetration by a penis gave of subjugation, and fellatio smacked of prostitution, self-abasement, and that disgusting misogynistic pornographic movie *Deep Throat*.

With no woman had he ever had it all. If his marriage to Tencha had been about sex without companionship, his marriage to Pru had been about companionship without sex. Companionship might be the prime ingredient in a marriage, but it should not be the only ingredient. Bombazine and Pru were companions who never quarreled. They were too companionable to quarrel. Maybe she'd gotten bored. Had money been a factor? Trevor had it and flaunted it, Trevor with his faux Victorian castle and $65,000 BMW and vintage wines and gourmet shopping sprees. His family had grown rich from building and operating aerospace systems in Cardiff. But Pru was well off too, so money wasn't it.

Whatever it was, losing her to a literary deconstructionist was like losing her to an Al Qaeda terrorist or New Aryan Brotherhood member. In one of his early novels Saul Bellow wrote that if a man hated you, he hated you for as many reasons as he could think of. Bombazine hated Dr. Trevor T. Merriman for more reasons than he could think of. That was disturbing, since Trevor's being a literary deconstructionist who stole his wife would have been reason enough. But he'd never confronted Trevor or challenged him. He took it out on Pru.

"Why does Trevor make everyone call him Doctor?" he'd asked her shortly after their divorce.

"Maybe because he's a PhD?"

"Almost every faculty member is. You're a PhD, I'm a PhD, the janitor is a PhD, the campus security guard is a PhD, and nobody calls anybody Doctor all the time. The students and teaching assistants call us Doctor because they have to. Outside the campus no PhD insists on being called Doctor except Trevor."

"It took him years to get his doctorate. He's proud of it. His dissertation was rejected twice."

"I would have guessed twelve or thirteen times."

"I notice you don't mind being called Professor."

"I don't insist on it. Students can call me anything but Dude. Trevor upbraids people who don't call him Doctor."

"You sound like a jealous husband."

"Jealous ex-husband."

"You weren't jealous. You were glad to get rid of me."

"Jesus Christ, Pru! How can you say that? I begged you not to leave!"

"You didn't put up much of a fight. You just didn't want to lose me to him."

"Why would I? He's such a pompous ass. Does he make you call him Doctor?"

"Of course not. How absurd."

"I asked him what deconstructionism meant and still get dizzy spells from his answer."

"Deconstruction is complicated. You're the one who used to say that making itself intelligible was suicide for any philosophy."

"Heidegger said that, not me. I said deconstructionists were out to destroy literature as we know it."

"Deconstruction is just a theory. It may be on the way out already. Trevor fears it's passé."

"I hope so. It confuses the hell out of my English majors. It makes them look for inconsistencies in a story or poem to demonstrate that nothing in the story means anything, including the story itself."

"That's so simplistic," Pru had objected. "Trevor says the point is not to show that the text means something. The point is, there need be no meaning. The text can mean anything you want it to because it means nothing. As in no one thing."

"Oh, that's great! *The Jungle* means nothing! *Moby Dick* means nothing! *Uncle Tom's Cabin* means nothing! We can't find meaning in literature, we can only dissect it like a goddam frog to demonstrate that it lacks meaning. Jesus, Pru, Trevor goes to deconstructionist conventions and subscribes to deconstructionist newsletters."

"So? I remember a time when you subscribed to *Screw*."

Bombazine flushed. "That was different. I didn't take that magazine seriously. And I never went to a *Screw* convention."

"No, but you went to a porn star convention."

"For research. I was doing a paper on integrating hardcore sex into mainstream cinema and creating an avante garde hybrid. I interviewed the director Alec de Renzy and the actor Ron Jeremy."

Pru threw back her head and laughed merrily. "You take Ron Jeremy seriously enough to interview him and then ridicule Trevor? Look at how generous Trevor has been to you."

"Sure. After seducing my wife and running off with her."

"No one ran off. I walked. Trevor cares about you. He read that letter you wrote to the *Times* about what a farce the Thanksgiving holiday is and why it should be discontinued. He's worried about you."

Bombazine saw red. "Is he? Tell him I read his letter in *Commentary* about deconstructing Shakespeare. He defended some scholar who thinks Hamlet is a disguised woman in love with Horatio. I'm worried about *him*."

"He has other qualities, too. He truly appreciates women. Sometimes I've thought that you don't."

"Just because I don't understand them doesn't mean I don't appreciate them."

"He's been a good husband to me, George."

So was I, Bombazine would have said had it been true. He had not been a good husband, but a lot of husbands were worse. In a breaking voice remorseful and self-pitying, he said, "I guess I wasn't a hard act to follow."

"I love you, George. I always will. But I'm in love with Trevor. I can't help it. People change with time."

"I didn't."

"Maybe that was the trouble. You didn't change and I did."

She was right, he realized today, his final day, remembering that conversation. It was an epiphany that arrived too late. He had not changed. For a moment his head swam as if he'd caught a fist to the jaw.

Neither had spoken. Pru broke the silence. "Hon, are you taking your blood thinners? And have you taken Argos to the vet for his shots?"

Chapter Ten: 8:08 a. m.

FATHERS AND SONS

As he stood trying to urinate into his gleaming white toilet (made of vitreous china), with its solid gold flush handle, he danced on one foot and then the other to get his trickle going. Argos moved into the doorway, sat on his haunches, and watched with great interest. Dogs peed at will, so Argos may not have understood why a man should take so long getting started. Bombazine didn't understand either. Now he felt a burning in his urethra. He gasped. Was it prostate cancer or just prostate trouble? A tremolo of dread vibrated up his spine. He would die tonight, he remembered. The question was moot.

He looked down and couldn't see his penis or his testicles. His big gut, round as the Buddha's, blocked his view. He'd been unable to see his privates while standing up for several years now. At a fitness club, a trainer had joked that he looked like Babe Ruth: big belly, flat butt. Bombazine wished he still looked that good. The Bambino never weighed 280.

Having finally urinated, he gave his genitals a shake — they hurt — and moved to his black sink. The other black sink had been Pru's and he dared not use it. What if she came back today? Everything had to be exactly as she'd left it. If she came back today, of course, he wouldn't kill himself tonight. Or ever, assuming that she meant to stay.

He stared into the ornate mirror Pru had framed with the silver dimpled faces of cherubim. Once he'd been handsome enough, and muscular, with a Ben Hur chest and a full head of curly black hair like Lord Byron's. Now his paunch defined him: he was pear-shaped, his face bloated, his jawline softened by jowls, his blue eyes bloodshot and bleary from drink, his cheeks ruddy and veined. He was getting boobs, too. Handfuls of loose fat around his nipples. Tits! Soon he'd need a bra, a 42 DDD.

Bombazine moved from his sink, stepped down into the shower, and turned the water on full blast. How good it felt! He shut his eyes tight and wished to be a kid again even though he hadn't enjoyed it that much the first time. How had he become an old man so quickly? His first thirty-five years had crept by, his second thirty-five had flown by. From the late forties he remembered soldiers (they did not include his father, who was 4-F with flat feet) returning from the war. He remembered songs by the Andrews Sisters and the Ink Spots and Vaughn Monroe. He remembered the polio scare and its iron lungs and its March of Dimes. And movies in which couples danced the jitterbug and a corny country waltz called "Put Your Little Foot." From the very early fifties he remembered party-line telephones and Fedora hats, cigarette holders and hula hoops, Gorgeous George and Rocky Marciano and Saturday afternoon Superman serials at the neighborhood theater. Kids doing tricks with yo-yos. Men smoking pipes. His family religiously listening to radio shows like "The Fat Man" and "Inner Sanctum" and "Fibber McGee and Molly" and "The Shadow" until his father bought their first TV in 1952; they soon become addicted to "Dragnet" and "I love Lucy" and "You Asked for it" and "Your Lucky Strike Hit Parade" and shows featuring puppets with names like Kukla and Ollie.

Since then he'd come all the way from the golden age of radio-TV to the digital age of high tech and lived to see iPhones no bigger than candy bar miraculously multitask as telephones, walkie talkies, computers, phonographs, radios, TV sets, timepieces, road maps, word processors, recording studios, dictionaries, encyclopedias, libraries, electronic mailmen, electronic mailwomen, and cameras that took and developed pictures and even made movies. Digital robotic automobiles that could drive themselves were said to be on the way, and he hoped never to ride in one, though it sounded like a good way to commit suicide. As with the accelerated film in a silent movie, things were happening too fast for Bombazine, who could not keep up and had stopped trying. For he, technophobic despite his computer addiction, despised Information Technology and the so-called Age of High Tech, with its ceaseless prolifera-tion of cellphones and iPhones and iPads and other portable gadgetry he blamed for the fact that bookstores and record stores were extinct now — nostalgic relics of yesteryear, like pay-telephone booths and drive-in movie theaters. Soon those toys would mean the end of reading and writing and literature itself. Thankfully, he would not live to see that. Or anything else after tonight.

He'd been not a baby boomer but a war baby, born the year of Pearl Harbor. His father Mirabeau Lamar Bombazine, a garrulous, cigar-smoking, gladhanding construction mogul, had once been the center on the Rice University football team and weighed 300 pounds. Then become a civil engineer and made a fortune building hideous strip malls in the suburbs of a humid venal boom town, Houston, with no zoning laws, aesthetic concerns, or ecological conscience. "Who cares about the goddam spotted owl when there's valuable money to be made?" was Mirabeau's response when his son George asked why he and his unconscionable developer cronies were willing to despoil the environment.

"Dad, I care about the spotted owl," Bombazine found the courage to respond.

"Why? Who give a goddam if spotted owls and lions and tigers and whales become extinct? What the hell use are they? I haven't set foot in a zoo in fifty years. Try eating a lion or a tiger. And who wears whale skin? Eskimos? I wouldn't care if the goddam polar bear became extinct tomorrow. There's no money made in keeping elephants or whales or polar bears or bottlenose dolphins or red-ass monkeys alive unless you run a water park or a zoo."

"Dad, the animals are our friends. I'm not sure we ought to eat them."

"Now you're a vegetarian? Fine, I'll eat your steak tonight. Jesus Christ, guy!"

"I'm not a vegetarian. But we should be stewards of the planet."

"Stewards my ass. That sounds like the liberal baloney

they teach you at school. Animals exist so we can eat 'em and wear 'em. That's what they're for. They fulfill our survival needs and make us money."

"Money's not everything, Dad."

"Maybe not, but you'll play hell without any. Money can't buy happiness, but it can sure rent it, and the more money you make, the longer you can rent it for and the happier you'll be. I kid you not."

"But Dad —"

"Case closed. I hate tree huggers and animal rights kooks. They oughta shoot 'em all. Don't become one."

Bombazine had loved his father very much but disliked him a great deal more. Fathers and sons always have some trouble, but Mirabeau Lamar Bombazine was the quintessential 1950s father, a bad one in most ways, a blustering Woody Hayes/Bobby Knight prototype stingy with praise for his son and lavish with criticism. (Catherine, who adored him, he ignored completely except to call her "dumb" and joke about her weight.) That George made straight A's in high school did not impress him. The one time he'd applauded his son came when George, a catcher on the baseball team, had tagged a head-first-sliding baserunner so hard with the ball that he'd fractured his cheekbone. Bombazine had been contrite and concerned, but Mirabeau had cheered with approval and raised his allowance. "Nice guys finish last," he'd explained. "That kid won't try to bowl a catcher over again. I kid you not. Head-first slides are stupid anyway."

Bombazine never forgave Mirabeau for being a bad father.

And Miguel would never forgive him for not being a father. It was axiomatic that sons who'd had bad relationships with their fathers did not become good fathers, just as a daughter who'd hated her mother never became the Mother of the Year. On NPR Bombazine had heard a rabbinical parenting expert aver that the harm a child can do a father is nothing compared to the harm a father can do a child. "We never stop being abused by our fathers," the rabbi concluded. "No matter what they do to us, we never stop loving them and looking up to them and seeking their approval and they never stop withholding it and letting us down when we need them the most." Guiltily, Bombazine had thought: "But Miguel has never sought my approval. The rabbi is not talking about me."

Bombazine's mother — a demure Southern belle from Texarkana named Mary Martha, the principal of a finishing school for girls who never raised her voice and cried readily as if always on the verge of tears — had named him George Noel Gordon after her favorite poet Lord Byron, whom she'd fancied more for his dimpled chin and curly black hair than for being a colossus of English literature. Her husband, who hated the name George, and wasn't keen on Noel, either, had wanted to name their son Mirabeau Lamar, after himself; but with fierce maternal pushback Mary Martha said absolutely not. It was the first battle with her husband she'd ever won and the last.

"Mirabeau B. Lamar was a great governor and a great man!" Bombazine's father was known to roar with Texas pride. "He tried to kill every Indian in Jefferson County and most of the Meskins and almost succeeded."

"Wonderful," his wife, who taught Texas history, had muttered contemptuously. "Genocide could've been his legacy."

"Did he kill 'em all?" little George, age ten and wide-eyed with wonderment, had asked.

"Unfortunately, no," his father laughed. "Some got away. The Meskins escaped to San Antonio. The Indians ran off to Oklahoma and struck oil and opened casinos and got rich and started callin' themselves Native Americans."

"Well, aren't Indians native Americans?" the boy inquired.

"Hell, no. They're not any kind of Americans. Goddam savages rowed over here from India in canoes. That's why we call 'em Indians. I wish we had killed 'em all."

Bombazine's parents died in the eighties—his father of a massive heart attack from overeating, overdrinking, overworking, and impotent rage at not being able to rent happiness any longer; his mother three years later from ovarian cancer. Was cancer hereditary? Dr. Fallopius said yes, in certain families it was, and had mentioned breast cancer but not ovarian. Bombazine's sister Catherine, convinced that all cancer was hereditary, had resigned herself to dying of it once she had it. Catherine was constantly getting pap smears and genetic tests and breast sonograms and volunteering for "trial" therapies and taking out insurance policies to pay for cancer treatments she might never need and probably wouldn't.

"I'll have the ovarian kind," she would sigh fatalistically. "You won't even have cancer, George." She made it sound like a failure of courage or abdication of responsibility. Catherine had always envied him. She'd even envied his marriages even though both of them had failed. Once she had been pretty. Growing up, she and Bombazine had been close. Too close. He could remember hot, sultry summer afternoons in the fifties when they were pre-teens, left alone in the big Tudor house in Houston's River Oaks. They would swim in the backyard pool or play catch in the driveway (Catherine was a tomboy) or romp on the beds. Catherine, bigger and a year older, won the wrestling matches, kneeling on his chest and pinning his shoulders to the mattress. Bombazine was embarrassed when the roughhousing gave him pipe-hard erections, but Catherine didn't seem to mind the rise in his Levis, which neither of them ever acknowledged.

She may, in fact, have taken pride in his arousals. It was her first close contact with boys. "Wanna rassle?" she would periodically suggest. The fun ended the afternoon Mirabeau came home early from the office and caught them wrestling in bed. With a curled index finger, he'd motioned Bombazine to another bedroom and closed the door. Then he'd backhanded him across the face hard enough to leave a red welt on his cheek.

"Ow!" Bombazine had squealed. "Jeez!"

"Hurts, don't it."

It was the only time Mirabeau ever struck his son except to spank him — words were his preferred punishment. "Now get this straight, guy," he'd then said in a muted voice. "There's a million little gals out there you can fool around with. Your sister is not one of them. Do I make myself clear?"

"Crystal," Bombazine said, blinking back tears. "Thanks."

"Don't get smart or I'll give you another smack."

Mirabeau had not said anything to Catherine, and when Bombazine told her what happened, she pretended not to understand. "I just don't see what the big deal was," she said innocently. "Why'd he hit you? You weren't doing anything wrong." She was playing dumb, a role that came naturally to her.

After high school he and Catherine had taken separate paths that seldom crossed. She had married a politically reactionary ne'er-do-well ten years her junior—a bank loan officer named Derek Evans who, having convinced her that he was a financial visionary, had managed to squander her inheritance on risky investments: a Blockbuster Video franchise in Juneau, a sports car rental agency in Tierra del Fuego, uranium mines in Paraguay. The last time Bombazine had seen Catherine, she'd become a fat old lady who smelled of stale sweat, a symptom of her neurasthenic anxiety. He hoped she would call today; maybe he should call her this afternoon? Maybe he should do a lot of things this afternoon. But why, he wondered now, was he brooding about the past when it was too late to atone? Did people about to die do that? Probably, for one was never free of the past. "Don't look back," the ageless black pitcher Satchel Paige had counseled. "Someone may be gaining on you."

Bombazine knew who was gaining on him. A figure on a motorcycle with a skeleton head, a black leather jacket, and a scythe.

Chapter Eleven: 8:14 a. m.

O What A Beautiful Morning

Argos trailing, Bombazine padded into the vast kitchen, headed for the espresso machine, which made a hissing noise when activated, and made himself a demitasse. Pru and Trevor had given him a latte machine along with the espresso machine, but he never used it. Lattes were a step too au courant.

This morning, of course, the mere thought of breakfast made him queasy. He'd never understood how death row convicts could enjoy that last meal they got to order. Could nothing ruin their appetites? He opened the fridge, which he still called the "icebox," and took out half a T-bone, prime beef cooked rare and, left over from last night, wrapped in foil. He tossed it into Argos's bowl. Argos loved T-bones, but this morning he wasn't interested; he took a sniff, walked off, stopped, turned, and regarded his master reproachfully, as though the meat were tainted. Again Bombazine thought: Does he sense what I'm going to do today? He may think I'm going to abandon him. I am. But Pru will take care of him. I can't take Argos with me...

He ambled into a living room also vast and minimally furnished: a black leather divan, a lamp, a coffee table, a cushy chair. The front door opened directly into the main living area; elsewhere in the living room, a short flight of stairs led down and a parallel short flight of stairs led upward. But every room in the house was bi-level, even the bathrooms and a small room containing just a washing machine and clothes dryer. In every room Bombazine was either stepping down or climbing up each time he moved, and Pru had laughed when he'd complained.

He flopped down on the black couch and finished his espresso. He'd have to walk Argos and throw him his Frisbee before J. J. arrived for their old guys' dip in the hot tub. At ten Conchita Maria Vargas, the tiny-waisted Peruvian illegal who looked like Penelope Cruz, would arrive to houseclean; when he left the world, he would not leave behind a dirty or messy house. There wasn't much to clean—the house was L-shaped and he never ventured into Pru's wing—but he paid Conchita Maria $80 every other week to clean it just to have some contact with a human being in the world outside. Even he needed that, and he enjoyed ogling her when she wasn't looking. She knew it too, he suspected.

He had to edit his suicide note, too. It needed pruning and polishing; it was wordy, maudlin, melodramatic. A suicide note should be short and businesslike and read as if dashed off by a Roman Stoic, an Epictetus, a Marcus Aurelius. The last letter he wrote had to be letter perfect. In Capote's simile, as tight and seamless as an orange. Who knew how many people might read and critique it?

Again he wondered why he was so calm. Being so brave. It wasn't like him. He leashed up Argos, found the Frisbee,

102

and they trotted outside. He gulped the purified sugar of the mountain air. It was a glorious Indian summer morn, cool (the afternoon would be warm) and sunny, with a clear aquamarine sky. He could not have asked for a nicer day to kill himself.

The house lay isolated in what locals called "the country" even though it was just a ten-minute drive from the campus and a fifteen-minute drive from The Village. On either side stretched a weedy lot half the size of a football field. His front yard was a quadrangle of pebbles. Parked on the gravelly street in front — there was no driveway or garage — was the silver Mercedes-Benz E-class hybrid Pru had given him for his sixty-ninth birthday. Another demeaning gift he'd accepted, but only after she'd sworn that Trevor had not contributed. Later Bombazine learned it had cost her $53,000.

The back yard, Pru's garden, was now a tangle of weeds, black banana plants, thorny pyracantha, yellowed agave blades, dead brown ferns hanging from tree branches, and decomposing fecal dumps courtesy of Argos. Bombazine seldom went out back; it made him feel guilty and he hated yardwork.

The house was ugly too. It was the perfect house for a recluse. If you want to live happy, live hidden, went the adage. He lived hidden but not happy. He was lonely. Pru urged him to go out, but where would he go? And why? Everything he needed — his medications and groceries and booze and office supplies and even the occasional restaurant meal — was delivered here, as were his stroker magazines: *Barely Legal* and *Finally 18* and *MILFS* and *40+*.

Thank God for the postal service and Amazon.com. On Sundays his *New York Times* got thrown.

The hideous lopsided house had a history. It was the only split-level ranch-style house for miles in any direction. "Split-level ranch style" sounded like an oxymoron, but there was such a thing. Amateurishly designed and hastily built in the fifties by a Vegas mafioso on the Witness Protection Program, the house had the crooked, lopsided look of melting plastic. With superstitious illogic, locals gossiped that the house was haunted after gunshots were heard from it one night and the mafioso's wife was seen no more. He himself had moved out in the dead of night. With his two children, media reported, he'd relocated to what he hoped would be safer witness protection elsewhere. But to no avail. A month later, in Farmington, New Mexico, he'd been shot to death.

For years the "haunted" house had languished unoccupied, going to seed, awaiting the wrecker's ball. When they'd married, Pru had rescued it—bought it for a cash pittance and paid to have it remodeled, rewired, repainted, refinished, reventilated, and redecorated without appreciably improving its appearance. Bombazine had begged her not to close on it; this was the only time she hadn't followed his counsel in an important matter except for her decision to divorce him and marry Dr. Trevor T. Merriman. Pru was a practical, levelheaded woman, the last person Bombazine thought would want such a house, but she had her quirky, whimsical side. The house was proof of that.

Today he walked Argos half a mile and too quickly tired. On the way back they stopped in a weed field and he unhooked the leash and tossed the dog a green plastic Frisbee. Alaskan Malamutes weren't noted for Frisbee skills, and Argos had lost a step with age, but he could still go get it. He may have thought he was a Border Collie or German Shorthead Pointer. With each of his running-and-leaping catches of the spinning disc, Bombazine applauded and yelled, "Good dog! Yessiree! Great catch, Argos!" Today the dog was at the top of his game; Bombazine would've filmed it had he not forgotten his iPhone 5S in the house. It wrenched his heart with a mean fist to realize that he would never toss Argos a Frisbee again.

Back at home, winded from the exercise, he lumbered out to the patio and set the hot tub for a scalding temperature. Then he collapsed on the black living room divan that had cost him $4000 and waited for his best friend other than Argos. With the Pandora device on his iPhone that activated speakers in every room and on the patio, he switched on a Country Western mix. In Houston he'd grown up with Country, and next to classical he loved no music more. He cherished the names of the older singers—Conway Twitty, Merle Haggard, Donna Fargo… Jessi Colter, Faron Young, Ernest Tubb, Johnny Cash … Shelly West, Country Charley Pride, Lefty Frizell, Ferlin Huskey, Lacy J. Dalton. No Nashville public relations flack could have dreamed up such names. They had to be real.

The doorbell rang. Argos barked, rose, and sprinted to the door. He recognized the smell of Old Spice aftershave. John Jacob Auchincloss had arrived. The day, Bombazine's last, was about to get really weird.

Chapter Twelve: 8:42 a. m.

JOHN JACOB AUCHINCLOSS

Argos loved John Jacob Auchincloss, or "J. J.," but it was unrequited love. Afraid of dogs, every time he came over the prissy old professor would shunt Argos aside with the point of the umbrella he used as a cane. "Mongrel, get thee hence!" he commanded today.

"He's not a mongrel," Bombazine objected. "He's a pure-bred Alaskan Malamute."

"I don't fancy dogs. They stink. They shit and just walk away from it. They sniff each other's asses the way liberal politicians do. They even lick their own assholes."

At Mount Olympus College J. J. held an august title: Distinguished Professor of Political Science. He was responsible for just one course — "The History of Modern Conservative Thought" — but it was so popular with students from rich Republican families that he had to teach five sections. J. J. was an eccentric fop who affected a British accent and hated liberals worse than Rush Limbaugh did. Politically to the right of Ethelred the Unready though to the left of Alaric the Visigoth, J. J. taught his classes that the poor, especially the blacks, were poor by choice and that the rich were rich because the cream always rises to the top. He taught that if you redistributed the wealth pie in equal slices on Saturday, the people who'd owned most of it on Friday would own it all by Monday morning. But everyone, J. J. added, might be rich were it not for government. "All government," he would quote H. L. Mencken, "in its essence is a conspiracy against the superior man: its one permanent object is to oppress and cripple him." In his lectures J. J. would invoke Jesus Christ. "In the parable of the talents," he preached to his classes, "Jesus upheld the profit motive. He praised the profitable servant who'd doubled his money and admonished the unprofitable servant who'd squandered his. Read Matthew: twenty-five. Contrary to liberal perversion of scripture, Jesus was a capitalist, not a socialist. He liked money and advocated making money. He was, after all, a Jew."

J. J. offered such notions as truths held to be self-evident, like those stated in the Declaration of Independence. It made no sense that Bombazine—a registered Democrat, former ADA member, Obama supporter, and MoveOn.org contributor—would like such a man, or that such a man would like him, but they'd liked each other right away. No one, not even they, understood why. "I suppose we make each other possible," J . J. ventured when asked. More than once, at his own peril, J. J. had defended Bombazine against the tenure committee at their ultraconservative private college, wielding his influence to ensure that Bombazine, an unabashed liberal, got treated fairly.

Bombazine and J. J. had been the campus odd couple, politically incompatible, the James Carville and Mary Matalin of Mount Olympus College. Physically J. J. resembled Mad magazine's Alfred E. Neuman and TV's Howdy Doody. He had their red hair (dyed — his hair was grey), freckled nose, jug ears, irregular teeth, and imbecilic "What Me Worry?" grin. Today he wore a seersucker suit with a white shirt, blue suspenders, and a red bow tie — the same outfit he wore every day, like a uniform. Every Wednesday morning since Pru's departure, he'd come over to soak in Bombazine's hot tub, soothe his creaky bag of bones, and denounce the President as a Muslim terrorist born in Kenya and about to impose Sharia law on the United States of America.

And now he was disrobing, leaving a trail of clothing behind him on the floor. Naked as a nudist, skinny as a cadaver, he hurried out to the patio, then stopped and whirled around. "What's that music playing?" he asked, making a face. "Country Western again? Last week, you played Homer and Jethro."

"You mean Flatt and Scruggs," Bombazine corrected him. "Their score from *Bonnie and Clyde*."

"My ears still ring from it. Play some music. Samuel Barber. But not the Adagio for Strings. I hear that everywhere. Even in church."

Bombazine laughed. "You haven't been to church since Joe McCarthy's funeral." He fiddled with the Pandora mechanism until he found a mix of Samuel Barber oeuvre. "How about *Music for a Scene from Shelley*?"

"It'll do. I had cocktails once with Barber and his husband Gian-Carlo Menotti and their son the Met conductor Thomas Schippers. It was before an Eastman-Rochester Symphony concert. Nice nuclear family." J. J. giggled. Before easing into the steaming hot water, he stretched in the morning air, raising his arms to the turquoise sky.

Repelled but fascinated, Bombazine gazed upon J. J.'s naked body as if beholding a prehistoric reptile. It was the worst body he'd ever seen belonging to a human being not a corpse. Loose skin hung in folds from the undersides of J. J.'s upper arms like fat from a turkey's neck. His caved-in chest was so thin Bombazine could count his ribs. His bony legs were bowed. He had a little pot belly like a pelican, and though his penis was smaller than an egg, his testicles hung almost to his knees. Stripping, Bombazine wondered if he looked as bad to J. J. as J. J. did to him.

Both men were big on reading, baseball, modern classical music, Mexican food, history, philosophy, political debate, and Scrabble. J. J. was perennial Mount Olympus College Scrabble champion. Bombazine suspected that J. J. had never played any games but Scrabble, bridge, checkers, and chess, but the old fussbucket knew his baseball backwards and forward. To him baseball was not just a sport but an intellectual hobby like ornithology or lepidoptery; his statistical knowledge was encyclopedic, his love for the game even deeper than that of his friend and fellow political ideologue George F. Will.

"Did the Dodgers win last night?" Bombazine asked this morning.

J. J. scoffed. "Who cares? The Dodgers ceased to be the Dodgers when they moved to La-La land. Yes, they won. They beat the Astros, nine to three."

As a Brooklyn Dodger fan in the fifties, J. J. had worshipped

Duke Snider, the silver-haired blue-eyed slugger who patrolled center field. "Duke was a better fielder than Mays or Mantle," J. J. would argue. "Christ, that man could jump! He had steel springs in his legs. He could soar through the air like Nijinsky. Now they've ruined baseball with their bloody pitch counts and designated hitters and instant replays."

"It's still the greatest game ever," Bombazine would say. Though Houston had been a St. Louis farm club in the fifties, he too had rooted for Brooklyn. He'd only become an L. A. fan when the Dodgers moved west.

J. J. shook his head. "The game is dying. There are no American players anymore. Even our blacks don't want to play baseball. The box scores read like the Santo Domingo telephone directory. Spic and Spanish. Everyone is Cruz and Perez and Lopez and Martinez and Gonzalez and Sanchez and Rodriguez."

Bombazine bristled—he still hated it when his friend got ethnic. "J. J., most Latino players come from families that were starving back home. Some have become philanthropists. St. Augustine said, 'Learn how much God has given you and from it take what you need; the remainder is needed by others.'"

J. J. harrumphed. "Augustine was black, so naturally he'd be for government handouts. Oh, I'm pulling your wanker, old chap. Latinos make good players, but like Stephen Spender, 'I think continually of those who were truly great.' The 'fifty-three Dodgers. Snider and Campanella and Robinson. Hodges and Reece and Furillo."

"That team lost to the Yanks in the World Series."

"Only because Billy Martin played over his head. I'm glad the big-nosed little dago drove off a cliff."

Bombazine felt a chill. Drove off a cliff. He'd forgotten about his rendezvous with death.

He tuned J. J. out and listened to the music. Barber's *Scene from Shelley* was dissonant yet romantic, swelling with passion and yearning. Shelley had drowned because he couldn't swim. A role model for the ages.

Death by Water.

J. J. claimed to be related to the storied New York/New England Auchincloss family, of which Jacqueline Bouvier had become a member, a stepdaughter, before becoming Jacqueline Kennedy and later Jacqueline Kennedy Onassis. He wore the distant kinship like a badge. "I sunbathed with Jackie once at the Cape," he would brag. "We had great fun. She was not nearly so pretty as in her photographs. That square jaw. She was photogenic, though. We enjoyed a Pernod on the beach at sunset." J. J. was always enjoying a Pernod or Mojito or some other exotic drink with some luminary at the Cape, at La Grenouille in Manhattan, L'Espalier in Boston, or Spago in Beverly Hills. Though he seldom left the campus, he'd be planning for lunch one week with Fox News's Roger Ailes in Manhattan and brunch the next week with William Kristol or Peggy Noonan in D. C.

Bombazine never called him on it. J. J. had attended Choate and Yale—that could be verified. He had written books about Russell Kirk and Edmund Burke and William F. Buckley—that too could be verified. And he may have been as comfortably well off as he claimed, though he drove

111

not a Bentley or Lexus or BMW but a Toyota Avalon that cost $35,000. He boasted that his former students ran the country as politicians, university chancellors, hedge funders, media moguls, lobbyists, bankers, corporation heads, and Wall Street felons. He was proud of them all. Especially the felons.

"Lovely morning," J. J. was saying. "How's your sex life?" He liked to pry about Bombazine's sex life even though he himself had none. The subject of his sex life was taboo. There were no women in his bed, nor men, nor boys or girls, and he was not fetishistic or bestial or onanistic or necrophilic. He was heterosexual but celibate. Bombazine suspected that J. J. was too ugly for anyone to go to bed with except a blind person. Conceivably he was asexual—a bookish ascetic who, were he not a professor, might have been a monk or Jesuit scholastic.

When Bombazine disclosed that Meridel Baxter was visiting him today, J. J. chortled, "Old chap, that randy wench needs a shagging and she fancies you. That's why she's coming."

"How would you know?"

"I met her at a cocktail party at your house. Remember? The little harlot even flirted with me. Clearly she's what one used to call a nymphomaniac. But attractive. There's a touch of Tuesday Weld about her. Give her a bonk."

"Mind your own business."

"You need a woman in your life. It's not healthy for you to be without one. I can, but you can't. Personally, I think the gash cause men more problems than they solve."

"The gash? Jesus, man, you sound like a misogynist."

"Mencken defined a misogynist as a man who hates

women as much as women do. How's Pru getting on with her new husband?"

"They seem to be making a go of it."

"*Tant pis*. I don't like Merriman. He's a limousine liberal. A bleeding heart do-gooder. He doesn't deserve Pru. The woman plays Haydn's cello concerto better than Jacqueline du Pre´. But I don't think you felt much passion for her."

"Who cares what you think?"

"It was that Mexican vixen who gave you the horn, as the Victorians put it. That wetback who crashed her Alfa Romeo. What was her name?"

"Tencha. She was no wetback. Her family was well off. She happened to be my wife and the mother of my son."

"Why in God's name did you marry a Mexican spitfire?"

Bombazine flared. "What the hell is a Mexican spitfire? An airplane? A Hollywood stereotype? With you everybody is an ethnic slur. Take it from me, that woman was no stereotype. She was a bona fide original."

"I apologize for the spitfire aspersion. I never met the lady. I was going by what you've told me about her. She sounds like a mythological she-monster. A Mexican Medusa."

"Don't talk about her."

"Why would you marry a Mexican national with so many red-blooded American white women available? It was unpatriotic. Even a Mexican American would have been preferable."

"Tencha had dual citizenship. Maybe even triple. Her family came from Spain."

"And how did your family take to her?"

Bombazine frowned. Ultimately, it had not gone well. Tencha had not allowed his parents to see Miguel. One of their worst fights had started when Tencha referred to his parents as white trash. "My mother reached out to her and thought she was beautiful," Bombazine told J. J. "My father suspected she was crazy."

"I know why you married the *bruja*. You were like that cripple Phillip in Maugham's *Of Human Bondage* and she was your Mildred."

"I'm not wild about that comparison."

"It wasn't because she got herself pregnant. Though that helped."

"She didn't get herself pregnant. I got her pregnant."

"Whatever. You're a timid soul and married her because she took you places you hadn't the bollocks to enter on your own."

Bombazine bridled. "What would you know about bollocks, you old eunuch?"

"She broke through your defenses and made life exciting and dangerous. But she would've killed you. Be thankful you got away."

"I said I don't want to talk about her."

"Have you heard from your son?"

"I don't want to talk about him, either. Indulge me. It's my birthday."

J. J. slapped his own forehad. "Christ on a bloody crutch — I forgot your gift! Breakfast is on me. Let's get out of this fucking hot water and go have some Christian Mexican food. I'm feeling faint and I'm famished…"

114

Chapter Thirteen: 8:59 a. m.

A MORBID CONTEST

On Wednesday mornings Bombazine and J. J. breakfasted at a self-styled "faith-based Christian Mexican food" restaurant, in The Village. Popular with Mount Olympus foodies, it was called Caramba! Its outlandish but original and certainly unique fare was touted in gastronomic guides to the area.

First they had to drop by J. J.'s office on the Old Campus to pick up J. J.'s birthday present for Bombazine. Except for Brigham Young in Utah and Bob Jones in South Carolina, Mount Olympus College was America's most politically conservative institution of higher learning. Archconservative Arizona was proud as punch of it. The Old Campus was the original one, built during the first Theodore Roosevelt administration. Its mock-baroque Gothic Revival architecture reflected the grandiose vision of a quintet of philanthropic oilmen, giddily optimistic about the nation's economy, especially the hunk of it they controlled. One campus historian told Bombazine, "Those robber barons had so much oil money they didn't know what to do with it. So the old bastards built a Gothic Revival college and named the buildings after themselves just to make themselves immortal."

Those five Gothic buildings—bizarrely out of place in the Sonoran desert—looked like the medieval cathedrals in silent movies. In 1906 they were tall enough to be called skyscrapers. By then, Gothic Revival architecture also blazoned the campuses of Princeton and Yale and Boston College and Notre Dame. The staircases were steep and endless, elevators rare, escalators nonexistent. In the thirties, an adjunct campus was built, unimaginatively called The New Campus; its utilitarian, mustard-colored, two-storied buildings looked like post offices or Deparment of Public Safety buildings; they clashed with The Old Campus's charcoal-grey temples. There was talk of constructing a kind of Berlin wall between Old Campus and New Campus, but nothing came of it.

Snobbishly, J. J. never set foot on The New Campus. His office was on the first floor of one of the original buildings, Ezekiel Carnegie Cornelius Hall. As a bevy of chattering coeds in maroon sweaters hurried past them in the hallway, he unlocked his door and he and Bombazine entered. Cramped and claustrophobic, J. J's windowless office lacked for bookshelves. Volumes were stacked four feet high along one wall, below framed photos of Duke Snider, Roy Campanella, Johnny Podres, and manager Walt Alston after the Dodgers' 1955 World Series victory over the Yankees. Adorning another wall was a poster collage of J. J.'s political deities: Edmund Burke, Russell Kirk, Senator Robert A. Taft, William F. Buckley, Ronald Reagan, Judge Robert Bork, Margaret Thatcher, Westbrook Pegler. The room was less office than portrait-and-poster gallery.

On the rear wall, behind J. J.'s desk, hung a huge gold-framed oil portrait of Wallace Stevens, the Hartford insurance exec and Taft conservative who was one of the premier American poets of the twentieth century. Bombazine's English majors had been in awe of Stevens' poems, especially those they couldn't understand. "The Man with the Blue Guitar," with its Picasso cubism, was one example. Needless to say, Bombazine had not taught or anthologized "Like Decorations in a Nigger Cemetery," though he admired it, but he did teach "The Emperor of Ice Cream," a student favorite for its title.

"Who says there've been no poets on our side?" J. J crowed, turning on the lights. "Look at Wallace Stevens."

"He was the only one. Unless you count Eliot and Pound."

J. J. moved to his desk and removed from the bottom drawer a flimsy little hardback book. "Happy Birthday," he said, handing it to Bombazine. "A first edition. I found it on a rare book Internet site."

The dusty volume, its pages loose and yellow, was *Lincoln: The Man*, Edgar Lee Masters' revisionist biography of the sixteenth president. Bombazine had read it years ago and wanted to burn it. A hatchet job, it read as if penned by a crank. Honest Abe corrupt? A tool of Yankee bankers? A covert racist? What about politics brought out the worst in people? Even people like Edgar Lee Masters? Since learning that Lincoln had been so depressed in his youth that he'd tried to kill himself, Bombazine had admired Lincoln more than ever.

"It wasn't cheap," J. J. said "It cost a king's ransom. The last first edition extant. A signed copy."

Bombazine was touched. "Thank you, J. J. I'll reread it and put it in my Masters collection."

"I started to get you Dexter Wallace's unexpurgated printing of *Spoon River Anthology*. It was so risqué that Masters had to use a nom de plume: Dexter Wallace. But they were asking three hundred dollars for it."

Bombazine doubted this—his own copy had cost $39.95 plus a shipping charge.

"Let's go get breakfast," said J. J. "The Village awaits us. Caramba!"

The actual name of "The Village," the tiny picturesque college town, was Thessalonki, named after a Greek city everyone assumed was Polish and usually misspelled. People loved The Village. Even the people who worked in The Village loved The Village, though no one got rich there. The Village was a state of mind, a fifties trip to Primrose Lane, a *Saturday Evening Post* cover, a turning back of the clock.

Main Street, its thoroughfare, was a row of ice cream and yoghurt parlors, souvenir shops, art galleries, and rare book stores that sold vintage comic books. There was also a liquor store, a tavern with live music every night, a Western Union office, a coffee house, health food grocery, bicycle shop, a little branch bank, and an old-fashioned movie theater, with just one screen and a balcony reached by climbing a red-carpeted stairway, that showed cult films like *Harold and Maude, Eraserhead, King of Hearts*.

Main Street's buildings, wooden and rickety and two-storied, had been repainted in soft pastels (blue, yellow, red, and green) that looked to melt together in the rosy morning light. Bombazine loved Main Street. Street traffic crept along, accommodating more bicycles than automobiles, and pedestrians had the right of way. On either side of the north end were sweet little cottages fronted by sweet little yards with white picket fences and gardens of impatiens and pansies and violets. Most of the homeowners were openly gay now, but thus far no one had tried to run them out of town or beat them up or kill them. A Villager was a Villager even if he was, in the lexicon of conservative college boys, a "perv."

The restaurant was a turquoise-colored shack with an orange porch, al fresco dining in back, and a history J. J. called an American success story. Caramba! had been opened as HUNG'S by a South Vietnamese refugee, Nguyen Van Hung, in 1975, when Saigon had fallen. After twelve years of war in Vietnam, nobody in America hungered for Vietnamese food, so Hung changed the fare to Mexican and touted his little shack as a "faith-based Christian" restaurant. He redecorated the walls with framed velvet paintings of the Sacred Heart of Jesus, La Virgen de Guadalupe, Our Lady of Lourdes, and Our Lady of Fatima. To standard Tex-Mex dishes like enchiladas and tacos Hung added Nuoc Mam fish sauce, sweet Saigonese chili gravy, and Vietnamese chicken curry. The spicy hybrid specials, which he got away with calling Christian Mexican food, caught on, and the little restaurant flourished. Hung still ran it with his wife, eighty-year-old mother, two daughters, a Vietnamese chef, and three Mexican cooks who may have been illegals.

Rumor had it that Hung was a millionaire and a registered Republican.

"God, I love capitalism," J. J. would say each time he'd retold the story, forgetting how often Bombazine had heard it. "And American capitalism is the best capitalism in the world. If the Jews hadn't invented capitalism Americans would have. Did you know that Mohamed Atta, that Egyptian terrorist who planned the World Trade Center attack, shopped at Walmart and ate at Pizza Hut the day before he flew the plane into the North Tower?"

"Is that an endorsement for Pizza Hut and Walmart?"

"I'm talking about capitalism. It has no borders. Could Hung have done this well in Hanoi or Haiphong?"

"Vietnam did pretty well once we got out. We shouldn't have gone in there in the first place. We killed two million Vietnamese and now we're trade partners. We lost a war to some commies in black pajamas who turned out to be bigger capitalists than we were."

"That's what I loved about that war!" J. J. smiled radiantly. "Vietnam prospered! We converted it to our way of life! We did the same thing for Germany and Japan. We made them economic superpowers. South Korea, too. Our warmongering is humane and altruistic. The countries we conquer always flourish no matter how many bombs we drop on them."

"We never conquered Vietnam."

"No, but we gained their respect by napalming their villages. The love came later."

Bombazine changed the subject. "Why does Hung call

it Christian Mexican food when it's Vietnamese Mexican food? Because of the holy card posters and velvet Jesuses?"

"Hung's a naturalized citizen and a patriot. Immigrants make the best patriots. America was founded by Christian immigrants."

"The founding fathers were Deists."

"Just Jefferson and Franklin for sure. The others were atheists. Hung's family was Buddhist. He's a Southern Baptist now. Everything is economics, George."

The restaurant was jam-packed, but they found a table near the double doors to the kitchen, through which drifted aromas savory and exotic; they made Bombazine's gorge rise. With a dull dread in the pit of his stomach, he had no appetite.

One of Hung's slim velvety daughters, who looked twenty but was twice that old, brought water and coffee. "I'll have the Saigonese *huevos rancheros* over easy," J. J. told her. "Soft but don't break the yellow, with crisp bacon, *frijoles refritos*, and *tortillas de mais*. I don't eat white flour. And I said crisp bacon, not crispy. I hate that nonword crispy; it started with Rice Krispies. Give me a Vietnamese chicken curry tamale on the side, *por favor*."

"Just coffee for me," said Bombazine. "Black."

When the waitress had gone, J. J. asked, "No food? Are you sick? I'm treating."

"I'm not hungry."

"You look like Robespierre on his trek to the guillotine."

"You don't look so great either."

"Didn't you like your birthday present?"

"I liked it very much."

J. J. was silent. Then: "Are you going on TV to publicize your book?"

"No one has asked me to."

"I love being on TV. Bill Buckley's 'Firing Line' was my debut. But I wouldn't put any stock in that screenplay business if I were you. Studio heads are Jews. Ditto the producers and screenwriters. All Jews. Even the "gaffers" and "best boys" are Jews. Those people will drink from your mind and then break your heart."

"Stop it. That's disgusting. You sound like Mel Gibson."

"Just don't expect much from them."

"I don't expect anything. It's a lark. I love movies."

"Are you still writing these days?"

"Yes," Bombazine lied. "I'm working on a new book."

"Good. You should continue to work even if you are re-tired. Voltaire said, '*Travaux nous sauve de trois grands maux ennui, le vice et le besoin.*' Work saves us from three great evils: boredom, vice, and need."

"He should have thrown in depression."

"What's your book about?"

"Suicide in literature. That's what I've named it." He was telling this lie because he wanted to hear J. J's thoughts about suicide.

"Suicide? The hell you say." J. J. sipped his coffee. "Have you read *The Savage God* by A. Alvarez?"

"I have."

"Didn't he commit suicide?"

"No. His parents did."

"Have you read Emile Durkheim's *Le Suicide*?"

"Twice," Bombazine said.

"How about Howard Kushner's *Self-Destruction in the Promised Land*?"

"Just once. Good suicide book. How do you know it?"

"What don't I know? Fascinating plot device, suicide. Shakespeare overused it. Many of his best characters did themselves in. Brutus, Cassius, Antony, Cleopatra, Enobarbus, Ophelia, Lady Macbeth, Othello..."

"And Romeo and Juliet. What's your feeling about suicide? In real life, I mean. The ethics of suicide."

J. J. furrowed his brows and sat up straight. His steamy hot plate of Christian Mexican food had arrived. He placed his cloth napkin in his lap and picked up his knife and fork and cleared his throat like a mayor about to address a banquet.

"Suicide," he said, "is the American way. We're a country of chronic suicides. Millions of Americans kill themselves with alcohol and tobacco and hard drugs and greasy fast foods and sugar and cholesterol. An equal number do it with prescription drugs—tranquilizers, sleeping pills, diet pills, pep pills, painkillers, Ritolin and Prozac and Paxil and Methedrine and aspirin. Half this country is clinically depressed or traumatically stressed or addicted to something and wants to die. To which I say 'Fine, die!' We're overpopulated anyway, having opened our borders to wetbacks and aliens who'll vote Democrat."

"I was hoping for a rational answer. Something worthy of an adult."

"Very well, old man. Listen up. Suicide is the ultimate act of valor. A deliberate suicide, when one is conscious of what one's doing, is heroic. They should award medals for it. It's much harder to kill yourself than someone else. That's why murderers outnumber suicides ten to one. The Greeks and Romans exalted suicide. Aristotle said there were times when to quit living is actually reasonable and decent and hanging on is the bloody disgrace. Socrates eagerly took the hemlock. Everybody in the *Antigone* commits suicide. Sophocles was an accidental suicide. He died trying to recite a long passage from the *Antigone* without pausing for breath."

"Apocryphal story. And I asked for an opinion, not a dissertation."

"I can't please you, can I. May I continue? The Japs still respect suicide —"

"The Japanese."

"Ah, so solly. *Gomen, gomenasai.* And then there are the Jews. No wickedness is attributed to Jews who've suicided. No judgment is pronounced. Judaism has the children of a male suicide say the Kaddish for him because the soul of a suicide needs prayers more than other dead kike souls do."

"You had me till you said kike. Stop it."

"I say it to annoy you."

"Well, don't. How do you know so much about Judaism?"

J. J. scowled. Chewing on a Vietnamese chicken curry tamale, he said, "Jews rule America, old chap. Didn't you know? We are now the United States of Israel. Marx, a Jew, was right: everything is economic. Jews have a low suicide rate because they succeed financially. But liberals as a group

124

have a high suicide rate. Except for limousine liberals, they're always broke. They're prone to suicide because they're nihilists and atheists and agnostics with no faith in a higher power than government."

"Rubbish."

"It's true. Liberals believe that with a benevolent nanny government nobody would want to commit suicide. They've never been to Scandinavia, where the suicide rate is sky-high because the government wipes your arse for you. Norman Mailer wrote that the real terror of the liberal spirit is suicide, not murder. Show me a list of writers who killed themselves and every one of them, if he or she had any politics, was some collectivist bleeding-heart do-gooder who found life too Darwinian to endure."

"I'll run and get that list. Save my seat."

J. J. smirked. "A tad sarcastic this morning, are we? You should be in a better mood on your birthday. Where was I? For many suicides the act expresses impatience to get on with what comes next. I doubt anything does, but I admire bravery. Hemingway was no coward. I just wish the old fool had found a less messy way to do himself in. A shotgun in his mouth? His poor wife Mary had to scrub the walls and ceiling. Papa was inconsiderate."

"I've never thought of Hemingway as overly intelligent."

"You've never written about Hemingway. People have heard of him."

"I wrote a postmortem when he killed himself. It was not a reverent reassessment."

They were silent. Bombazine felt a stab of guilt about Pru.

125

His suicide would hurt her. In a seventies best seller, he'd read that suicide was a Fuck You sign waved in the faces of those the suicide loved. He did not want to hurt Pru or wave a sign in her face. But he had to drown himself tonight. Pru would understand. His suicide note would explain it.

J. J. signaled for more coffee. "The number of lefty writers who killed themselves is astonishing. Hemingway. Hart Crane. Sylvia Plath. Romaine Gary..."

"And Romaine Gary's wife Jean Seberg."

"Stick to writers. Add Virginia Woolf."

"And Cesare Pavese," said Bombazine. "He wrote the shortest suicide note: 'No more words. An act. I'll never write again.' Nine words."

"Brevity is the soul of wit."

"Add Arthur Koestler, Ross Lockridge, Jr., Yukio Mishima --"

"William Inge," J. J. said. "John Kennedy Toole."

"Anne Sexton. Good poet."

"So-so poet," J. J. opined. "Joseph Conrad tried to kill himself but failed. Damned fool shot himself in the chest. Novelists are poor marksmen."

"Malcolm Lowry was a probable suicide. Overdosed on his meds."

"He meant to. Hunter S. Thompson also. And Richard Brautigan. And didn't your Italian Hebe friend Primo Levi kill himself?"

"The coroner thought so. They weren't sure. It might have been an accident."

"He doesn't qualify," J. J. said. 'Scratch him. Throw in Randall Jarrell. No, that idiot walked in front of a Mack truck. But he'd been hospitalized for depression and slashed his wrists, so he qualifies. Poets have the highest incidence of suicides. Twenty percent."

"How do you know so much about suicide?" Bombazine asked.

"I know a great deal about everything. More names, please."

"Abraham Lincoln. He'd thought about it."

"Is that what Masters says?"

"He doesn't have to," said Bombazine. "It's documented."

"Lincoln was not a writer."

"He wasn't? Who wrote the fucking Gettysburg Address?"

"Name some more real writers."

"Thomas Chatterton," Bombazine remembered. "And Jerzy Kosinski. And the Scottish poet John Davidson. And John Gould Fletcher."

"Whoa," J. J. interrupted. "Who the bloody hell was John Gould Fletcher?"

"Only the first Southern poet to win a Pulitzer. He drowned himself in a pond in Arkansas."

"Oh." J. J. faked a frown and nodded gravely. "I thought he might be another of those poets you write about that no one's ever heard of. Arkansas, you say? I had an offer to teach in Fayetteville. Turned it down, though the pay was good. Students a tad slow, one would think. All that inbreeding…"

The conversation continued as a morbid contest to see who could name the most authors who'd suicided. Given his research, Bombazine had the edge. "Stefan Zweig and his wife committed suicide together," he said. "Barbiturate overdoses. John Berryman, whose father had committed suicide, jumped off a bridge into the Mississippi River."

J. J. said, "Charles Jackson, the alcoholic who wrote *The Lost Weekend*, committed suicide. He was in some Baptist dry state on a Sunday and couldn't get a drink. And did I mention the Russian poet Vladimir Mayakovsky?"

"No. And I forgot Kurt Cobain."

J. J shook his head. "Damn it, man, we're talking writers, not rock stars. What did Kurt Cobain ever write?"

"Just all the songs for Nirvana. The best rock band of Generation X."

"That's not setting the bar terribly high. Next you'll give me Abbie Hoffman."

"I will. He was a major historical figure of the sixties. He wrote *Steal this Book*."

"And many larcenous hippies did. Bookstores refused to carry it."

"Gentermen, good morning. How nice to see you."

Little Nguyen Van Hung, the restaurant owner, hovered over them. He bowed with a smile. In his sixties, Hung was still razor thin with the hard, wiry body of a young man. He stood barely five feet tall and looked as if he could run a four-minute mile.

"You fearing okay?" he asked. "Food good?"

"Delicious, Nguyen," J. J. said. "Best Christian Mexican food in Christendom."

"Wonderful food," agreed Bombazine.

"Then why you not eat?" Hung asked him.

"Not hungry this morning."

"It's his birthday," J. J. said.

"How old?" asked Hung.

"Seventy," Bombazine said.

"Seventy!" Hung bowed formally. "No charge today. Your breakfast is on house, gentermen."

"Absolutely not," J. J. protested, but the diminutive Asian stiffened and J. J. reconsidered. "Well, thank you, Nguyen."

"No, thank you," said Hung. "*Cam o'n ong.*" He pointed upward. "Thank Jesus."

J. J. clasped his hands. "Muchas gracias, hay-soos."

Hung bowed formally. "Happy Birthday, Pwofessor Bombazine. Seventy not old." He shuffled off toward the kitchen.

"Christ, man," reprimanded Bombazine, "I can't believe you did that. All I had was coffee. You let him comp your breakfast."

J. J. was staring toward the front door. "Don't look now," he said tightly, "but your ex-wife just walked in with her husband."

Chapter Fourteen: 9:43 a. m.

"A BLOODY AWKWARD ENCOUNTER"

The Merrimans, Trevor and Pru, looked to be dressed for a chamber music concert, not breakfast. Pru wore dark slacks and a dark jacket, Trevor a tweed coat with leather elbow patches, a white dress shirt, a black knit tie. Bombazine and J. J. rose. Bombazine gave Pru the desultory hug one gives an ex-wife who's left him for another man and then shook hands with that man, whose touch made his flesh crawl. Surprising for an academic, Trevor's grip was like iron; he did not know his own strength. Bombazine squeezed back as hard as he could. His right hand would hurt later on.

"I'd ask you to join us," he said, "but we were on our way out."

"How are you, George?" Trevor asked.

"Not bad. And you?"

"Happy as a clam, good as gold, and fit as a fiddle."

Wincing, Bombazine remembered that for an English professor the man was inordinately fond of clichés. What shit luck, he thought. What were the odds of this encounter on his last morning on earth?

Pru studied him with a frown, edged closer, and lightly

poked his shoulder. "I need to talk to you," she murmured. "I'll come by this morning."

"Do. It's your house."

She continued to frown. He frowned back. Her hair was too short, clipped in a gamine's pixie cut, and faintly visible along her upper lip was the down of a mustache. Pru did not shave or wax her face or legs or thighs or mons pubis or under her arms or anywhere. If men could grow facial hair, she asked, why couldn't women? She did not pluck her heavy Frida Kahlo eyebrows or use depilatories or lipstick or powder or rouge or deodorants or skin creams or fragrances. Au naturel, she dressed not up but down.

"You look marvelous," J. J. told her nevertheless.

"My love," said Trevor, "I think Nguyen has found us a table. Way over there, darling. It was grand seeing you, George. You too, J. J."

"Right," J. J. droned. "*Doctor* Merriman."

As the couple drifted off, J. J. said, "A bloody awkward encounter, I must say."

"Let's get out of here." Bombazine left a five dollar tip for Hung's daughter.

On the ride back, he chided J. J. "You shouldn't have called him Doctor like that."

"Why not? The man loves being called Doctor. He didn't hear the hostility."

"He's not deaf."

"He doesn't listen. He irked me by calling Pru 'my love' and 'darling' right in front of you."

"Why should it bother you? It didn't bother me."

"It should have."

"It bothered me a little."

"It ought to have bothered you a lot."

"Okay, it bothered me a lot. What should I have done? Challenge him to a duel?"

"You're in a horrid mood, old sport. Take some Prozac. Buy some Tampons. Are we on for Scrabble tomorrow?"

"Maybe," Bombazine said. He would play Scrabble tomorrow if he didn't kill himself tonight. Remembering his plan, he shivered anew.

J. J. dropped him off at the house and sped away, like a teenager, with a moaning of gears and a spray of pebbles; he was an awful driver. Bombazine went inside and flopped down on the black leather couch. He was expecting the young Peruvian cleaning woman who came on Wednesdays at this time, but still brooding about Trevor's calling Pru "my love" and "darling." It was silly, of course. J. J. loved to instigate. Let's you and him fight while I watch.

Pru had not mentioned his birthday. Had she forgotten it? Pru never forgot birthdays. Did he want her back? More than ever. And if he got her back, would they be happier this time around? Probably not. Reconciliations never worked for very long. He wished they hadn't run into her. And this morning she was coming by. He should want to see her one last time. But he didn't.

Now he hurt more than before. It was Trevor's fault. The possibility that for all his faults Trevor was a good person, thoughtful and compassionate and generous, gave Bombazine another reason to hate him. It was okay to hate a bad person, but hating a fundamentally good one made Bombazine feel guilty even if the person was a fool. He disliked people who made him feel guilty for disliking them. Trevor delivered Meals on Wheels to the very old and disabled throughout the Mount Olympus area. Trevor read to the blind at a state facility in Big Town and visited burn victims at the veteran's ward. Trevor sponsored and coached a Little League team even though he had no kids, had never played baseball (being Welsh), and didn't know a double play from a double entendre. At Thanksgiving, his favorite holiday, he cooked and served turkey dinners at a homeless shelter, and at Christmas he wrapped and delivered gifts for torture victims and played the bagpipes in the Salvation Army band.

Trevor was so kind and generous it was revolting. And he wasn't particular about it. Even Bombazine found himself on the receiving end of Trevor's largesse. Soon after marrying Pru, Trevor began coming by the house with her, his arms filled with bags and boxes of warm freshly cooked shrimp Arnaud or coquilles Saint-Jacques au gratin or lobster thermidor or boeuf bourguignon. He also brought cases of wines with names like Chateau Latour and Medoc Grand Cru and Lafite Rothschild. For Argos he'd bring cans of gourmet dog food lumpy with chunks of low-fat *pâté de foie gras* and gluten-free beef tenderloin.

Bombazine continued to brood about Dr. Trevor T. Merriman. Might the man be tormented with guilt and concern for the husband whose wife he had stolen? He should be. Pru's concern was genuine; everything about Pru was. But was Trevor's genuine? Whose idea were the CARE packages, the haute cuisine, the fine wines? Did they think he was destitute and starving? Did they know he was suicidal? The proud, manly, right thing to do would've been to politely refuse the handouts and help Trevor tote the packages back out to his $65,000 BMW X-Drive sedan. But Bombazine was fond of shrimp Arnaud and lobster thermidor and boeuf bourguignon and coquilles Saint-Jacques au gratin, and was not a gourmet cook. He could not cook at all. He would end up eating every bite of the food and drinking every drop of the wine and loathing himself later on.

When Trevor was new to the English Department, Bombazine had stopped by his office to introduce himself. He didn't understand deconstructionism and wanted to learn about it from an adherent, a true believer. Trevor invited him to sit down and spent thirty minutes trying to explain it, smiling like a charitable missionary teaching a Papuan tribesman Esperanto. "In simplest terms, George," Trevor had begun, "deconstructionism is both a philosophical movement and a theory of literary criticism. It questions our traditional assumptions about language, certainty, and truth. It asserts that words are inherently irreconcilable and should not be used as a search for some specific meaning or message."

"So far that's as clear as mud. But go on."

Trevor's helpful smile never wavered. "Deconstruction primarily applies to the written word, but we also use deconstructive techniques to deconstruct political and cultural concepts, systems, institutions, and long-held assumptions that may be incorrect and need deconstructing." The last word made him chuckle, as if he'd said something clever.

"What sort of long-held assumptions? Like capitalism is the only economic system that works?"

"Well, yes. But one could get more basic than that."

"How about 'The Earth is Round?' Or 'Two Plus Two Equal Four?'"

"That may be *too* basic." But Trevor gave a hopeful, encouraging look. "Am I going too fast? Are you getting this?"

"Run it by me again."

"Be happy to," Trevor said, but now his smile was gone. He raked his fingers through his thick shock of red hair. "Take literary deconstructionism. It's a theory of textual analysis holding that a text has no stable reference or inherent meaning and calling into question our assumptions about language's ability to represent reality as we know it. It's as simple as that, really."

Bombazine made a face. It may have been as simple as that, but it wasn't simple to him. His lips moved soundlessly as he tried to reconstruct Trevor's deconstructing. He couldn't.

"Or put it this way," Trevor tried again, barely concealing his impatience now. "Deconstructionism is a technique of literary analysis holding that meaning results more from the differences between words rather than from any direct reference to the things words supposedly stand for. All sorts of new meanings can be created by taking apart— deconstructing—the structure of language we use and ridding ourselves of the assumption that words have some fixed reference point beyond themselves."

Bombazine had meant to ask what also made deconstructionism a philosophical movement and not just a theory of literary criticism, but he decided not to. "Okay, Trevor," he said. "And just what the fuck is its purpose?"

Trevor was stunned. "Why, to simplify and expedite our understanding of language and literature and life," he replied. "And George — why did you say fuck?"

Now the doorbell chimed. Bombazine bounced up from the couch and hurried to the door, hoping it was Pru. But it was Conchita Maria Vargas, the slender young Peruvian domestic who looked like Penelope Cruz and for whose body he covertly lusted. Conchita Maria was in a panic. She had her three-year-old son out in the car, she explained in breathless broken English cum hand gestures. The boy had an ear ache and she had to take him to the emergency room ("*la sala de urgencia*"). She could not clean the house today.

Bombazine nodded. "*Si*, Conchita — it's okay, *esta bien, no te preocupes.* See to your *hijo.* He reached in his pocket, gave her four twenties, and sent her on her way. What the hell, he told himself. Where you're going tonight, you can't take it with you. What was eighty bucks to a man with so few hours to live?

He shuffled to the kitchen to check on Argos. The old dog lay motionless, asleep on his side beside his bowl, snoring lightly. The half a T-bone steak remained untouched. "What is this, a hunger strike?" Bombazine softly asked. "Listen, dog, do you have any idea what that steak cost me? Twelve dollars! Your half cost six. It's prime beef. If you want Alpo, I'll give you Alpo." He bent down, removed the steak from the bowl, and returned it to the fridge. He opened a ten-pound bag of dry Alpo and filled the bowl to the brim. He would serve Argos the steak again for dinner. Or put it in a fancy bowl and leave it when he headed for Mount Make-out just before ten, never to return.

Chapter Fifteen: 10:13 a. m

THE POLITICAL JUNKIE

Midmorning.
 Twelve hours to live and time being wasted.

He plopped down in front of his Apple iMac in the library to check his e-mail. He spent too much time at his computer even though he knew it was unhealthy — mentally, emotionally, spiritually, and physically unhealthy."The people recognize themselves in their commodities," the New Left political theorist Herbert Marcuse wrote in the sixties. "They find their soul in their automobile, hi-fi set, split-level home, and kitchen equipment." They do, Herbert, agreed Bombazine. Especially in their split-level home. There I seek my soul in my hard drive. I spend most of my day at my computer in my split-level home trying to find my soul. I haven't found it yet, but I'm still looking.

He had fourteen new messages. He began with the spam, the junk mail, the daily offers for boner pills, penile implants and vacuum pumps, arthritis painkillers, blood pressure kits, and hair restoration. Back braces. Hearing aids. Catheters. Prepaid cremations. Online dating and square dancing for seniors. Today he received audiovisual congratulations (a choir sang him Handel's Hallelujah Chorus) for having won $978,000 in a contest (though he hadn't entered any contests) and had only to send a $49.95 money order or his credit card number to cover transaction expenses and receive his winnings tomorrow.

Bombazine felt his high blood pressure rise even higher. Dangerously so. Being old made you a target for every kind of scam—it was another indignity you endured as a punishment for staying alive too long in a country that worshipped at the altar of youth. Like the comedian Rodney Dangerfield, the elderly got no respect. Female clerks at the grocery store in Big Town called Bombazine "Sweetie." Male clerks at the liquor stores called him "young man" and recently one had asked him, with a wink, if he was old enough to buy his Scotch without showing an I.D.

"Do I look like a young man to you?" he'd asked the clerk.

"No, sir," the clerk, a young man, replied with a sheepish grin.

"Then why did you call me 'young man,' you patronizing little asswipe?"

He didn't shop at that liquor store again. He had his booze delivered to the house from the liquor store in the Village. Today's e-mail also included pleas for money liberal politicians needed if they and other liberal politicians were to be elected or reelected. There were liberal petitions to sign, too, and liberal websites like MoveOn.com and SumOfUs.com needing money in order to survive and ask for more money.

Then he saw the message he dreaded.

He had hoped not to get it but another from the same person. It came from his thirty-five-year-old son Miguel, just out of rehab in Provincetown, Massachusetts, where he owned a floral shop. It was the same birthday greeting, word for word, that Miguel sent him every year. Bombazine wondered if Miguel saved it on his computer and had some app or droid that mailed it automatically:

"Unhappy birthday, La Bamba. I do not love you. I do not like you. *Te detesto!* Why did you have to be my father? What did I do to deserve you? *Besa mi culo, viejo! Cuantos años tienes?* How old are you now? *Cien años?* Over a hundred? Why will you not die? You have polluted the earth for too long. It is time you died and went to hell. One day I may kill you. You ruined my life, motherfucker. *Chinga tu madre!*

Feliz cumpleaños, adios,

--*Tu hijo*, Miguel

p. s. I may have to call you collect tonight. Be there."

Bombazine sighed and shook his head. A deep sadness made his eyes water. Any hateful ten year old could have written this. The letter never changed, he knew it by heart, yet every year he read every word. At least the boy—or manchild—remembered his birthday. Of course, Bombazine knew what Miguel's collect call would be about. Miguel was broke and needed money for the floral shop he jointly owned with his butch lover-partner Dimitri, a

Russian ex-con.

Miguel was a certified civil engineer who'd never worked as an engineer, civil or uncivil. He'd earned a B. S. in engineering and immediately become a florist. Dimitri, an immigrant from Novosibirsk in the former Soviet Union, had been a loan shark, a breaker of arms and legs, and later a resident of Bay State Correctional Center in Norfolk, Massachusetts; he now headed up the floral shop's collections agency; delinquent accounts were rare.

From his estranged sister Catherine in Carmel, California, Bombazine did not expect an e-mail asking for money. Catherine telephoned on his birthday to ask for it. Like Miguel, she was always broke. She worked as a telemarketer for bargain vacation cruises. As mentioned earlier, everything she'd inherited from their parents had disappeared after she'd married Derek Evans, an investment banker and Tea Party activist indicted in 2008 for derivatives fraud. Now Derek tossed newspapers (the *Monterey County Herald*, the *Carmel Pine Cone*) onto suburban lawns from his Volvo. He was a pain in the neck who always had one—a herniated disc, a stenosis, a whiplash trauma requiring expensive neck surgery that never got performed. Husband and wife barely managed to make ends meet while contributing generously to Tea Party candidates and Sunday morning televangelists.

Nevertheless, Bombazine hoped for a call from his sister. It would be the last time he'd talk to her. Maybe he should call her, he thought.

His sole uplifting e-mail message came from a former student, Holly Teasdale; she was on the campus today. For

141

her dissertation on Edgar Lee Masters in her doctoral program at the University of New Mexico, Holly was using the Special Collections Library at Mount Olympus College; it contained new material Bombazine had unearthed in 1998. Holly wanted to show him what she'd written about Masters and talk about his forthcoming book.

"I'll be in the cafeteria in Harding Hall at noon," she wrote. "Can we have lunch? My treat. I hope I'm not imposing. I need quotes from you. I will give attribution. I don't trust my advisers the way I trust you. You are still the best teacher I ever had. Pardon the short notice. Hope you can meet me. Can't wait to see you again."

Bombazine remembered Holly Teasdale. A tall, big-boned, somewhat masculine redhead with a temper. Husky, buxom in the extreme, she'd tried to conceal a bosom bigger than Dolly Parton's with baggy woolen sweaters. The attempt was unsuccessful. She'd organized campus demonstrations demanding that the college build a battered women's shelter. That also failed, but Holly, vocal and volatile, had fought a good fight.

She'd come to his rescue one evening when he was onstage, open to attack, in the auditorium of Ezekiel Carnegie Cornelius Hall; he was addressing a packed house of English majors, professors, administrators, teaching assistants, and grad students on the subject of Edgar Lee Masters. The college may have been conservative, but its lefty fringe was loud and rude: a long-haired male heckler had risen halfway through Bombazine's address and shouted, "This is bullshit! Masters is just another dead white straight Euro-American male! Why don't you talk about gay or lesbian or transgender nonwhite writers from somewhere besides Europe or America who are alive? Get off the fucking stage, man!"

There were gasps and boos, but a few cheers also, and some whistling and handclapping. Bombazine tried to defend himself, but his voice shook: "In nineteen-sixty-nine at Columbia I wrote my doctoral thesis on Langston Hughes, a black poet known to be gay and very much alive at the time. Yes, he was American, but nobody's perfect. Last month on this stage I read from J. M. Coetzee's book *In the Heart of the Country*. Coetzee was born in South Africa and grew up in Cape Town and moved to Australia. How does that make him European or American? And by the way, he's still alive."

"Coetzee won the Nobel!" the heckler shouted. "He's a lapdog of the literary establishment! Fuck Coetzee and fuck you! Go home!"

Some audience members began to chant, "Go HOME... Go HOME" and Bombazine felt his knees buckle. A big redhead in a heavy sweater and baggy overalls jumped up on the stage and grabbed the mike from him.

"Shut up!" she screamed. "You bunch of ASSHOLES! Professor Bombazine introduced me to black and gay and lesbian authors from all over the world! None were chicks with dicks as far as I know, but so what? If you want to study trannies, go on the Internet. You don't like Professor Bombazine's lecture? Fine, get the hell out of here. I want to hear the rest of it. Any questions?"

There were no questions. The heckler and the chanters

were mute. Holly's tirade had inspired shock and awe. Bombazine was allowed to continue. When he finished, he received a standing ovation.

Leaving the building, he looked for the redhead, wanting to thank her, but couldn't find her. Having forgotten her name, he asked one of the teaching assistants. "Teasdale," the young man said. "Holly Teasdale. She's a little crazy, but she's got balls."

Remembering that day, he was again grateful and felt his pulse quicken. He sent a reply, accepting Holly's invitation. He wondered when Pru would arrive and hoped her visit would not interfere with his lunch date or vice-versa. It was now midmorning and the best he'd felt all day.

He had time to catch up with today's news. Except on weekends, when his Sunday *Times* arrived, he got his news from MSNBC-TV or Jon Stewart in the evening and his Internet provider in the morning. The Internet dispatches were sensational headlines, sound bites, thirty-word articles, mug shots, YouTube videos, rumors, teasers, and ads that sometimes blocked his view of what little there was to read. This morning's headlines were more depressing than usual. He'd hoped for an inspiring story for his last day on earth and didn't get one. The lead headline read NEW TRIAL SOUGHT FOR EXECUTED 14-YEAR-OLD. Bombazine skipped that story along with one headed TODDLER KILLS PARENTS WHILE PLAYING WITH HANDGUN, both of which would have upset him. He read the other stories, each a short paragraph:

- Governor Elmer Combs of Colorado had lost his governorship in a recall election for urging that the Fed not print IN GOD WE TRUST on money. Combs felt it dishonored the Deity. Reviled as an atheist even though he was a Pentecostal minister, he was ousted from office in a landslide vote.

- A Planned Parenthood clinic in Mississippi had been bombed, killing seven people, because abortions were said to be performed there even though abortions were not performed there and never had been.

- In Memphis a white policeman had killed a black twelve-year-old boy wearing a hoodie for taking a red SONY Walkman out of his jacket as the policeman tried to stop and frisk him. The Walkman looked like a red pistol, the policeman explained, so he'd shot the boy eight times in self-defense. No action was taken against him.

- In San Antonio an eighty-year-old man was arrested on misdemeanor charges and fined $2000 for giving food to a homeless beggar. The City Council had just passed a law illegalizing the feeding of beggars, bums, panhandlers, vagrants, loiterers, carriers of I WILL WORK FOR FOOD signs, illegal aliens, legal aliens, and hoboes wiping windshields at traffic-light intersections. It was also illegal to give them money — that, the Council members explained, only encouraged their drug use; besides, nobody in Texas was hungry unless they chose to be; America was the only country in the world where the poor people were fat, and Texas had the fattest poor people in the nation.

Sick at heart, Bombazine felt his spirits droop. His knee began to ache; his back was stiff from sitting at his computer; again he looked forward to killing himself. Was America losing her mind? Six decades ago, Philip Roth had complained that no satirist could lampoon the Eisenhower-McCarthy fifties, whose hysteria could not be trumped with satirical exaggeration. Today that era seemed like a gilded age of enlightenment and restraint. The inmates had taken over the asylum. Guns outnumbered people, and demonstrably the populace felt safer if Uzis and AK-47s and AR-15s were available at Target and Krogers and WalMart. Now one could take a gun to church, school, into a bar or an airport, and anywhere else except a courtroom.

He began his letter to the editor protesting the Colorado governor's recall, remembering what Luther said in 1517 as he nailed his 95 Theses to the door of All Saints Church: *"You are responsible not only for what you say but for what you don't say."* Prior to his Army service in the sixties, Bombazine hadn't said much. He was above politics — they were a swamp in which power-hungry philistines slithered like alligators and fed on one another. Politics revolted him. His father, a Strom Thurmond Dixiecrat, had hated Roosevelt

146

and Truman and Kennedy but loved Nixon until he started the EPA; his mother was apolitical except for liking the Kennedys, especially Jackie, and distrusting Nixon because he was shifty-eyed and always had a five o'clock shadow.

Bombazine had gotten hooked on politics in the late sixties. To avoid the draft, he'd enrolled in R.O.T.C. at Rice and earned a commission as a Second Lieutenant. He'd spent two years at a pencil-pushing desk job in the Pentagon, editing ARs (Army Regulations) and writing PIO (Public Information Office) dispatches for the Public Affairs Media Relations Division. He still remembered the address: 1500 Army, Pentagon, Washington, D. C. 20310-1500.

Patriotically, loyally, with a blind faith in American exceptionalism, he had supported the Vietnam War, fearing the U. S. would lose Vietnam (even though the U. S. never had Vietnam) and trigger a collapse, like a row of dominoes, that would color the Far Eastern world red, as in Red Chinese, and invite a nuclear attack on the United States by Beijing and Moscow. Even the generals at the Pentagon found that funny. Bombazine would hear them joke about how the Army's kazillion-dollar weapon systems were obsolete before they got off the drawing boards. Congress knew it, too, as did the President, but the systems had to be built anyway: money had been spent on them and jobs depended on them.

His military service had afforded him an insider's view of the war from the basement of the Pentagon; Bombazine turned against it and supported Eugene McCarthy, and then Bobby Kennedy, in 1968. He became what his father feared he would and prayed he wouldn't: a liberal. Each year since, he'd moved further left despite Churchill's dictum that age and maturity should make one conservative. In graduate school at Columbia after his discharge, Bombazine wore long hair and a bushy beard and sandals and vigorously protested the war. For him the early seventies were the sixties he'd missed out on. He would've enjoyed the late seventies even more had he not become a college academic and married what Dostoyevsky would've called a demonic woman.

The seventies had been his favorite decade. Culturally they'd begun as a licentious era of hardcore porn (*Deep Throat, Behind the Green Door*) and surprisingly good post-Beatles music (Cat Stevens, Carly Simon, Chicago, Moody Blues, Elton John) and rednecks finally smoking grass and growing their hair long. Bombazine had experimented with mind-expanding drugs, consciousness-raising encounter groups, and recreational sex, including an occasional threesome. He read *Penthouse* and Carlos Castaneda and Germaine Greer and Hesse's *Steppenwolf*. Having disliked Nixon, he relished every afternoon of Watergate, rushing home to watch its televised proceedings the way a housewife would to catch her favorite soap.

In the 1976 election he backed Jimmy Carter and still remembered the little peanut farmer as too honest for the office and the unluckiest president in American history. Carter's successor — an amiable dolt, a likable actor cast as an American president — would be the luckiest. By then the seventies had become the eighties and the nation begun to regress, dumb itself down, abandon the lessons of the sixties and revert to its former bad behavior. The 1980 assassination, in Manhattan, of Beatle John Lennon foreshadowed what was to come—a retrograde era in which Americans could again be comfortable with their prejudices and contempt for the poor. "Greed is good," a character in an Oscar-winning movie would reassure audiences, and they nodded, albeit reluctantly, in agreement. Yeah, greed was good after all.

Bombazine was proofing his letter protesting the Colorado governor's recall when the doorbell chimed. He rose and headed for the door, but Argos, roused from lethargy, was there already, whining with joy. Argos had missed Pru even more than his master did.

Chapter Sixteen: 10:47 a. m.

DEAR PRUDENCE

The three of them — Pru, Bombazine, and Argos — went into the kitchen. The divorced husband and wife sat down at the table at which they'd shared hundreds of breakfasts, and the dog sat underneath it. Pru had arrived with a large birthday card in a red envelope and an oblong-shaped box wrapped in shiny gold paper, with a fancy blue bow. Bombazine shook the present and guessed what it was.

"From the Merrimans," Pru said with a shy smile. "Happy Birthday, Georgie."

Bombazine clawed away the paper and tossed it aside. The gift was a bottle of twenty-year-old Talisker single-malt Scotch that must have cost a hundred dollars. "Marvelous," he said. "Talisker is the only distillery on the island of Skye. Thank you both. Shall we have a nip?"

"Thanks, I'll pass. Read the card."

Bombazine complied. It was a generic birthday greeting, but below Pru's signature Trevor had scrawled his name and scribbled, "We love you, fella. Happy 70th. Many happy returns. Don't do anything we wouldn't do." Bombazine felt his gorge rise.

"Nice card," he said with effort. "Very… nice."

"He's not a bad guy, George."

"No, he's not. Tell him thank you."

They were silent. "My sweet, you're looking well," he said, though he disliked the gamine hairstyle.

"You aren't," she said. "Forgive me, but you look like a man on his way to the gallows. You have that haunted look."

J. J. had said that too. Bombazine remembered his Bobby Burns: "*O wad some power the giftie gie us / To see oursels as ithers see us.*"

"What's wrong?" asked Pru.

"Nothing. Why must something be wrong?"

"Something is. I noticed it in the restaurant this morning."

Rien ne pese tant qu'un secret, he thought. Nothing weighs more than a secret. I'm only about to kill myself, he wanted to say, mouthing the words and almost saying them.

He asked, "What's happening with your music?"

She brightened. "The Mount Olympus symphony is playing *Don Quixote* next month and I'm the soloist. They call it a tone poem, but it's a cello concerto." She'd pronounced it "Kee-HO-tay," in the true Spanish, rather than the anglicized "Quicks-Oat" of college English departments.

"That may be Strauss's best tone poem," Bombazine said.

"You must come."

"I will," he lied.

They talked of this and that. She couldn't wait for *Return to Spoon River* to be published. The property taxes on the house were due—had he taken care of them? She'd noticed some cracks in the wood above the front porch and worried about foundation problems. And was he going to clear and

151

replant the garden? Or pay someone to? And didn't Conchita Maria clean the house on Wednesdays? Had she come already?

She sounded like a wife planning to return home. His heart swelled with hope. He explained about the cleaning woman.

Pru laughed. "Georgie, that wasn't her son in the car. She doesn't have a son. She doesn't have any children. It may have been a nephew. Did you pay her?"

"I did."

"She fleeced you. Are you going to dock her next time?"

"Of course not."

Pru smiled affectionately. "You're really such a softie. Doesn't she look like Penelope Cruz?"

"I haven't noticed."

"Yes, you have. I know about you and Latin women." She paused, as if wanting it back. They never discussed Tencha.

Pru asked, "Have you heard from Miguel?"

"Today. The usual birthday greeting."

"The crazy hateful e-mail? I'm sorry. It's his way of saying he loves you."

"I wish he'd find some other way."

"If he didn't care about you, you'd never hear from him. When someone keeps yelling 'I hate you! I hate you!' don't you know what that means?"

"That he hates me?"

"That he loves you. Men are so literal. I got a sweet note from Miguel. He asked for some money and we sent him a check. He wants a sex change operation."

"Great. I wanted a daughter anyway."

"He said his partner Dimitri was sick. I invited them for Christmas."

"What did he say?"

"He can't come. It's a busy time at his floral shop. Remember, he's my stepson. I helped raise him."

"Rear him. One raises cattle."

"Sorry." She flushed and tried to smile. "He's not you, George. He's had to rebel against you. Who was that Irish poet you used to quote about parenting?"

"Brendan Francis. '*Parents can be fairly criticized for anything with one exception – their children's behavior.*'"

"Why didn't you take it to heart? You think you failed as a father?"

"I know I did."

"I mean by leaving. Are you ever sorry you left?"

An odd question after such a long time, it rankled him. "No," he lied. "Are you?"

She pretended not to understand and he didn't pursue it. He went on: "Miguel is still punishing me. He'll never stop. Why did he become a florist? We gave him a terrific education. He earned a degree in civil engineering. He became a florist to spite me. What if I'd earned my English degrees and then become a hairdresser to spite my father?"

"Miguel thinks you've never loved him."

"Well, he knows you do. You brought out the best in him. Such as it was."

"I tried to be a mother, not a stepmother. But he missed Tencha, and he had father issues. He's Oedipal."

"Big time."

"He thinks you were relieved when he left home."

"I was."

"He's still angry. I had problems with him too. But I tried to understand his anger. He's transparent and pathetic and vulnerable. I gave him unconditional love. Your love may have been the other kind. 'Children begin by loving their parents. After a time, they judge them. They rarely if ever forgive them.' You used to quote that."

"Oscar Wilde. Miguel has never forgiven me for Tencha's death. Or for leaving her."

"He thinks you left them. Children never forgive the parent who leaves."

And husbands never forgive the wife who does, Bombazine wanted to add. "Tencha was an erratic mother," he said. "She was kind and loving with strangers. She parked Miguel with Mexican nannies or her witch of a mother while she traveled and partied and shopped."

"All the same, Miguel feels that she stayed and you didn't. What's happening with your screenplay for the Masters movie?"

"The studio is Lionsgate now. Meridel's flying in this afternoon. She wants us to Skype my agent and my editor."

Tongue in cheek, Pru gave a smirk. "She has to fly here to do that? Why can't she Skype them in New York and include you on the video call?"

"I don't know. I told her not to come."

"Is she staying here?"

"No. She has a friend in The Village."

"She just wants to see you. Be careful. That woman's a man eater."

"Lucky me," he said. But he was grateful for the hint of jealousy.

"Did you hear from Catherine?"

"Not yet."

"Be kind to her, George. She's your sister. She hasn't had an easy life."

"Who has?"

They were silent. Pru asked, "Are you finally enjoying having the house to yourself? You used to say it was haunted."

"I never said that. The locals did. They never found that woman who disappeared. She's not here. Argos would have sniffed her by now and dug her up."

"You told me you heard a woman singing Verdi one night."

"Eileen Farrell. I got drunk and left a tape on the stereo and it replayed again and again. I like our house. I liked it better when you were here."

"Do you ever get out?"

"All the time. I'm having lunch today with a former student. She e-mailed me. It's nice when students remember you."

"Lots of women are after you today."

Bombazine's heart jumped. "Present company included?"

A faux pas. Her face fell, she seemed embarrassed. Under the table Argos growled, as if to rebuke him.

"Don't do that," she said.

"I was kidding," he croaked.

She looked away.

He added, "But I need to ask you something."

"Ask."

"Is there a chance you'll ever come back?"

Her look was pitying. "I'm married, George."

"You were married to me."

"Stop."

"I'm sorry. I've had a rough day."

"You seem a little desperate. But you won't tell me what's wrong." She changed the subject. "Argos is unhappy too. What's wrong with him?"

"I don't know. He won't eat. He misses you."

"Don't lay a guilt trip. I've been gone a while. You probably aren't feeding him right. Are you giving him healthy food with protein and fiber and not rich cheeses and T-bones marbled with fat?"

"He hasn't long to live. I want him to enjoy himself."

"He seems strange. You're strange, Argos is strange, and J. J. was snide to Trevor at the restaurant for no reason. What an odd-looking creature that man is. Trevor doesn't like him."

"A two-way street. I thought Trevor liked everyone."

"Trevor loves everyone. There's a difference. John Jacob is not a likable man."

"I like him."

"And why, I can't imagine. I've heard that course he teaches at the college borders on a neofascism worse than Ezra Pound's. He's so far right he's left."

"He's a Tory. But who else would I play Scrabble with?"

"Whom else," she corrected. "Gotcha. I hope he's not the only person you see. Try to get out more. You need sunshine. Vitamin D. You're wan and pale. Are you writing?"

"Yes," he fibbed. "A book."

"What's it about?"

"Suicide in literature."

"Sounds depressing. Are you still writing letters to the newspaper op-ed pages?"

"I am."

"I hope you've quit raving about Thanksgiving. I know you had unhappy Thanksgivings as a child, but that was ages ago. The holiday was not to blame."

"I've quit writing about Thanksgiving. But I'm still politically active."

"Oh, Georgie. Your activism consists of letters to the editor and reading left wing blogs."

"I send money to the Brady Campaign."

"I wish you were active. Get out and canvas. Distribute leaflets. Knock on doors."

"There are no houses around here. May I ask what you're doing?"

"Writing a cello concerto. I'll dedicate it to you. Maybe Yo-Yo Ma will record it if we pay him enough."

"I'd rather you recorded it. You play better than he does. You're better than Gregor Piatagorsky. You're the tops."

Her smile was forgiving. "And you're the sweetest," she said, rising. "I do miss you, Georgie." She stood and gave him a hug. "Enjoy your birthday. I should have baked you a cake."

"I'd rather have the Scotch. Give my best to Trevor. Tell him thanks."

After she'd gone, Bombazine felt more like killing himself than ever. He was tempted to break open the Scotch and take a belt. Pru was never coming back and it depressed him to learn that after all these years she thought he shouldn't have left but stuck it out with Tencha and Miguel. Or had he heard her correctly? It was not the day to revisit that.

What a day this had been. And it was still early.

Chapter Seventeen: 11:29 a. m.

A LETTER TO THE EDITOR

He returned to his iMac to finish the letter he would e-mail to five newspapers, including the *New York Times* and *Washington Post*, and four magazines (*Time, The Nation, The New Republic*, and *Rolling Stone*). He had written so many letters to the *New York Times* that the editors probably thought he was a crank. They had published two of them.

Once again he saw politics as a drug he, a political junkie, was addicted to, a virus to which he had succumbed, an unhealthy habit like pornography. Twenty-four-hour cable news was partly to blame, having turned politics into entertainment, a blood sport that competed for ratings with ESPN and the major networks. If politics was a virus, politicians were chronic, often fatal victims: they had to lie to get elected and lie again to get reelected and soon, as Truman said of Nixon, they couldn't tell when they were lying from when they were telling the truth. "*a politician is an arse*," e. e. cummings wrote, "*upon which everyone has sat except a man.*" Or a woman, one would add today. Though female politicians were less likely to be pathological liars. But no one was immune. Politics were ubiquitous, inescapable, and intrinsically evil, Bombazine had decided. It made people who were intelligent and educated and normally sensible talk and behave like dangerously fanatical lunatics.

He was no lunatic, not yet anyway, but even he was mildly infected. His heart raced with indignation as he typed fast but accurately: "Dear Editor: I am outraged that Governor Combs of Colorado was recalled for wanting to remove God's name from our money. Do we worship the almighty dollar so much that God must endorse it like a check? IN GOD WE TRUST cannot be found anywhere in our Constitution or Bill of Rights. The motto arose in 1956 from the shameful Red Scare of the demagogic Senator Joseph McCarthy of Wisconsin. It is contrary to the separation of church and state guaranteed by the First Amendment. Governor Combs is absolutely right about the issue. Conservative Colorado Christians should read 1 Timothy 6:10: *'For the love of money is the root of all evil.'* Why would you think that God wants His name printed on the root of all evil? In Matthew 6:24 Jesus said *'Ye cannot serve God and Mammon at the same time.'* I doubt that the Deity we worship in Judeo-Christian and Muslim traditions considers it an honor to have His name printed on filthy germ-ridden coins and paper. It is blasphemous and insulting—an affront to God whether He exists or not. Jesus threw the money changers out of the temple. Why would you think he'd want to see his father's name on the fin or the sawbuck or the dollar bill?"

Bombazine reread and spell-checked and proofread the letter and clicked SEND. He'd thought of copying it to J. J., but didn't. Occasionally J. J. would concede that progressives were half right on an issue — gun safety was one — but demand an ungrantable concession in return. "Possibly," J. J. would say, "the NRA is unreasonable about guns in bars and schools and churches and airports. But you liberals should let us have all the guns we want because we let you have you all the pornography you want. I can't pass a newsstand without seeing a magazine cover showing a woman with her knees spread wide and wearing no bloomers. Innocent children can look right up her lady garden."

"J. J.," Bombazine had countered, "that may be the worst argument against gun control I've ever heard."

With the help of a liter of Scotch, Bombazine and J. J. would engage in political donnybrooks that lasted till dawn. The nance would ask, "Do you know who the two worst philosophers in history were? Not Marx and Engels. Not Machiavelli and Neitzche. *Locke and Rousseau.* And Rousseau was worse than Locke. We have that little frog to thank for the myth of the noble savage, the absurd idea that man is unselfish by nature. Man is totally selfish by nature. Take a baby. His five senses are the limits of his universe and most of us never outgrow that stage. Locke and Rousseau and Thomas More and that lard-ass Aquinas created the liberal belief in utopias. The liberal belief in utopias gave us Marx's Dictatorship of the Proletariat and the Kremlin and the Gestapo and Hitler's Third Reich and Kennedy's New Frontier and Johnson's Great Society. And the Peace Corps."

"I almost joined the Peace Corps," Bombazine protested. "Strike that one."

"Dishasters all." Drunk now, J. J drained his drink and

belched. "Name me one liberal utopia that worked. The utopian fantasy made liberals love revolutions—another romantic idiocy, since the dialectic of a revolution always results in a shtate of affairs worsh than what the rebels rebelled against. Look at the aftermath of the French Revolution and the Russian Revolution and Mao's Cultural Revolution and Castro's Cuban Revolution and —"

"The American Revolution turned out well."

"Don't pull my wankie. Well for whom? We've been the blood-thirstiest nation in history. Do you know how many people we've killed in wars since seventeen-seventy-six? More than the Black Death and Stalin." J. J.'s head lolled, drunkenly, from side to side, and his speech was slurred. "Let's shay England had won the Revolutionary War. We'd have remained a British colony until the Crown realized what an unwieldy, ungovernable pain in the arsh we were and begged us to declare our independence. They still have that problem with Northern Ireland. The world would be safer if we'd shtayed a British colony."

"That's treasonous and you're drunk. You don't cherish our democracy?"

"Do you? Mencken called democrashy a pathetic belief in the collective wisdom of individual ignorance."

"What about that American exceptionalism you righties brag about?"

"Rationalized rubbish. Like the divine right of kings in the seventeenth century and manifest destiny in the nineteenth. Religious patriotism. Theocracy. God is on our shide. Is there more Scotch?"

Getting drunk himself, Bombazine had wanted to argue more, defend America as the only nation in history to pass laws against its own greed and racism and genocides and xenophobias and oppression of native minorities, blacks, women, gay men, lesbians, transgenders, immigrants, atheists, anarchists, communists, Hispanics, and classical music lovers. It was a rare role reversal—the liberal Bombazine waving the flag, the conservative J. J. wanting to burn it. Bombazine would've argued all night, but J. J. passed out.

The morning was flying by now and he had to meet Holly Teasdale at noon. Picturing her flaming auburn hair and farmgirl face and heavy breasts lit a concupiscent flame like a pilot light in his groin. I'm still alive, he thought. The girl he remembered was a milkmaid painted by Rubens or Vermeer. How nice it would be to escort the milkmaid to his haystack for the final fuck of his life before he left for Mount Makeout tonight. The Carthagenians had bedded their women before riding off to die in valiant combat with the Greeks.

He told Argos good-bye and left for the campus. It was close to noon. Every minute precious now. If all the world was a stage, death waited for him in the wings. Holly once had rescued him from a mob. Might she rescue him today from something worse?

Chapter Eighteen: 11:59 a. m.

HOLLY, HOLLY

The Warren G. Harding Student Center on the New Campus was a two-storied mustard-colored edifice whose brick facade had the look of a state building in a totalitarian country. Inside it looked like a shopping mall. It was a shopping mall. Its stores provided students and faculty instant access to the overpriced designer brands of every necessity and many luxuries.

Fast food booths, serving up exotic fare like Mongolian barbecue, rattlesnake sandwiches, and menudo, were interspersed with a Wendy's, a Jack in the Box, a McDonald's, Starbucks, Pizza Hut, and beer tavern. There was also a basement cafeteria noted for low-cal organic Blue Plate Specials devoid of sodium, trans fats, cholesterol, gluten, sugar, or flavor. For most students the formica-tabled cafeteria was just a coffee shop, cheaper than the Starbucks down the hall, where they could read, schmooze, hang out, hunch over their laptops, debate the existence of God, and exchange cheat sheets for upcoming tests. Few students or faculty members ate the Blue Plate Specials unless they were crash dieting or health fanatics.

Holly Teasdale, with a big smile and a wild gleam in her eyes, was waiting when Bombazine arrived. They hugged chastely. In her twenties now, Holly sported a new look. She'd lost weight. She was as buxom as ever and wore the same loose-fitting overalls, but today she'd doffed her baggy sweater and donned a blue denim shirt (with the top buttons open) that may have shrunk from hot machine washings. Bombazine tried, without success, to ignore her freckled cleavage. Holly was sexy now.

They hurried to the serving line. Today's Blue Plate Special was organic baked chicken breast with organic baked okra, organic mashed potatoes, and an organic green bean casserole baked to a crisp. Unthinking, Bombazine chose it; Holly ordered a spinach salad with sprouts and goat cheese and a fat-free oil-and-vinegar dressing containing neither oil nor vinegar. She tried to treat, but Bombazine wouldn't let her.

They found a table large enough to accommodate all the books, papers, and notes in her satchel. Momentarily Bombazine's eyes roamed the room and took in the latest crop of uncharactered young faces and firm, athletic, well-dressed bodies, plus a few hippie types — unwashed, unkempt, with stringy long hair — thrown in as a salute to a fabled decade fifty years earlier. Bombazine had loved his students, even those he'd had to flunk, and he missed them.

He and Holly chatted like old friends reunited after many years, though it had not been many, and he was temporarily able to forget that this lunch would be his last. "How's your lovely wife, Professor?" she asked with genuine interest. "I took her music appreciation course. She introduced me to Palestrina and Pergolesi."

"We divorced, Holly. I live alone now. I was a good house-keeper. She let me keep the house."

Holly tried to smile; the joke was old and he hoped she hadn't heard the note of self-pity in his voice. "I hear," she said, "that your new book on Masters might become a movie based on *Spoon River*?"

Amazing, he thought, how fast rumors traveled. "A canard," he chuckled. "Inaccurate on several counts. I wish it were true."

"I'll buy your book as soon as it's out. Are you still teaching?"

"Retired. William James said, 'What an awful trade that of professor is — paid to talk, talk, talk. It would be an awful universe if everything could be converted into words, words, words.'"

"I think teaching is a wonderful trade. I only hope I'm half as good at it as you were."

"I miss it, Holly. Even the worst days."

"What do you miss most?"

"That dramatic moment when you see a student awaken for the first time. A light bulb comes on in his or her head. You see the eyes unglaze and you know you've reached that person. Maybe changed his or her life."

Holly seemed to glow. "I remember that moment," she said. "You made it happen for me."

"I remember the day you saved me from a lynch mob. You jumped up on the stage. I never got to thank you."

She blushed and took a bite of salad. "I totally lost it," she said, chewing. "I would've killed for you. You were

166

my hero. I guess having a crush on your sexy English prof wasn't very original."

"Well," he blurted, "I'm not your English prof now."

It was a mistake—blood drained from her fair chubby cheeks; she looked away in embarrassment, as if he'd belched or farted. She wore the face Pru had shown him this morning for making the same mistake. A pitying look. He'd thought both women were flirting and they weren't.

"I'm kidding," he mumbled.

But the rapport was broken. Holly seemed flustered. Awkwardly, without looking at him, she bent forward to slide a sheaf of notes his way. "Maybe we should get to work," she said.

A glimpse of her milkmaid's cleavage, with its twin white pillows, plucked a string in his loins. He wanted her. *Dr. Fallopius*, he thought, *there's still procreational fluid in my tank.* Taking charge, he said, "Why don't we eat first."

"Whatever you say. My mind is a mess these days. I'm operating two shelters for battered women. One in Albuquerque, one in Santa Fe."

"That's wonderful, Holly."

She began to prattle, as if to restore the earlier mood. Bombazine tuned out for a few moments and then tuned in again. "I work on my dissertation at night," she was saying. "Which means I never sleep. I mean, I should sleep, but I can't 'cause I get so mad at Academia. The Midwest Tradition in literature is ignored by scholars. That drives me nuts, you know? It's always, like, the New Englanders and the Southerners but never the Midwesterners."

"You're absolutely right." Unable to control himself, he stole another peek at her cleavage.

"I'm sorry—I should shut up and let you talk. Did you ever meet Masters?"

He laughed. "I'm not that old, Holly. Masters died in a nursing home in Pennsylvania in nineteen-fifty. I was just a boy. In the seventies I met his son Hardin at a Masters family reunion in Mason County, Illinois. Hardin was the first name of Masters' father too."

She lifted a forkful of salad to her mouth. "What a strange man Masters was," she said, shaking her head. "Did you know he lived and wrote for a while at the Chelsea Hotel in Manhattan?"

"On West Twenty-third. Many writers did. Even I did. The Chelsea is full of literary ghosts."

"In my dissertation I'm, like, having trouble reconciling Masters the poet with Masters the lawyer and biographer."

"Join the club."

"Why aren't you eating?"

"I'm working up an appetite."

"Why do you keep looking at me?"

That startled him. "I'm sorry. I guess I like to look at pretty girls."

Blushing, she was silent. Then: "I'm glad you found those suppressed poems by Masters for your new book. But he was, like, a bad guy sometimes? In his politics. That awful book he wrote about Lincoln."

"Masters was politically confused. A populist conservative. His father had been a liberal Democrat."

168

She mumbled something he couldn't hear.

"I'm sorry?" he asked

"You're doing it again. Looking at me."

He turned his head away and wondered if he should apologize. His nerves thrummed with annoyance. His mood had changed. The cafeteria was filling up, getting loud. The music piped in—some contemporary grunge—was distracting. He wondered who the group was. Sick Puppies? Nine-inch Nails? Flaming Lips? Today's bands had bizarre names. When he managed to stay awake past ten-thirty, he tried to watch the musical guests on "Saturday Night Live" but needed closed captions for the lyrics. What he heard wasn't singing but shouting.

"Holly," he said, "I don't think we can get our work done here. It's noisy. Why don't you come over tonight?"

She frowned. "Over where?"

"My house. We could have dinner and work on your dissertation."

"With just the two of us there?"

He paused. "Well, no. My dog will be there."

Holly put down her salad fork and looked about to cry.

"What's the matter?"

"You too?" she whimpered in a child's voice. "Even you?"

"Even me what?"

Holly glared. Her cheeks had reddened. She cleared her throat indignantly, swallowed, and regarded him as she might a stranger who'd propositioned her. She brushed a strand of hair away from her forehead. When she spoke her voice was tremulous: "You're divorced and living alone and you're asking me over to your house? At night?"

He hesitated. "Well, yes. Is that inappropriate?"

"So you can fuck me?"

That shocked him. "What? Who said I wanted —?"

"You want to. I can tell. We both know what would happen if I came."

"We do?" Again he felt the tingle below his belt. Only now it was unwelcome.

"Don't tell me you don't want to," she said.

"I hadn't thought about it." Not true, but what else could he say? "All I know is, I grill a delicious Porterhouse. Unless you're vegetarian."

"Be serious."

"I could grill veggie burgers…"

"Stop."

"Pizza? I can call out for a vegetarian pizza from the Village." Now he was rattled.

"You don't think I'm attractive?" she barked. "Is that what you're saying?"

He looked around uneasily. "Lower your voice, Holly. I find you very attractive. But I thought you wanted to work on your dissertation."

"Why can't we do that here?"

"I told you. It's noisy."

"And what would happen after we worked on it at your house? I can't trust you. I can't trust any of you. Why do you keep leering at my breasts? Haven't you ever seen a full-figured woman before? A woman with a big chest?"

"I wasn't leering —"

"You were." Even her neck was mottled now, in a rashlike blush. "You were ogling me."

"I'm sorry —"

"I get this all the time."

"Holly… Holly…" He looked away and shook his head. He felt trapped and angry and disrespected. She had turned into another person. A crazy one. Her mood had swung so abruptly and violently that he had no idea how to handle it. This lunch was a disaster he wanted to be over with.

"I'm sorry," he repeated. "I didn't realize I was staring."

"You're a dirty old man."

"What? Holly, that's not fair —"

"Let me tell you something, Professor." Her mouth quivered and for a moment she could not get the words out: "I've been invited to dinner at the homes of three unmarried doctoral advisers and every one of them had something extracurricular in mind. Fucking me. They thought they were entitled. You know, like movie producers with a casting couch? One of them got naked and chased me around his living room."

Her glower could have turned a man to a pillar of salt. Rage distorted her face — she looked deranged. Bombazine had not touched his organic baked chicken and organic okra and organic mashed potatoes and he wasn't going to. He wanted to bolt.

She went on: "If you're wondering if they 'got a little,' the answer is no."

"I wasn't wondering that."

"You were. I don't trust you."

He would try one last time. Slowly, evenly, he said, "I just thought we might enjoy a pleasant evening together. I could have pizza delivered and we could work on your dissertation and that's all. I have to be somewhere at ten."

"Pizza? You think you can buy me with pizza?"

"We can go out for dinner. Someplace really nice."

That too came out wrong. When she spoke her voice was piercing enough to shatter a glass: "A teacher sexually harassing a student is like a doctor sexually harassing a patient!"

People could hear. "Shh! I'm not harassing you, Holly. I told you — I'm not a teacher anymore."

"It's okay for you to sexually harass me because you're not a teacher? I had such respect for you! You were my favorite teacher!"

"Holly, stop —"

"Go to HELL!" She rose awkwardly, gathered up her satchel, papers, and books and bundled them in her arms. She backed away from the table, eyes glistening with tears, sheets of paper dropping. "First my father and now you!" she sobbed. "And by the way — I'm a lesbian." She rushed out of the cafeteria, bumping aside a black busboy carrying a tray.

He thought of going after her but decided no. A table of students nearby who'd been watching looked away. Bombazine gazed up at the ceiling and took a deep breath. He remembered the teaching assistant's implying that Holly was crazy. The girl needed help, Bombazine thought; she was paranoid, and hadn't he known about her temper? Parentally abused, sexually confused, a postfeminist Sylvia Plath with Daddy issues. No wonder she built battered women's shelters. She was a battered woman.

But he had been at fault too. He had been ogling her. He did desire her. It must've been obvious; she'd caught him peeking in her top drawer and he had hinted that he was romantically available. She had not come on to him, he had come on to her. Maybe he really was a dirty old man. Not Masters' Petit the Poet but Eliot's Prufrock: "*What if one, settling a pillow by her head, should say: 'That is not what I meant at all; that is not it, at all.'*"

He ought to be ashamed, he told himself, but he was shameless. Today he would kill for sex with a woman. Or at least phone an escort service. He'd never fooled around with his students or former students, but he knew professors who did. It was accepted. Affairs and sometime marriages resulted. Why couldn't he have gotten a break today? Young women Holly's age were sexually active and some of them liked older men and fucked their teachers. Why did she have to be a basket-case paranoid lesbian?

Awash in self-revulsion, he thought, *I'm disgusting*. It was an epiphany. "You're a dirty old man." That accusation was an echo.

He rose with arthritic stiffness. His eyes stung and watered. The room swam. Everyone in here was looking at him, pitying him, embarrassed for him. A few students and T.A.'s ("Hey, isn't that Doctor Bombazine?") surely recognized him. He staggered out of the cafeteria like an old drunk, weaving his way through a path of tables, leaving his Organic Blue Plate Special untouched.

Chapter Nineteen: 1:21 p. m.

ALL IN THE FAMILY

Home again.

Half the day, his last day, was gone. Yet much remained to be done. The ugly scene with Holly Teasdale in the Harding Student Center cafeteria had left him feeling even more despondent than before, and he still had nine hours to kill before he could kill himself. But he would adhere to the program. Take his time. Exercise grace under pressure. Papa Hemingway's hands had not shaken as he loaded his double-barreled twelve-gauge shotgun that fateful day in 1961. Bombazine was sure of it.

His publicist—blonde, vivacious Meridel Baxter—would be here soon. Ever full of surprises, fun to be around, she made him wish he were twenty years younger. She was mercurial and unpredictable, but he knew she liked sex and food. Sex, especially. Such was the word on her. For this afternoon she had scheduled a Skype conference with his New York contacts—his agent and his book editor—and he needed to be at his best even if nothing came of it.

But why was she really stopping by? He wasn't up to dealing with her. His head felt heavy and started to droop. His knee ached and there was a bitter taste in his mouth. He should eat something and take a nap, he told himself. Maybe have a drink first—break open the Talisker Pru and Trevor had given him for his birthday. In the thirteenth century St. Thomas Aquinas wrote that sorrow can be alleviated by a bath, a glass of wine, and a good sleep. Scotch was a better antidepressant than wine, and having showered this morning, he could skip the bath and just grab a nap.

But he would skip the Scotch, too. He couldn't be tipsy when Meridel Baxter arrived. Dealing with her and the other New Yorkers would require sobriety, sharp focus, mental celerity, unslurred speech. There could be no coming on to her, either, much as he'd like to. He wondered if she knew he fantasized about her. Probably. How and where had he found her? He had forgotten. It must've been through Babs. They were tight, like sisters under the skin, but not above stabbing each other in the back. Babs thought Meridel exceeded her duties as a publicist and wanted *her* job too. Babs was probably right.

He trudged to the kitchen to check on Argos. The old dog was napping near his bowl and hadn't touched his dry Alpo. Why wouldn't Argos eat? Argos loved to eat. Was he sick?

Bombazine decided to skip the nap. Actually, he wanted to skip the whole afternoon and drive up to Mount Makeout right now. Most men would—just to get it over with— but he wouldn't. The thing had to be done a certain way, according to schedule. He dragged himself into the library and plopped down on the swivel chair at his computer. He tried to write another letter to the editor but couldn't even think of an issue to be outraged about. He was at loose ends.

Maybe I should watch some porn, he told himself. It would be for the last time. If he could get off, it would relax him; he hoped his prostate cancer had not made ejaculation impossible. One benefit of the cyber revolution had been that now he could watch pornography, which he preferred to call erotica, at any time of the day or night in the privacy of his home and not have to drive to some sleazy theater and watch it with a bunch of creeps and perverts, degenerates and dirty old men in raincoats. He had never watched it when Pru was around. Pru called porn "woman-hate" and "depersonalizing" and an "abomination." She didn't like porn.

It was showtime. He began to surf the XXX-rated sites. Normally he watched a Classics website of seventies porn, with stars like Marilyn Chambers, Annette Haven, Georgina Spelvin, John Leslie, Jamie Gillis, and John C. (Johnny Wadd) Holmes. The seventies were porn's Golden Age: its best movies, shot in 35 mm., had plots and budgets and were made with film crews and the latest technical equipment. Some were funny, even intentionally funny, and others delivered a message. One classic, *The Devil in Miss Jones*, a morality tale, was reviewed as a serious movie by New York *Herald Tribune* critic Judith Crist. There had even been talk of hardcore art films: Rabelais, D. H. Lawrence, Henry Miller's *Rosy Crucifixion*, the bawdy *Canterbury Tales*. It was fun to imagine what a director with the talent (if not the mindset) of a Steven Spielberg or Martin Scorsese or Woody Allen could accomplish with hardcore sex scenes in their movies. But in the eighties, that retrograde decade of greed, profiteering pornographers arrived with videocams and videotape to make movies on the cheap again, and the dream of a brave new world of erotic cinema worthy of an Aubrey Beardsley or Anthony Christian or Courbet was flushed down the toilet. Where the bluenoses felt it belonged anyway.

Nostalgically, having savored the seventies, he often revisited seventies porn, but today called for something more bizarre to rev up his engine. He surfed the porn web sites until he found one, TABOO FILTHY KINKY INCEST, that sounded promising. The short-short movie he downloaded, *Incest Is Best*, shot with a videocam, began with a pigtailed, gum-chewing teenager in bra and panties lying across her bed, surrounded by stuffed teddy bears, reading *Cosmo*, and playing with herself. Without knocking, her mother—a buxom blonde matron—entered the room and recoiled in shock. Indignant, hands on hips, she demanded an explanation. Shamed, embarrassed, the teenager covered her eyes with her hands and broke into tears.

She was the worst actress Bombazine had ever seen except for the woman who played her mother; in fairness, however, the mother's mortification and the daughter's humiliation were meant to seem feigned. There was no worse actor than a bad actor playing a bad actor, and this movie had two of them. "You naughty little slut," the mother scolded as she unzipped her skirt. "Promise me you'll never play with yourself again and I'll teach you how to do it right. Move over."

Then both females were naked and the mother was teaching the daughter how to find her "G-spot." Whereupon the door burst open and Junior, the girl's barechested teenage brother, interrupted the instruction. "Holy SHIT!" he exclaimed. "Mom! Sis! What the heck is going on?"

Junior, another execrable actor, was wide-eyed with shock, but with minimal prodding the two females coaxed him out of his jeans, onto the bed. "It's all right—it's all in the family," the mother reassured him. After some cursory foreplay, the naked threesome became a tangle of arms and legs and heads in an orgy of nonstop licking and sucking and fucking. Once everyone had gotten off (Junior twice), Mom snuggled up to him from one side and Sis from the other, both wearing contented smiles. Lying with an arm around each, Junior grinned cretinously at the camera. "Incest is best," he said to it.

The movie left Bombazine cold. He had not touched himself a single time. It had been the most revolting, least elevating pornography he'd ever watched, having not just failed to arouse him but deepened his depression. It was the kind of smut that gave smut a bad name and could turn a man against porn. For the briefest of moments he'd understood what it was about porn that so offended bluenoses and prudes that they were willing to repeal the First Amendment to get it banned from cable TV.

He felt a queasiness that bordered on disgust. A profound sadness, an emptiness. Perhaps, it occurred to him, his last day on earth called for something spiritual. Maybe he should be watching a documentary on the life of Mother Angelica or St. Francis of Assisi on the Catholic Network. But something religious might give him second thoughts about tonight.

He cursed softly, channel-surfed, and found the BASEBALL TODAY website previewing the National League Championship Series between the Cardinals and Dodgers that began today. The winner would go to the World Series, the first one he would miss since the early fifties, and he was still a Dodger fan at heart.

The phone rang; he cursed again and grabbed for the receiver. "Bombazine," he growled.

"Happy Birthday, George," droned a woman's bored voice. There was no love in it but something quite the opposite. "What are you up to, little brother..."

Catherine sounded down. Catherine always sounded down. "Hey, Sis," he said. "I was hoping you'd call today. What's wrong?"

"What isn't? I hate my life, that's what's wrong. Derek and I can't make ends meet."

"Is he still throwing newspapers?"

"Yes. And he has an afternoon job at the church. In the accounting office."

"The accounting office? Is that a good place for him?" In 2008 Catherine's banker husband had barely escaped indictment for approving unlawful loans to dummy corporations.

"Don't be mean about Derek, George. He sweeps up. Janitorial work. His neck has been killing him. He has another stenosis. He'll need surgery that will cost an arm and a leg. We have no health insurance."

"No Medicare?"

"Derek's only sixty-one."

"How about the A.C.A?"

"Obamacare? Are you kidding? Derek wants it repealed. He would die first. He has his pride."

"Disability assistance, then. Bum neck, one arm, one leg…"

Silence.

Then: "Was that supposed to be funny?"

"Not really. I'm sorry."

"You've always been mean about Derek. Why?"

"He must be the only investment banker in America without health insurance."

"He's not a banker anymore. I told you, we're having a rough time. Derek didn't marry a rich woman with a big house to live in. Our house has a mortgage."

"I'm no longer married, Catherine. Start spreadin' the news."

"You've got a big house to live in rent-free. You don't own that house."

She'd always seen him as the fortunate one and always managed to make him feel guilty. She didn't know about his cancer and he wasn't going to tell her. Or that in a few hours he would kill himself. She would lecture him about the cancer (though secretly envying him for it) and not believe the other because she saw him as a coward.

"You don't worry about us," she added.

He didn't. Not much, anyway. "I do worry about you," he told her, "but I have other concerns too."

"Like what? Your damned old dog? Or yourself? Honestly, you're so detached. Not just from your family but everyone. You don't relate to people. You're, like, some outer space alien. There's something missing in your makeup."

"Thank you. Did you call to tell me that?"

"I called to wish you Happy Birthday. And ask you something really important."

He felt his chest tighten. "What," he said warily.

"Don't you think I should've inherited more from Mom and Dad?"

"Come on, Sis. That old chestnut again? You got your half."

"I should've gotten more than half when we sold the farm in Arkansas."

"We agreed to abide by the will."

"Derek thinks I should contact a lawyer. It was me who looked after Mom when she was dying of cancer. You were gone. I tended to the farm while you were off writing books and reading your scholarly papers and touring Europe and getting famous."

"I never got famous, Catherine."

"You wrote a novel."

"Nobody read it."

"I did. Only because you wrote it. It was about junior officers in the Pentagon. It was bad."

"It wasn't that bad."

"It was pretty bad. I hear you're involved with Hollywood now."

"Where'd you hear that? I'm not." If she thought he was doing all right, she would ask for money.

"How's Miguel?"

"Thirty-five years old now."

"I didn't ask how old he was. I asked how he was."

"He's getting married. To a man. I seldom hear from him."

"I'm not surprised. I'd hate to have you for a father. You're a bad enough brother, you know?"

It was the sort of thing he didn't need to hear today of all days. "Why am I bad?" he asked irritably.

"I told you. You're a cold fish. A scholar who lives in an ivy tower."

"Ivory tower. And I'm retired. Not a scholar anymore."

"You always correct me. It's one of the things I hate about you. Remember, you went to better schools than I did."

"Because I made better grades and did better on tests."

"I had the common sense. Derek wishes you Happy Birthday too. Even though you've never liked him."

"Who says I've never liked him?"

"He does. He thinks it's because he's a Tea Party conservative."

"He's wrong. That's not the only reason."

"See? I knew you hated him! You've never approved of him."

"You never liked my wives, Catherine."

"You have such terrible taste in wives. First that crazy Mexican woman who killed herself. Then a feminist hairy legger who won't pluck the whiskers off her chin."

"Don't disrespect my wives. Tencha's dead and Pru's gone."

"Don't badmouth Derek, then."

"It's a deal. Are you still going to Weight Watchers?"

"I'm doing the Scarsdale Diet." Her tone softened: "I want to be pretty again. You used to think I was pretty."

"Didn't Scarsdale die?"

Catherine sighed. "Scarsdale is a place, George. You're so out of touch. The man who invented the Scarsdale diet was Herman Tarnower."

"Right. Didn't someone murder him?"

"Yes, but so what? I've lost weight, if that's what you're asking. Fifty pounds. Starving will do that to you. Could you loan us some money?"

"Lend you some money," he corrected her.

"All right, lend. God damn it."

Here she goes, he thought. It was her M. O. First she'd scold him and make him feel guilty. Then put the touch on him. Then make him feel guilty again if he said no.

"We always pay you back," she reminded him.

"You never pay me back."

"We always intend to."

"How much do you need," he said, anxious to end the conversation before she asked for anything else.

"Ten thousand?"

"Jesus, Catherine. That's a lot."

"You can spare it. There must be some money laying around from your rich ex-wives."

"Lying around."

"Oh, fuck that. Derek and I are in trouble. We're family, George. For once in your life, be generous. Give us something."

"Now you're demanding a gift? I thought it was *my* birthday."

"Do you know how hard it is for me to ask you for money?"

"No, but I wish it were harder."

"Ten thousand can't be that much to you. You've got your

royalties and a full professor's pension and Social Security and you're married to a rich woman."

"We're divorced. I told you she left me."

"I'm not surprised. You're such a selfish bastard. Clueless and thoughtless and selfish."

That again. It was like a refrain. Who had said it earlier? With just a few hours to live, he did not need condemnations.

"Please help us," Catherine entreated.

"I'll see what I can do."

"At one time you and I were close. Have you forgotten those days?"

"I have to run, Catherine. Someone's coming over."

"Remember all that rassling we used to do?"

"Got to run. Thank you for remembering my birthday."

"I always do. Don't forget about the money." She rang off.

Her call left a foul aftertaste. "*You're such a selfish bastard.*" He was? He had never thought of himself as selfish. He was no bountiful Santa Claus with a bag of gifts like Dr. Trevor T. Merriman carried around, but he wasn't any more selfish than the average husband. "*You're a cold fish.*" What did she base that on? "*There's something missing in your makeup.*" There is? What? He wondered how Catherine would take the news of his suicide. Once she'd stopped crying, if she did cry, she would ask when his will would be read and if it needed probate.

He remembered how passionately Tencha had hated Catherine. It had inspired her cruelest letter. He lumbered to his desk, unlocked it, and rifled around until he found the letter; in it Tencha referred to Catherine as a pig, hog, sow, and vari-

ous other farm animals and implied that Catherine had incestuous feelings for him. Again her Spanish, or Spanglish, had
a flair: "La Bamba: *¡Tu hermana Catherine, es la peor Jorge!* She
makes me sick just to look at her. *Es tal cual un cerdito – pert-
enece a una pocilga. A un chiquero. ¡Es evidente que tiene una rel-
ación malsana contigo!* You know what I am talking about and
it is disgusting to me. *Y eso es porque no tiene ningún hombre
en su vida.* I feel sorry for her. I try to be kind to her. *Pero ese
MARICONCITO con el que está casada ¡La gorda de tu hermana
es muy zorra, Georgio! ¿Sabes lo que eso significa? Muy zorra!*"

She was reviling not just Catherine but him. Hoping to
hurt him. Tencha had ended up hating him. Why? Catherine hated him too. How many other women hated him? He
wondered how he'd managed to enrage every woman in
his life, not just his sister and wives but a parade of par-
amours in serially monogamous single file, perfectly decent
women he'd led on, let down, left behind. Women he had
loved, women who'd loved him. Yet he didn't see himself
as a misogynist or chauvinist or unconscionable prick or
any other of the things they'd called him when he'd left.
True, he had not been attentive and thoughtful in the little
ways women were said to appreciate; but that, he rationalized, was because he was an academic, a scholar more
concerned with matters like Eliot's objective correlative and
Edmund Wilson's notebooks and journals and diaries than
with making a woman feel needed and cherished at every
waking moment. The ironic thing was, he'd needed and
cherished and appreciated them all. And been faithful to
each in his fashion before going on to the next.

He scanned another of Tencha's letters. In it she'd accused his family of looking down on her because she was Mexican when she was not Mexican but aristocratic Castillian Spanish from Madrid—a pedigree far superior to the "white-trash Pecos River peasantry" whence he came, he whose father was developing ugly shopping strips in Houston while hers was acquiring and developing half of San Luis Potosi.

Furiously scrawled with such force that there were scratches and holes in the paper, the letter ended: "*¡Tu familia no me quiere Jorge!.¿Crees que no lo sé? Se atreven a menospreciarme porque soy hispana. Escucha gringo, ¡Yo vengo de la nobleza! ¡Mi piel es tan blanca como la tuya! ¡Mis antepasados eran reyes y emperatrices y sacerdotisas!* Kings and emperors and priests, do you understand? *Mis abuelos vinieron a México de Madrid--eran aristócratas Castellanos.* I have blue blood in my veins, La Bamba! My people are better than your people! *Vivieron en palacios mientras que tus ancestros vivieron en carretas cubiertas, que se bañaban en el río Pecos, en Texas y sacrificando a los pobres indios mestizos. Tú provienes de gentuza, Jorge. Tu padre construyó centros comerciales en Houston, Texas.* Ugly shopping centers for the white trash and poor Mayates. *¿Por qué me casé contigo? Adios,* La Bamba! Go to hell!"

He tossed the letter aside. Why had there been a Tencha Villa-Lobos in his life? Be careful what you ask for—you will surely get it, went the saying, but he had neither wanted a Tencha nor asked for one. Had she been a fantasy incarnate, an answered prayer? In later years when he talked about her, which was seldom, since it was painful, people did not believe that such a person had actually existed. Sometimes even he couldn't believe it. They accused him of embellishing, exaggerating, and he could hardly blame them: Tencha belonged in those movies about sexual obsessives like *Play Misty for Me* and *Fatal Attraction*.

Now the doorbell was ringing and Argos was howling like a timberwolf. Bombazine knew who it was. He rushed to the front door, stumbling like a schoolboy in his haste.

———

Panting from exertion, painfully trying to smile, his blonde publicist stood on the porch clutching a bulging burlap bag, large brown leather purse, and silver briefcase that contained a laptop. "I'm here," Meridel Baxter announced. "Move aside. Jeez, what a bumpy flight... I brought food and wine... I'm thirsty and hungry... let's have lunch and get to work."

She pushed past him. "And before I forget," she added. "Happy Birthday."

Chapter Twenty: 2:37 p. m.

MERIDEL, BABS AND MOTHERWELL

In the kitchen they unpacked the burlap bag, which contained six lobster egg rolls and two bottles of a Chinese rice wine, Sheung Jing, that Bombazine had never heard of. He wondered where Meridel had gotten such fare. Surely not at the airport. They sat at the table and she began to eat and drink with gusto. Bombazine nursed a glass of wine. He still wasn't hungry. His dread came and went and right now he felt it full-force.

"What's wrong?" Meridel asked, feeling it too. "Eat," she commanded with her mouth full, pointing to the egg rolls. "Eat, drink, and be merry."

For tonight I die? he thought. "In a while," he said.

She looked around, then gave a laugh and a wave of her braceleted wrist. "This house is so not you."

"This isn't your first time here."

"It seems weirder today. Abandoned. Spooky. Like nobody lives here, not even you. Or a spirit does."

"A ghost maybe" he said. "A mobster from Vegas on the witness protection program lived here with his wife and kids. She mysteriously disappeared, he took the kids and split. Maybe she's buried under the house. There's no cellar."

"That's creepy, babe."

"It's an urban myth. Or a rural myth."

"Don't you get lonely?" "

"Sometimes."

"All these empty rooms. Even our voices echo. Awful place. No offense, baby."

"None taken."

"You could buy some furniture. That would help."

"I'm a minimalist when it comes to decor."

"That's obvious."

Meridel's couture, as always, was kooky chic. A mauve turtleneck sweater; a loose turquoise gypsy skirt of some crinkly lightweight material (chiffon, perhaps); and knee-high black leather boots. Her beiege-blonde hair, the color of fine German lager, was gathered in a teenage ponytail. According to Bombazine's agent Babs Katz, Meridel began having work done at thirteen to win beauty contests. In her forties now, her body looked as hard and firm as a cheerleader's. She jogged, she worked out in spas, rode an exercise bike in her New York office, and owned second-degree belts in Jiu Jitsu and Taekwondo. Twice married and divorced but childless, she'd once been (Babs gossiped) a "swinger" — a regular at Studio 54 and the notorious Plato's Retreat, the Studio 54 of Sex. Bombazine believed the Studio 54 rumor — everybody hip had gone there — but disbelieved the Plato's Retreat. Meridel would have been a child then.

He'd never made a pass at her — not just because he'd been married but because he didn't want to embarrass himself. What would a sexpot swinger, or ex-swinger, want with a geriatric? It would have been unprofessional, too: an unwritten law of publishing forbade dalliances between authors and their editors, agents, and publicists. They were considered incestuous. Writers had enough problems with those people already.

It had taken him a while to understand the difference between an agent and a publicist, and Meridel did not clarify matters by acting like his agent, infuriating Babs in the process. The fact that a publicist is an agent—a public relations agent—confused him further. Publicists arranged an author's media bookings and promotions and public appearances like signings and readings, but agents could do those things too. Sometimes the publicist worked for a publishing house, as its "publicity director," but more often independently. Agents marketed an author's work to publishers, though they could double as publicists. Often the agent and the publicist were the same person. Some authors dispensed with agents, others with publicists, and a few got by with neither. Agents mostly worked behind the scenes and rarely made public statements about their clients, while publicists sought out the spotlight and never shut up about them. Meridel did and said whatever she wanted, infuriating Babs to no end.

"Babs" Katz, whom they would conference today, was an effusive upper-East Sider in her early fifties, so obese that she had to buy two seats on commercial air flights to accommodate her girth. Babs didn't fly much. Savvy and aggressive, she prided herself on the fact that she made money for Bombazine even though he wrote books about authors nobody had read. Babs was terrific at finding publishers for his freshman literature anthologies and getting them adopted at huge universities like UCLA and Penn State, where readership was guaranteed.

In Manhattan Babs and Meridel lunched and shopped together and clawed at one another with catty remarks. Apart, they said even worse things about each other. When they fought, it was not over Bombazine but for him; each thought she was indispensable to him. His stature in the groves of Academe had lent them prestige, especially back in the days when his reviews were appearing in *The New York Review of Books*. Now they fought to protect him as they tried to promote him and keep his name alive.

"They both want you," J. J. had explained. "Why not give them a shag?"

"Separately or together? Don't be ridiculous."

"All right, not the fat one. Bang the little blonde."

"Worry about your own sex life."

"What sex life?"

"I talked to Babs this morning," Meridel was saying now as she munched on a lobster egg roll. "Our conference call is set for three-fifteen. It's important that you and she and I are on the same page before we talk to your editor at Grove/Atlantic. What's his name? Linus Motherfuck?"

"Lionel Motherwell."

"Oh, yes. He edited your novel. He must be terribly old by now."

"He is. He uses two canes. Why are we talking to him?"

"He's tight with Izzy Tannenbaum at Lionsgate. They do

the Met together when Izzy's in New York. They love Italian opera. Verdi, Puccini…"

"Israel Tannebaum? The studio head? We're conferencing him?"

"Not today. He's in London filming with Jennifer Lawrence and Gary Ross." Meridel drained the wine in her glass. "Your editor recommended us to Izzy. He has clout and pull."

"I don't like it," Bombazine said. "Too many names. I need a dramatis personae and a flow chart."

"Bad attitude! That's why I had to fly in and hold your hand. This call is crucial, babe. You need to be in on it."

He eyed her levelly. "I'm not sure I want in on it."

She stared back in disbelief. "Now listen, Lord Byron. I've stuck by you. I've gotten you promotional gigs nobody else could've, not even that sow Babs. I've been your agent-in-waiting. I've been your friend and fan. I've read every word you've written, and believe me, that was a labor of love because some of your books weren't exactly page turners. I pushed and hawked them for you."

"Thank you. I think."

"So don't tell me you're bailing on the best gig we've ever had. At least talk to the movie people."

"All right. But I'm not commiting to anything."

"You won't have to." She dabbed at her mouth with a white cloth napkin and left a red smudge on it. "At least not today."

"You really want in on that movie, don't you."

"Don't you?" She flashed a canny smile. "Tell you what.

192

Let's make a deal. Don't bail and I'll give you the best birthday present you'll get today. Something naughty."

He felt his heart jump in his chest.

She was watching him with amusement. No, he told himself. She's teasing. "What's the present?" he had to ask.

"Cooperate and find out."

Something stirred below his belt that hadn't stirred while he was watching *All in the Family*. Could she mean… ? He hoped this wasn't a "that is not what I meant at all; that is not it at all" moment because he couldn't handle another one. Today of all days, how could he turn down a come-on from a beige-blonde cougar with the hard body of a cheerleader?

The day had come alive for him. His dread moved away.

Curled up at Meridel's feet, licking her leather boots, Argos vied for attention. She reached down and petted him. "Your dog looks like a wolf," she said. "Is he a Husky? Those blue eyes are to die for. You should write a novel about him. Izzy could make a movie of it. Dog movies are in, you know. Jeff Bridges just made one. So did Paul Walker and Owen Wilson and Richard Gere."

"Let's hope *Spoon River Anthology* is in."

Meridel chortled. "I remember those poems from high school. Isn't there one about a corpse complaining that two teenagers screw on his tombstone every night?"

"There is. The epitaph for A. D. Blood, the village bluenose. He'd closed down the saloons and brothels and kept the townsfolk from playing cards."

"He deserved to have teenagers fuck on his grave." She

193

licked two greasy fingertips. "I'm through, baby. Let's move to the living room and talk. We've got ten minutes to kill."

—w— —w—

The conference call with Babs and Motherwell in New York got off to a rocky start. First Bombazine and Meridel couldn't agree on whether to videoconference using Skype. With Skype one could talk to, see, and be seen by up to twenty-five persons at once. But he'd never Skyped and didn't know how. Meridel assured him that she could Skype because she'd recently bought Linux, the latest version of its operating system, and her laptop came equipped with a handy "Enable Skype Video" option.

Bombazine solemnly frowned and nodded, though she might as well have been explaining macroscopic quantum theory to a Tasmanian bushman. He hated cyberspeak. "Wonderful," he said. "Skype it is. You do it."

Removing her laptop from its silver case, Meridel reconsidered. "Actually, I'm not up to seeing Babs," she decided. "Don't ask why. I don't want to Skype her."

"All right, we won't."

"It's because the poor dear is a beast now. A whale. Her weight is off the charts. You haven't seen her lately. She has an eating disorder. It depresses me." Meridel shuddered and replaced the laptop in its case. "We'll do an old-fashioned conference call."

Bombazine tried to remember how old-fashioned conference calls worked; nowadays it was hard for him to remember how anything high tech worked. The direct telephone

phone number of the first party, Babs, would be dialed; once she'd answered, a flash/recall button would be pressed and the direct phone number of the second party, Lionel, would be dialed; while Lionel's phone was ringing, the flash/recall button would be pressed again and connect all three parties. It was a simple process, and they contacted Babs, who'd been expecting the call, right away. But when Motherwell's direct number was dialed, the connection broke and they had to start over.

On the second try, Babs laughed: "What happened? Never mind. Meridel, darling, how are you? It's been ages."

"Babs, I spoke to you this morning."

"It's been ages since I've seen you. Have you missed me?"

"Darling, no."

"Lunch next week at Bergdorf's?"

"I'm Bergdorfed out. Think of someplace else."

"The Brasserie?"

"Tommy Bahama," Meridel said.

"Oh, good, let's do Tommy. I've heard their salade nicoise with seared tuna and artichokes and anchovies is to die for. I'm on a diet."

"It's about time," said Meridel.

"You know, darling, there are times when I don't like you?"

"Can we get on with the call!" Bombazine groused over the phone in the kitchen. He switched to Extended Speaker Phone so the call could be heard all over the house and he could pace. Clearly, this conference would take some time.

"My, my," Babs cooed. "That sounds like our Georgie. How are you, Georgie?"

"Not good, actually."

"Why not? I'm working out a deal with Lionsgate. I'm getting you either a small option or a consulting fee."

"Is that all?" Meridel sounded disappointed.

"Is that all? Darling, this movie could become a classic. Look at that cast. Keira Knightley starred in *Pride and Prejudice* and Ang Lee directed a big Jane Austen movie. I forget which one. Lionsgate may bring in Miramax for financing. Georgie, they might want you to rewrite the screenplay. I hope so. It'll mean more money."

"We'll think about it," Meridel said before Bombazine could reply.

Babs snickered "What's this we, darling? Did you marry Georgie without telling me? You're his flack, remember? I'm his agent.'"

"Don't pull rank," Meridel said. "Have you gotten with the screenwriters?"

"Not yet, sweetie. These things take time. But what's there to 'think about?' I was talking to Georgie, not you."

"Leave me out of it," Bombazine interjected.

Meridel said, "I hate doing business with Canada. Lionsgate is Canadian. Canada has too much government regulation."

"Not your problem," Babs told her. "Making a movie is cheaper in Canada. Lionsgate's getting rich with their *Hunger Games*. We're not in this for the money anyway."

Meridel asked, "What are we in it for?"

"Prestige, darling. And all that fun we can have. Actually, we're doing it for Georgie."

"No, you're not," Bombazine objected. "Don't do it for me."

"Let's get Motherlode on the horn," Meridel said.

"Well, ring him," Babs snapped. "And it's Motherwell, not Motherlode."

Meridel pressed the flash/recall button and the editor's phone rang. It was not Motherwell who answered but his executive assistant, ShaNika, who was black and six feet tall and looked like a Vogue model. Bombazine had seen her.

"I'm so sorry," ShaNika said. "Mr. Motherwell is in a meeting."

"Well, get him out of it," Babs ordered. "Tell him it's Katzie and I've got George Bombazine on the line for a conference."

"And me," added Meridel in a huff. "Meridel Baxter. Tell him Meridel is on the line too."

"He may not remember who that is," Babs murmured.

"Please hold," ShaNika requested.

The next thing they heard was Muzak—violins playing a Barry Manilow song from the seventies. "Lionel does this," Babs told the others in a muffled voice. "He's not in a meeting. The son of a bitch makes you cool your heels."

They waited longer. Finally ShaNika announced, "Mr. Motherwell is available now."

"It's about time," Babs said.

Motherwell, who'd edited Bombazine's biographies and his sixties novel *In the Belly of the Pentagon*, sounded cordial, but something in his voice rang false. "Sorry about the wait, gang. Hi, Georgio. How are things in Culture Gulch, Arizona? Oh, I'm kidding."

"Hello, Lionel," Bombazine said lifelessly. "How are you?" He pictured Motherwell—a handsome silver-haired man, older than himself, who looked like the actor Christopher Plummer.

"I'm good," replied Motherwell. "Our pub date for the new anthology is fifteen November. We've booked a signing afternoon at Barnes and Noble Fifth Avenue. Surely Meridel told you? We're throwing a shindig for you afterward. Nothing mucho grande, but the max for a Barnes and Noble party. So get out there and hawk *Return to Spoon River*. I may order a bigger first run: five thousand copies. Do whatever Babs and Meridel say. Give readings and signings at colleges and book clubs and bookstores and nursing homes and Shriners conventions and prisons."

"Talk about the screenplay," Bombazine said.

"The screenplay." Motherwell repeated the words as if they were foreign to him. "The screenplay."

"Lionel, this is Babs. Cut the crap. What's happening with Lionsgate?"

The editor hesitated. "Babs, how are you? I assume you mean the movie they're making of *Spoon River*."

"No, I mean the remake of *Casblanca*. Talk to me, Lionel."

"Don't stall, Lionel," Meridel said. "This is Baxter. Why are you stalling?"

Motherwell sighed. "My dear girl, no one is stalling. I'm trying to field your questions. You did a nice job for Georgio with Barnes and Noble, by the way. They love *Return to Spoon River*. Now, is everyone sitting down?"

"Bad news," Bombazine grumbled.

"I'm afraid so," Motherwell said. "Lionsgate bailed. The plug was pulled. The project is dead in the water."

"What?" shrilled Babs.

"What?" Meridel gasped.

"Gang, I'm sorry," Motherwell said.

Silence.

"Lionel," Meridel said tightly, "how the fuck long have you known this?"

"For three minutes. I just got off the horn with Izzy in London."

"Shit!" said Meridel.

"Shit!" echoed Babs.

"Shit happens," said Motherwell.

Babs asked, "What happened?"

"Many things," sighed the editor. "Lionsgate is having union problems in Toronto. Santa Barbara got cold feet. Brad Pitt walked because of a contractual commitment with Plan B Productions. When Matt Damon heard Brad Pitt walked, he walked. And when George Clooney heard that Brad Pitt and Matt Damon walked, guess what he did?"

"Walked," Bombazine said.

Meridel asked, "What about Miramax, Lionel? Any interest?"

"None. They were never on board. That was just a rumor. I was misinformed."

"It appears," said Babs, "that you were misinformed about a lot of things, sweetie."

"I was."

"And you misinformed us," Meridel reminded him.

Motherwell replied, "I gave you the misinformation I received."

"We didn't want misinformation," Meridel snapped.

"Now listen, girl," Motherwell lisped. "Don't kill the messenger. It's like the Iraq war. We were all wrong."

Meridel scoffed. "We weren't all wrong about the Iraq war."

"Well, shit..." sighed Babs.

"There's more shit," said Motherwell. "Izzy said the Masters estate was raising cain about copyright permission and film rights. I think they wanted money and they weren't going to get it from him. He told them, 'Go shtup yourselves, you goddam greedy goyim! *Gai feifen ahfen yam!* Go peddle your fish elsewhere! I don't just make movies, I make money.' Pardon the ethnic impression, but that's what he said."

"Lionel," Babs said, "you must've known. This can't be news to you."

"I was always skeptical about the project," Motherwell said.

"That's not true," countered Meridel. "And you know it."

"It's my fault," Babs said. "As Georgie's agent, I should've dealt with the studios directly. I trusted you, Lionel."

Bombazine wanted to kill himself but also wanted to be involved in making an art movie. He was vastly relieved and bitterly disappointed. He felt his mood careen like Shelley's sailboat in that fatal thunderstorm. But at least one thing was certain now.

He could drown himself tonight.

"Lionel," he intruded, "this is George. I'm curious. Did the project ever really stand a chance?"

Silence.

200

"It was a long shot," the editor finally disclosed. "Izzy never liked it. He's leery of art films. A graveyard in the Midwest and six tombstones and everything a flashback? He thought it was a horror movie. When he found out otherwise, he had a hissy and the screenwriters revolted and told me they wanted you aboard. So Izzy fired the screenwriters. I might have talked him into it if the cast hadn't walked and the Masters estate hadn't bitched. But the books Izzy wants to make movies of are Young Adult potboilers and graphic novels about iron robots fighting Middle Eastern terrorists. I love Izzy, we do the Met together, but the poor dear doesn't know Spoon River from Moon River. George, I'm sorry if I gave you false hopes. It was never a fait accompli. Remember your signing for *Return to Spoon River* at Barnes and Noble Fifth. Gang I have to run. ShaNika just handed me a note. E. L. James is here. Have you guys read *Fifty Shades of Gray*? They're making a movie of it."

Chapter Twenty-One: 3:39 p. m.

A KISS BEFORE DYING

Ever so slightly, hardly at all, Bombazine was more dis-appointed than relieved. But as Truman Capote wrote, there is peace in certainty, and now he could be certain that no screenplay rewrite or movie consultation or other distrac-tion would postpone his mission until Thanksgiving. Tonight would be the night to accomplish it; the die was cast.

He flopped down on the black leather divan in the living room; the conference call had exhausted him even though he'd contributed nothing to it. Meridel was stomping about the living room in her black boots, hands clasped behind her waist like a general who's just learned that his troops have surrendered. "Damn," she kept repeating. "Damn, damn, damn."

"I expected this," he said in a voice of calm resignation. "It was always a long shot."

"You did not expect it."

"It was just a dream. A fantasy."

"No. We got jerked around."

"It wasn't your fault. It wasn't anyone's."

"I don't like to lose. That fucking Lionel. That fucking Tannenbaum." She marched to the kitchen and returned with a wineglass filled to the brim with Chinese rice wine, along with a Wedgewood saucer she planned to use for an ashtray. She clawed open a pack of mentholated Marlboro Lights 100s and lit one with her sterling silver lighter.

Bombazine jumped up to stop her. "My house is a no smoking zone, Meridel. *Ne fumez pas s'il vous plait.*"

"Sue me. I smoke when I'm frustrated and I'm frustrated."

"In that case, give me a cigarette. We'll kill ourselves together."

She handed him one and lit it for him. Bombazine hadn't smoked in years, having quit to lower his blood pressure. The puff he took made him dizzy and he snuffed out the cigarette in the saucer.

"I never liked menthols," he said, making a face,

They sat together on the sofa. She took a deep pull, blew a jet of smoke, and smiled at him fixedly, accusingly. "Tell me why," she said, "I get the feeling you're glad the project is dead?"

"Part of me is glad."

"Why?"

"It's personal."

"Oh, for Christ's sake." She blew smoke into his face. "What does that mean? It could have been fun."

"I know."

"Why are you acting weird? You've been weird all day. What's wrong?"

"I'm always like this on my birthday. Maybe I don't want to get any older."

"Who does? How old are you?"

"Too old for you. I told you earlier."

"I like older men. I'd fuck Clint Eastwood or Sean Connery in a New York minute."

"So would millions of other women."

"That's a little mean. Don't make me feel badly."

"Bad," he corrected her "Feel bad."

"The grammarian. And I was trying to make you feel good. I'm so disappointed. I was up for today and now I feel like shit warmed over."

"Does that mean I don't get my birthday present?"

Her face softened as she remembered. She pursed her lips. Her eyes roamed the. room as if someone were hiding in it. "Do you still want it?"

"I do."

"Are we expecting any visitors?"

"None."

"Are you sure?"

"Positive."

"Are all the doors locked?"

"Tightly. What's my present? A striptease, I hope."

"No, this." She crushed out her cigarette and set the saucer on the coffee table. She wrapped her arms around his neck and kissed him hard on the mouth. Her breath smelled of wine and smoke, but her mouth had the deliciously sweet taste of bubblegum or Big Red Cream Soda. She drew back and then kissed him again, harder, turning her head sideways and filling his mouth with her tongue.

The kiss seemed to go on forever, like kisses in Hitchcock movies where the camera slowly circles the lovers and circles them again, a little faster, and then whirls about them as violin music on the track soars to a fever pitch.

When she finally pulled away, her lipstick was smeared and her eyes were wide, as if her behavior had shocked her. Regaining composure, she smoothed her sweater front and cleared her throat and tried to smile.

"Whew," she said. "How was it?"

"Not bad. Is that all?" He was trying to be blasé. He felt lightheaded, a little dizzy. Fortunately he was sitting, not standing, or he might have toppled over.

"What do you mean, 'Is that all?' You were expecting more?" Meridel seemed offended, as if a bum had asked for a blow job. It was the look Holly Teasdale had given him at lunch when she thought he was coming on to her. It was the look Pru had given him earlier, for the same reason. *"That is not what I meant at all."* Maybe he really was J. Alfred Prufrock.

"I was joking," he said feebly.

"It wasn't funny."

"I know. I'm sorry."

"It hurt my feelings. Do you think I kiss just any man like that?"

"Holly, I don't know why I said it. Please don't be angry."

She was gaping at him in disbelief, and he realized his mistake.

"Holly?" she said. "Who the fuck is Holly?"

"I meant Meridel. I'm sorry—I was with a girl named Holly earlier. I don't know what I'm saying. I'm not myself today."

She eyed him doubtfully. Her stare was pitying. In a dull voice she said, "I have to go to the bathroom."

He leapt up from the couch and pointed toward the half bath in the alcove where the two wings of the house intersected. She rose and slowly headed toward it, gypsy chiffon skirt rustling, black leather boots squeaking, shoulders back, head high. A haughty queen en route to the chamber pot.

He did not want to wait until tonight. He wanted to die now. He had botched things again. The afternoon was ruined. Nothing today had gone right, things just got worse and worse, and time was running out.

God damn you, he cursed himself. You senile addle-brained Alzheimeric old fuckup. You'd fuck up a wet dream. Calling Meridel "Holly!" Holly was still on your mind. Why? What happened with Holly was not your fault. The girl was crazy. He wondered what he could he do or say to atone to Meridel for the gaffe and salvage the afternoon. It had been a great kiss. He was grateful for a kiss before dying from a younger woman before he went to his watery grave. Especially a juicy wet kiss that tasted of wine and smoke and Big Red Cream Soda. He'd wanted another. Kissing was something that not just any woman did well. Most women, in his experience, were good at kissing back but not good at kissing—you had to kiss them first. Meridel was good at both. He'd asked "Is that all?" because he'd wanted more, lots more.

She was taking her time in the bathroom. He hoped she wasn't sick. His mind wandered. He worried about Argos—where he was, what he was up to, whether he'd eaten. As if reluctant to intrude on a romantic tête-a-tête, the tactful dog was making himself scarce. He noticed that Meridel had left her pack of Marlboro Lights 100s and silver lighter on the coffee table, next to her half-full glass of wine. Feeling oral, he thought about lighting another cigarette and taking another puff just for the hell of it. And draining the wine. But he needed a real drink. He yearned to break open the twenty-year-old single malt Pru had brought over. When Meridel returned, if she ever did, he would offer her a Scotch and soda.

What could be taking her so long? Had she discovered an escape hatch? He should check on her. He would knock on the bathroom door. He forced himself up from the couch and at that moment she reappeared. He sat back down. Actually, he collapsed. She was not wearing anything.

Not only was she not wearing any clothes, she was not wearing her rings or wristwatch or turquoise necklace or gold bracelet and earrings or anything on her feet or in her hair. She was not wearing any anything. Like Botticelli's Venus or Goya's Naked Maja or Lady Godiva or *Playboy's* Miss September, Meridel was totally, unabashedly naked.

She sauntered toward him. Her face was without expression. O my God, he thought. Here she comes. Is she an angel sent from heaven as a sign? Do I take her to the bedroom? I do. I have to. She's not teasing. She flew across the country to go to bed with me today.

He cleared his throat. "Meridel," he said with the stern tone a father might take with an immodest daughter, "Meridel, you have no clothes on."

207

"I know," she said in a breathless Marilyn Monroe voice. "You wanted a striptease and I skipped the preliminaries." She parted her moist lips, touched the back of her head with one hand, struck a pose, and preened. She shook her hair loose. Then, with the seductiveness of a concubine at a sex trade auction, she drew closer and stopped ten feet from the coffee table to give him a close look at the merchandise. He had been to bed with at least fifty women and none, not even Tencha, had looked better with her clothes off than on. Meridel did. Clothed she was pretty, naked she was gorgeous.

It was as if she'd planted a body double in the bathroom and it was the double he beheld. Never had he noticed the sensuous curve of her lips, which had the texture of marzipan, or the hazel-green of her eyes, which blazed like jewels. She had applied fresh makeup and undone her ponytail to let her beige-blonde hair fall to her shoulders. Her breasts were small but firm, the areolae not pink but brown. Her skin glowed with the translucence of alabaster. Her neatly trimmed mons pubis was a perfect little triangle, its pelt matching the champagne hue of her hair. She had become a girl in her mid-twenties.

Like a fashion model, hand on hip, she executed a turn — first this way, then that, then completely around. Her ass, a masterpiece Velazquez would've paid a thousand Castilian ducats to paint in the seventeenth century, revealed a dimple high on either cheek, near the hip, and he remembered that she worked out in a spa, rode an exercise bicycle in her office, and earned belts in martial art disciplines.

Surely a minute inspection would reveal hints of middle age — wrinkles on the backs of her thighs, cellulite lumps on her buttocks, loose flab here and there — but from where he sat now she had a perfect body.

Facing him squarely, she stopped and arched an eyebrow as if awaiting a response. Applause, perhaps. A stamping of his feet. An appreciative whoop. But he was catatonic, mute with awe. He could not applaud or stamp his feet or whoop. He could barely breathe.

He feared he was having a stroke. His response, when it came, was to say, "O Meridel. O my God, Meridel. Look at you. You're trying to seduce me." Now he was the dumb Graduate, seeing Mrs. Robinson naked. But this time the younger person was seducing the older one.

His open-mouthed shock tickled her. The blank fashion-model gaze yielded to a smile, and she could not keep from laughing.

"What's funny?" he croaked.

"You. Listen, Georgie, if you don't take me to bed right now, I'm going to feel pretty foolish standing here like this..."

Chapter Twenty-Two: 4:02 p.m.

"Sex Is Fun—Or Hell"

As he led her by the hand to his king-sized bed in the master bedroom, he couldn't believe what was happening. Surely he would wake up at any moment. Her appearing nude was like something out of a movie he'd seen—a real movie, not a porno—but he couldn't remember which movie, or what followed. Finally something good was happening today. The question was, could he rise to the occasion? He had not been to bed with anyone but Pru in twenty years, and not with her in the past five. He was seventy years old, with benign prostate hypertrophy, prostate cancer, a limp dick and no Viagra.

This is the last time I'll ever go to bed with a woman, he realized. That hurt more than the idea of killing himself. There was no doubt he would take the plunge tonight. He had no reason to put it off till Thanksgiving. Waiting until ten would take forever—six hours—and the only thing that might tempt him to postpone it would be a wild, pagan, bacchanalic romp with Meridel, followed by a mutual declaration of true love and commitment. But how could sex between a cougar with a teenage body and a codger with prostate cancer be wild and pagan and bacchanalic?

He ought to be nervous and was. A lot might be riding on his performance. He felt pressured, under the gun, vulnerably self-conscious. Given the shape he was in and the shape she was in, he couldn't let her see him naked. Before removing his clothes, he yanked the cord on the blinds at the window, shutting out the afternoon light and leaving the room semi-dark. Wordlessly he slipped into bed and cuddled with her. His feet felt icy. His prick, soft and small, a tiny sponge, had retracted into his scrota. Whereas Meridel emitted heat like a stove. "Sex is Fun—or Hell," he remembered. Something from a Salinger short story. Would sex with Meridel be fun or hell? He was about to find out.

With a chuckle he asked, "Are you sure I'm not taking advantage of you?"

"I did have too much wine. After three Bloody Marys on the flight. And this is crazy and unprofessional. But I'm glad it's happening."

"Why? I'm an old man on Medicare."

"Don't talk. Make love to me."

"You're ravishing," he said, talking anyway. "You're *Playboy* gorgeous. But I can't promise anything."

"Me neither. I'm tipsy. Do as much or as little as you like. I'll do anything you want. You're not my first senior citizen."

He liked the sound of that, it took some pressure off. He began his foreplay as best as he could remember it, hoping that like playing Beethoven's "Fur Elise" or riding a bike, it would come back to him automatically. He liked to make love slowly. "It matters not how slowly you go," Confucius said, "as long as you do not stop." Who could be sure Confucius hadn't been talking about sex? Even Confucius got laid. Bombazine lay on his left side and Meridel on her back as he nuzzled her playfully, his lips brushing her mouth and neck and shoulders. This is what it all comes down to, he thought. Eros and Thanatos on one's last day. Sex and death. First we lust for one and then for the other...

"George, where did you go? I just had the feeling you were adding numbers in your head."

"Now who's talking too much?" He kissed her on the mouth. It was not an Alfred Hitchcock kiss like those they'd shared earlier, but neither was it playful. It meant business.

Meridel didn't need much foreplay. She had gotten wet too fast—maybe back in the living room—and he had to slow things down and hope for a boner pretty soon if one was materializing. His penis, having reemerged from safe haven in his scrota, was stirring.

They kissed some more. "Ah, you're sweet," she whispered. "Sweet, sweet..."

"You are," he said, wishing she'd shut up.

"I want you inside me."

"In due time," he whispered, impatient with her impatience. He took her hand and put it on his cock. He'd been bluffing when he said "in due time." That was assuming a lot. But on his flaccid member Meridel's fluttering fingers felt like his own. Most women did not know how to play with a man's pecker. Now his blood was flowing and his procreational fluid, as Fallopius called it, had surely heard the call. Could he get even half hard, he might slip it in and work it up...

Heartened by the possibility, that fresh hope, he hadn't realized that someone was in the room with them. Argos had infiltrated and posted himself at the door like a sentry. The marbles of his eyes glowed blue in the semidark as he watched, intently and quietly, refusing to pant even though his long tongue hung out; his face showed puzzled concern. Argos had never watched Bombazine and Pru make love, perhaps because they so rarely had.

Aware of the dog, Meridel began to laugh and he had to call time out. "Shoo!" he whispered loudly. He made to rise from the bed and chase Argos out, but Meridel stopped him. "Let him stay. It makes things kind of kinky."

"Argos is a voyeur," Bombazine joked. "Usually he brings a camera." Meridel's laughter was like wind chimes; glancing at the dog, he laughed too.

He resumed his foreplay and she continued to foreplay with his cock, but the mood was broken. Comic relief had taken its toll; his rope refused to rise. Meridel stroked his penis gently, squeezed it firmly, tapped it like a Morse code operator, trilled it like a pianist, and bending forward rubbed it between the palms of her hands as if it were a rolling pin. Nothing worked.

He lay back, closed his eyes, and heard Dr. Fallopius say, "Sex ain't everything. At your age it ain't anything..." But now what he felt were not hands or fingers on his cock but the soft warmth of a mouth and the licking of a tongue. Meridel evidently was a fellatrix par excellence—in a former life she might've been the head (no pun intended) courtesan in the harem of Louis XV or Charles II. She blew and

213

sucked, kissed and spat, whipped his member with her hair, and talked to it as if it had an identity of its own and just needed coaxing. Smiling dreamily, eyes shut, Bombazine began to enjoy himself, and soon he was as happy as any pasha, sultan, or raj. Only one problem remained.

He still wasn't hard.

Halfway, yes. Semi-tumescent, yes. But not hard enough to enter the portal of the promised land. After ten minutes, Meridel's head rose from its labors. Her face was a question mark.

"I can't," he answered. "I'm sorry."

"Hey, it happens," Meridel consoled. "Maybe it's me."

"No. There's something I haven't told you."

"Don't. No true confessions. You tasted good. A little salty, but good."

Reared to be gallant, a gentleman as well as a scholar, he could not let things end there. That he couldn't get off didn't mean she couldn't. "It's my turn to head south," he announced. "There's something I can still do."

—⁓— —⁓—

Though out of practice, Bombazine was an accomplished cunnilinguist who'd been trained by an expert. In 1967, on Thompson Street in Manhattan's West Village, with the Army behind him and graduate school at Columbia ahead, he'd lived for two months with Irenka Wozniak, a forty-year-old Polish lesbian choreographer. She had performed with the Merce Cunningham and Alvin Ailey dance troupes. Double jointed, contortionistic, supple as rubber, Irenka could bend her body into pretzel-like shapes. She could perform autocunnilingus, she boasted, but when Bombazine too eagerly asked to see that, she indignantly refused. Irenka had agreed to live with him because he looked like her brother Wladyslaw, an anticommunist labor organizer behind bars in Warsaw; she showed him an old Polaroid of Wladyslaw, handsome and smiling and confident, and he saw the resemblance. Irenka and Wladyslaw had grown up hungry and destitute in Warsaw's Marszalkowska Housing District. Fantasizing (Bombazine suspected) that he was Wlyadslaw, Irenka instructed him in the art, craft, and science of pussy eating, something the callow conventional young Bombazine had never done. He proved a quick study, a bright, capable novice thirsty for knowledge.

Now, with his face buried in Meridel's golden fur. Bombazine remembered Irenka. Her spirit was in the room, standing beside the bed, watching with Argos, mutely coaching her old novice.

Playfully, Meridel asked, "Do you mind if I smoke while you eat?"

"Yes, I do," he grunted.

"I'm kidding. My smokes are in the living room anyway."

"Lie back and hush," he ordered. "I used to be good at this."

He had not lost the knack — it really was like riding a bike, and one didn't need an erection for it. The secret, he remembered, was to enjoy it. It was a return to the womb, the miraculous beginning, the source of human life, the supreme déjà vu. If truth were told, we all want to go back there. But if you were only performing the act as a favor, a service, a distasteful act of supplication, the woman would know.

Gently lapping away like a cat might a bowl of cream, he was grateful for her pubic pelt even though it tickled his nose. Bombazine disliked shaved pudenda. It was the style now, but to him there was nothing more fascinating than a woman's pubic bush; it made a statement about her just as much as the hair on her head did, and there was something pedophilic about making love to a woman with the hairless crotch of a ten-year-old girl.

Meridel's promiment labia, unusually large lips sweet as fresh ambrosia, were fit for the gods. Given her spicy diet, Tencha's juices had been hot, *muy caliente*, a *salsa picante*. Tencha had not enjoyed oral sex but tolerated receiving it as a concession to his gringo depravity. (Her reciprocating was out of the question, fellatio being a practice she associated with street *putas* in Nuevo Laredo.) Pru disapproved of oral sex too, and fellatio especially, though Bombazine's skilled tongue had given her powerful orgasms that embarrassed her.

"Please don't stop," Meridel murmured. "You're hired."

"You couldn't afford me," he said, coming up for air.

Now he had reached the clitoral stage. Third base, heading home. Meridel was delaying her orgasm, teetering on the brink but holding back, as if approaching an earthquaking climax of 5.0 on the Richter Scale. With his right hand he slipped three fingers into her, thrust them to and fro like a phallus, moved them up and down, rotated them in a clockwise motion, massaged her clit with his thumb and forefinger, and gingerly penetrated her anus with his right thumb. That made her gasp. Her orgasm, when it came, was violent, as if she'd been flung across the room. She arched her back, gave an ear-piercing whoop, and bucked like a bronco, smashing her pelvis against his face with such force that he feared she might break his nose or split his lip. Argos barked, concerned that his master was in trouble.

Meridel came and came in paroxysms more like convulsions than releases — she came, as the Rolling Stones would have it, in colors. And then lay deadly still. He continued to kiss her inner thighs. He was relieved when finally she gave his hair a tug, the signal to stop.

"Come on up," she murmured. "Just hold me a while. With me up here and you down there, a girl starts to feel left out..."

Bombazine's jaw ached, his tongue was numb, his fingers were sticky, his gums sore, his balls blue. In his youth, that's what they'd called not getting off. Blue Balls. He wondered if they still called it that.

Her voice was husky and sleepy. "It's been ages since I've been eaten out like that."

That rankled — he would've preferred to hear that she had never been eaten out like that. But what did it matter? He was a bottom-line old schooler whose mission was not accomplished. She had begged to be fucked and he had not been able to penetrate her. Getting a woman off the way he had was cheating.

Both tired now, they cuddled with her head nestled on his

shoulder, her fingers toying with his chest hairs. He hoped she wouldn't fall asleep. He had to get rid of her soon. There were last-minute things to do. He glanced up at Pru's antique grandfather clock. Five-thirty. Ample time, but now he wanted her gone.

She was purring with contentment. Drowsily, she asked, "Who is she?"

"Who is who?'

"The girl whose name you called me earlier."

"Holly? A former student I had lunch with today."

"I was so mad I started to leave."

"I was afraid you'd climbed out the bathroom window."

"I started to. Why didn't you want to go to California or Canada with me and Babs and help make that movie?"

"There's something more important I have to do here."

"What is it?"

"I'd rather not say."

They were silent.

"You're mysterious, George Bombazine. Maybe that's why you float my boat. I'm sorry you didn't get off. It's not fair."

"It wasn't your fault. It was mine."

"Want to go again? I know tricks we could try."

"Not today."

"Maybe it was the where. In this room, on this bed, you made love to your wife. Was that the problem?"

"The house is hers, the bed is mine. I don't want to talk about her."

"Then we won't."

"I'm sorry I wasn't able to perform."

218

She laughed. "Jesus, babe. You make me come like a tsunami and then you apologize?"

"It's a guy thing."

"It's a macho thing. Grow up. Be happy that I'm happy. Usually I don't get off."

It was becoming tiresome and he let it go. Holding hands, they continued to lie supine but apart, perfectly still, twin corpses in a wide casket. He squeezed her hand, she squeezed back. He had nothing against post-coital intimacy, but today he could hear the clock ticking. Another chill crept up his backbone.

"George," she said in a voice that might have come from a child, "do you think I'm an airhead?"

"Of course not. Why would I?"

She pulled herself up and positioned her back against the headboard. "Be honest with me. You think I'm all about Gucci shoes and perfectly fab East Side restaurants and hawking books Hollywood might want. When I was talking to Babs, we could hear you sighing in the kitchen. I could almost see you rolling your eyes. You think I'm an airhead."

"Everyone was playing a role this afternoon."

"I'm not just a bottle blonde bimbo flack. That's the role I play but not who I am. I went to Barnard on a scholarship. I was summa cum laude. My I.Q. is one fifty. I majored in journalism and edited the newspaper and the yearbook. When I graduated I wanted to be Tina Brown."

"Keep trying. Everyone in publishing is a woman now."

"Motherwell's not," Meridel said.

"Yes, he is."

219

"The big shots are still men. Doubleday hired me out of Barnard to read the slush pile of unsolicited manuscripts that come through the transom. I ended up as a flack. That was ages ago. Do you know how old I am?"

"Babs said forty-five."

"That cunt. I'm forty-four. Speaking of Babs, I didn't want to Skype her because I didn't want to see her."

"You said that. You just pretend to be friends?"

"In five years, if I stop dieting and working out, I'll look like her. I'm going to be her. She's retiring. She's a foodie with an eating disorder. She's also a closet alcoholic with rheumatoid arthritis, like poor Kathleen Turner. That's why she's obese. She was gorgeous once."

"I know. She's told me."

"She wants me to take over her agency. I can be your agent."

"Glad to have you aboard, Baxter." His response was desultory—he could barely conceal his impatience. He glanced at the clock again.

"I've been your agent all along. You've had two agents and it's driven Babs crazy. Her clients will transfer to me and I'll keep mine. I'll be your publicist and your agent."

"And this means you'll look like Babs?"

"I drink and eat too much. I'm getting old. This business ages you. For a man, forty-four is young. For me it means I'm a woman of a certain age. Do you know what I have to do to maintain this body? Soon it'll be dermoplasty, rhinoplasty, botox…"

It was depressing, and he didn't want to hear any more.

"Nonsense, Meridel. You'll always be desirable."

"I can't have children. I've had two abortions and a hysterectomy. I was married twice. Hubby Number One was rich but gay and ran off with our chauffeur. Hubby Two was rich but snorted coke twenty-four-seven and went to jail for importing it from Colombia. We lived on Park Avenue and had a yacht and a chef and a masseuse. Now I have a one-bedroom in Soho and nobody. You wouldn't believe how many nights I sit home alone, wishing a man would call me. Any man. Even one I don't know, an obscene caller, I wouldn't care as long as he'd take me to dinner at Sardi's and the theatre and then take me home and fuck my brains out.

"Some nights," she added, "I think about going the Marilyn route."

He felt the spinal chill again. "Don't talk like that."

"I'd never do it. I just think about it."

Suicide was pandemic, he thought. The Savage God went everywhere, looking for supplicants. She was not helping to alleviate his dread or make him want to go on living. She was baring her soul to him. He knew he should be sympathetic, but this was not the time for it. Momentarily he was ashamed. How to get rid of her?

"We can't do this again," she said.

He hesitated. "Do what?"

"Hop into bed. It's unprofessional. I want to be your publicist and your agent and your friend, but I can't be your lover too. For years I fantasized about going to bed with you and now I have. Speaking for myself, it was fun. But I can't go to bed with you again."

"Jesus, why would you want to? I was impotent."

"So what? I've been to bed with enough older dudes to know that needn't matter. There are a thousand things two people can do in bed besides fuck, and we did one of them. I loved it and I'd love to do it again. But we can't."

"All right, we can't." I especially can't, he thought.

"I need to make sure you understand. If anything, I enjoyed it too much. But I can't afford to get addicted to you."

"Meridel, please. I understand." He wondered if tomorrow she would feel responsible for his suicide. He hoped not.

"So you agree with me?"

"Of course," he said. "We shouldn't do this again. But thank you for today. You were fabulous and I can't tell you how much it meant to me. It'll be the nicest birthday present I get."

"I should hope so."

"I wish I could ask you to stay the night. But I can't."

"I couldn't. My friend Karla is waiting for me in the Village. It's late... I should call her... Jesus, where are my fucking clothes..."

—⁓— —⁓—

Once she'd gone, Bombazine wondered whether going to bed with her hadn't been the worst mistake he'd made all day — and he'd made some big ones. After his nightmarish lunch with Holly Teasdale, it hadn't seemed possible the day could get worse, but it had. And not because Meridel said she didn't want to go to bed with him again. Or be-

222

cause she'd painted such a depressing portrait of her own life before she left. No, it was because he hadn't been able to get it up; he would never have a sexier sex partner and never have another day when he'd wanted and needed a woman so badly. Yet he had failed. Only a fuck could've made him want to stay alive any longer, and he'd been denied one. Sex with Meridel had not been hell, but neither had it been fun, and it had left him feeling emptier than before.

He had failed at everything he'd tried to do on the most crucial day of his life. With twenty-twenty vision he saw ("*I read the news today oh boy*") that he had nothing to live for. His fate was sealed. How had Yeats prayed for death? "*Consume my heart away / Sick with desire and fastened to a dying animal, / It knows not what it is.*" Yeats knew.

He checked the time. Ten of six. Four hours to go.

Chapter Twenty-Three: 6:01 p. m.

A Game Of Scrabble

There were still things to do. Last minute things. Earlier, the hours had crept by; now the afternoon was gone and it was evening. But before doing anything else, he needed to rest. He was drained, weary, fatigued. Weak from hunger yet unable to eat. The effort he'd expended by taking Meridel to bed had worn him out. It was a tired, bedraggled old man with a swollen belly and defeated face he beheld now in the mirror. Though wanting to nap, he could not stay in the bedroom—it smelled of Meridel. Her hair, skin, perfume, and pussy. He remade the bed, staggered to the living room, and collapsed on the black leather couch. He tried but couldn't doze off. Though exhausted, he was too excited about dying in a few hours, and too edgy from his Blue Balls, to relax.

He checked on Argos. He found the dog out back, digging up something in Pru's withered garden. Again he thought of Eliot, the dour poet of death, writing about some freshly buried corpse in "The Waste Land." How did it go? "*Oh keep the dog far hence, that's friend to men, / Or with his nails he'll dig it up again.*" Was Argos digging up the body of the Vegas mafioso's wife? No, he would've done that long ago.

Argos was probably hungry, having not eaten the Alpo in his bowl, and digging up a bone he'd buried. He led Argos into the kitchen, dumped the Alpo into the garbage, took from the fridge a slab of English Stilton, cut off a hunk, and tossed it into the bowl. If he wouldn't eat the Stilton or the Alpo, he was sick and Bombazine would have to mention that in the suicide note he left for Pru.

He walked away, giving the dog a chance to sniff the cheese and eat it when no one was looking. Some dogs (though Argos had never been one) wouldn't eat if you were watching. Appended to the suicide note he'd leave would be updated information about Argos's vaccination and heartworm pill regimen. He'd also reassure Pru that he'd remitted payment for every outstanding bill, including those for the security alarm system and the Sunday *Times* delivery. And paid the property taxes. And made a few changes in his will, which were largely to her benefit. The house's foundation problems would have to wait. He would add that he had clothes ready for pickup at the dry cleaners; in the appended note he'd asked that Pru dispose of his wardrobe any way she wished — an estate sale or the Salvation Army or Goodwill or Haven for the Homeless. Trevor could help. Trevor was skilled at that sort of thing. In his element.

He shambled into the library, sat down at his computer, and spent half an hour polishing his suicide note to Pru, adding things, deleting others, proofreading everything. The last letter he'd write couldn't have typos or grammatical errors like dangling participles. It needed cutting — it was verbose. Loquacious. Nobody would be moved to tears by a suicide note that went on and on and on. Eventually, like those gawkers who end up yelling "Jump!" at the suicidal fool on the skyscraper ledge, a reader would wish you'd go ahead and kill yourself and get it over with. Encouraging him to write, Gore Vidal had told Bombazine, "Write something even if it's just a suicide note!" Well, now he had written one. Its close was sentimental, but in his experience women were not averse to sentimentality if it seemed genuine and affectionate. Women, he had learned, would remember how you said good-bye to them.

He reread the note for the tenth time: Dear Prudence: *My darling, I did myself in not because I had to but because I should. I refused to live without you any longer. You were my everything, but please don't feel guilty. I'm sorry to have done it without telling you, my love, but it was time. I have prostate cancer that would have killed me unless I underwent radiation treatments that sounded messy and unpleasant and a bother. What seventy-year-old scholar wants to wear "Depends"? Woody Allen said he wasn't afraid of death but didn't want to be there when it happened. I didn't want to be there when I died of cancer. Or became so depressed I HAD to suicide. I hear the pain of clinical depression is excruciating and intolerable, and I'm pretty depressed already. I chose to cross the River Styx right now. Call me proactive. Tell Trevor I said good-bye — for a deconstructionist he really isn't such a bad guy. Thank him for the Scotch again. I'm sorry I didn't make you happy and I hope he does.*

Ciao, mi amor. L'amero per sempre. Finish that cello concerto you're writing for me.

Love, Georgie

226

He spent the next half hour editing and revising it. Should he have referred to himself as a scholar? He was a scholar, but wasn't it pompous to call yourself one? It was like calling yourself an intellectual. Trevor T. Merriman, of course, would call himself an intellectual and a scholar in the same sentence. Bombazine had been a scholar, an eminent one, and an intellectual, a teacher, a biographer, literary historian, anthologist, critic, mentor, novelist, and lecturer. Only as an anthologist had he made money, compiling the works of men and women infinitely more gifted than himself. As an author he'd made little money, but what was it Montesquieu said about authors? *"An author is a fool who, not content with boring those he lives with, insists on boring future generations."* Bombazine hoped his books would remain in print long enough to bore future generations.

He changed the word scholar to professor and hunkered down at his computer, struggling to remember if there was anything else he needed to say or anyone else he needed to say it to. He'd talked to Catherine already, though he hadn't told her goodbye, and he couldn't say goodbye to J. J. because that old fool would rush over here to talk him out of it and probably have an accident on the way. Even under normal circumstances J. J. was a bad driver. As for Miguel, who'd said he'd call this evening, should he prepare his son for the dire news that would reach him tomorrow? He decided no. It would make their last conversation melodramatic, and Miguel thought he was a drama queen already. Miguel would accuse him of trying to lay a guilt trip on him.

Argos was barking. Someone was coming up the walk. They had a visitor, an uninvited guest. Shit!

Bombazine scampered to the front door and arrived as the bell rang. From the frenetic way the dog was behaving and the overpowering smell of Old Spice aftershave, Bombazine knew who it was before he yanked the door open.

———— ————

A crestfallen John Jacob Auchincloss stood on the porch, clutching his boxed Scrabble set and a red hardcover Scrabble dictionary. His Alfred E. Neuman face had a desperate, imploring look and his mismatched eyes shone with tears.

Bombazine moved aside to admit him. Christ, he thought. What now? Not a good night for an impromptu visit. "Yes?" he curtly asked.

J. J. didn't answer. Argos greeted him with the slobbering affection he always did. But instead of poking the dog away with his umbrella, J. J. tossed it aside, lay down the Scrabble set and dictionary, and squatted to rub Argos's head and snout with loving tenderness. That was a clue that something was wrong, hideously out of joint; never before had J. J. been loving or affectionate to Argos.

"All right, what?" Bombazine demanded. "What's up?"

Rising, J. J. announced, "I need to play Scrabble."

"Your memory has atrophied. We play on Thursdays. Today is Wednesday. I just saw you this morning, remember?"

J. J.'s gaze was blank. He looked unkempt and disheveled and needed a shave. Beneath his seersucker sport coat, his white dress shirt, normally clean and crisp, was soiled and rumpled. His red bow tie was askew and he had forgotten to wear his blue suspenders.

"Are you drunk?" Bombazine asked.

J. J. reeled as he rose to his full height. "I've had a drink, yes, and I want to play Scrabble. I bloody well know what day it is, but I need to be with someone. Let's play one game. Indulge me."

Bombazine sighed. "All right. One game. I have somewhere to go."

"May I ask where?"

"The River Styx. Hades. Actually, the River X."

"Play me one game and I'll leave you to find your Charon. I promise."

They went into the library and sat down at their usual table. Bombazine was nonplussed. Appearing out of the blue on the wrong night was not like J. J. The man was a robotic droid who did not deviate from his program. When had he ever admitted the need to be with someone? He prided himself on his self-sufficiency, independence, and inhuman lack of feeling. This was a J. J. Bombazine had never seen before, and that was disconcerting.

They set up the game. They always used J. J.'s set because its base had a swivel and its plastic board slots were brightly colored. (Bombazine's set was old, with a flat cardboard, no slots, dull colors.) Each man drew a letter from a brown paper bag of tiles. J. J. drew a C and Bombazine an R, which meant J. J. would play first and Bombazine would keep score.

Bombazine was a good player, but J. J. was Mount Olym-

229

pus College champion. Having memorized the Scrabble dictionary, J. J. was a master at deploying tiny words like aa and za and ae and qat and xu and xi and qi the way a general might deploy infantrymen in battle. J. J. was also adept at "bingos" — playing all seven tiles for a fifty-point bonus.

They dispensed with a timer, preferring to play slowly, deliberately, like Fischer playing chess with Spasky in the seventies. Tonight J. J. took longer than usual to assemble the tiles on his rack. His eventual play — the word MELT-ING — was indeed a bingo and earned him 76 points, counting the bonus. Bombazine noticed that his fingers shook as he played his letters. J. J.'s fingers never shook.

"Nice," Bombazine complimented, jotting down the score. "Usually it takes you two or three turns to bingo."

J. J. was regarding him morosely, almost tragically, like a family member about to impart to another family member bad news about a third family member. His lips quivered and a nerve beneath his right eye twitched. When he spoke, his piping voice sounded like a girl's:

"George, the Duke is dead."

"What duke? Oh. You mean Snider."

"The immortal Duke of Flatbush is dead. The greatest center fielder of all time." J. J. burst into sobs and covered his face with both hands.

Bombazine reached across the table and gently patted his friend's arm. "J. J.," he consoled, "the Duke died back in February. Seven months ago. You called me the day it happened."

"I know," J. J. whimpered, removing his hands from his wet cheeks. "But tonight it finally hit me. The implications of it. A nation lives and dies with its heroes. Americans will always remember what they were doing when they heard the Duke had died." He closed his eyes and began to blubber like a child again.

Dammit to hell, thought Bombazine. He picks tonight of all nights to have a nervous breakdown? What luck is mine.

J. J pulled a powder-blue silk handkerchief out of the breast pocket of his sport coat, dabbed at his eyes, and blew his nose. "I met him, you know," he sniffled. "At Forbes Field before a Dodger-Pirates game. He let me come on the outfield grass and have a picture taken with him. The Duke hugged me, George. He put his arm around my shoulder. A batboy took the picture. I have it in a lock box at the bank."

"Could we get back to our game?"

J. J. cried, "Dammit, man, I'm cracking up and you want to play Scrabble? Do you think it's a joke? Oh, Christ..."

Bombazine recoiled. He had no idea how to handle this. It was unnerving to watch someone he'd always thought of as an impregnable tower of strength and unfeeling topple before his eyes and disintegrate. He desperately wants my help and I should help him, Bombazine thought. But tonight I can't. I have to get rid of him.

"For God's sake, J. J. Pull yourself together. Do you want a drink?"

"I thought you'd never ask."

Bombazine rose, went to the kitchen, and returned with the bottle of Talisker and a pair of tumblers, an ice cube in each. "One drink," he said, pouring Scotch into the glasses, "and that's all. You've caught me on a bad night."

J. J. smiled imploringly, a little desperately. "You are not a kind man, George. Or a compassionate one. Do you know that?"

"It's what people keep telling me. Shall we play while we drink?"

"Bugger the Scrabble. Let's drink. Tonight I couldn't beat *you*."

"Not even with a seventy-six point lead?"

"I concede the game," J. J. muttered. "You win." Tears trickled down his hollow cheeks. With trembling cobweb fingers he gathered his letters from the board and dropped them into the brown paper bag.

"Cheers," he said cheerlessly, raising his glass.

For a while neither spoke. They drank. "All right," Bombazine said. "Tell me why you're putting me through this."

"I had a metaphysical experience. An epiphany."

"Meaning?"

"I stared into the void of nothingness tonight. The existential abyss."

Bombazine kept himself from laughing. "And who did you see there? Whom, rather. Whom did you see? Heidegger? Sartre? Kierkegaard? Camus?"

"I had a revelation about myself. I'm a hoax, George. A charlatan. A sham. A caricature. A *gascon*. A poseur. A nothing."

"Stop. Humility doesn't become you."

"I'm an empty suit."

"You mean you didn't know that?" Bombazine decided to keep things playful; some lighthearted banter might help.

232

"People don't know it, but I'm a fussy pretentious old quacksalver and a mountebank. You're probably not familiar with those terms, but they fit me to a T."

"I'm familiar with mountebank. Quacksalver I'm not sure about."

"Tonight I consulted my huge old Funk and Wagnall's dictionary for the definition of the word MERETRICIOUS. It described me."

Bombazine laughed. "Actually, you're worse than meretricious. I found your picture in the New Unexpurgated Random House Dictionary of the English Language above the word POPINJAY."

J. J. nodded miserably, like a suspect admitting a crime. "Yes, I'm one of those too. The world may think I'm great, but tonight I realized how small and inconsequential I really am."

"What made you realize it?"

"A pint of Scotch on an empty stomach. Tell me, what's the use of living?"

"I've been wondering that myself."

"There's something you don't know about me that you should."

Bombazine held his breath. Oh, no, he thought. He's got cancer too.

"I'm Jewish," J. J. confessed. "Just a fraction. An eighth. I'm an octo-Hebe."

"Well," Bombazine said after letting that sink in, "I hear Hitler was Jewish too. No wonder you know so much about Judaism. I'd never have guessed it, though, considering what a jackbooted old Nazi you pretend to be."

233

J. J. gulped his drink, drained it, and with a trembling hand poured another. "I must say, this Talisker is tasty. Wonderful peat nose. It must have cost a Tudor King's ransom. Who gave it to you?"

"Trevor and Pru. It's a birthday gift."

J. J. was able to laugh through his tears. "Marvelous," he said. "A man who gives you Scotch like this must be forgiven even if he did steal your wife. Did your publicist come today?"

"She left an hour ago."

"You gave her a shag, I hope."

"I tried. Wasn't up to it. We did some other things."

"May I ask which?"

"You may not."

J. J. nodded pensively. "Tell me, my friend, don't you ever wonder why I don't have a sex life?"

"I only wonder why I don't."

"Someday I'll tell you why I don't."

"Not a Hemingway war wound, I hope?"

J. J. hesitated as if unsure whether to laugh or start crying again. "Old sport, do you know what you are? A pinko faggot peacenik commie towelhead-loving one-world-socialist America hater."

Bombazine breathed relief. That was more like it. J. J. was his old self again.

"Old chap, let's drink more Scotch. I'm starting to feel better."

Bombazine snatched the bottle away. "Negative," he said. "I don't want to have to drive you home."

"God damn it, man, I'm in pain. At least tell me how to change my life. I want to die."

"Join the club."

"Don't be glib about this. Help me, you son of a bitch."

Anger flashed like a bright light in Bombazine's brain. "All right," he said. "Do as I say. Stop teaching that neo-fascist course at the college. Recant. Repent. Admit your're Jewish. Brag about it. Tell it to the world. Become a liberal. It's not too late to save your soul. For what doth it profit a man —"

"Oh, bugger that. Shove that preaching up your arse. Did I ever tell you I used to be a liberal? A socialist, actually. When I was young. Do you want to hear what happened?"

"Yes, but not tonight. There are things I have to do. It's time you hit the road." Bombazine rose and extended his hand to help J. J. up.

"Wait. Will you help them make that *Spoon River* movie?"

"They cancelled it."

J. J. shook his head. "*Merde… tant pis… Je suis desolé, old man. Mais je te l'avais bien dit.* I told you I was skeptical. How's the book coming?"

"What book?"

"The one you're writing about suicide. You mentioned it at breakfast this morning."

"Oh. That book. It's… coming right along."

"I've thought about suicide." J. J. sniffled. "Does that surprise you?"

Hell, no, Bombazine thought. It's endemic. "J. J., everyone our age has thought about suicide," he said.

"I decided against it. With Bill Buckley and Chris Hitchens and Bob Novak dead, there are just three eloquent, witty, erudite conservatives left. I'm one and George F. Will and Charlie Krauthammer are the others."

"You guys won't win any beauty contests."

"My country needs me alive. And conservative."

"I need you alive too, you old fascist. Let's hit the road."

"Besides, I wouldn't have the bollocks to kill myself any more than you would."

"Don't be so sure about me."

"Did you know suicide is no longer a crime in Canada?"

"Didn't know it ever was. What did Canadians used to do, arrest the corpse?"

"I hate my life, George. But that doesn't mean I don't love life. Moliere said, '*Le plus grand faible des hommes, c'est l'amour qu'ils ont de la vie.*' If only I had a life to love. I have no life. I need to get a life. I wish Sartre were still alive. I met him, you know. On the Champs-Elysees. We drank Pernod martinis. He chain-smoked. That's probably what killed him. That and French-kissing Simone de Beauvoir."

"Let's go, J. J."

"On that note I'll say goodnight." J. J. stood up and almost fell. He regained his balance, thrust forth his jaw, and squared his shoulders. "Come with me to my car. I drank too bloody fast."

"You drank too bloody much."

Revived by the cool night air, J. J. wobbled and stumbled without falling down and made it to his Toyota Avalon. Bombazine, trailing, carried the Scrabble set and dictionary. Once behind the wheel, the drunk seemed to sober up. "Thanks for the Scotch, old chap. I just needed a nip and someone to talk to. I'm sorry about all that *Sturm und Drang* earlier."

"I'm sorry I wasn't more help."

"You weren't any help. But I didn't need any. Forget those things I said."

Bombazine reached through the open window and gave his friend's shoulder a squeeze. "Not to worry, John Jacob. I'm glad you came. How else could I beat you at Scrabble?"

"Will I see you tomorrow?"

"I don't think so. Not tomorrow. Drive safely."

As he sped away, J. J. yelled, "Don't tell anyone I'm Jewish."

Chapter Twenty-Four: 8:49 p.m.

FAMOUS LAST WORDS

Bombazine felt guilty about how cooly and dismissively he had dealt with J. J. And since friends did not let friends drive drunk, shouldn't he have driven him home? J. J. had been drunker than he'd ever seen him, and his pain seemed genuine. But he hadn't far to drive and the traffic was light. Tomorrow J. J. would face a far worse existential crisis, learning that he'd lost his best and only friend. He would gaze into the abyss again.

At the moment, however, Bombazine could not afford to fret about J. J. He had to wait for Miguel's call. He would wait until nine forty-five. If Miguel hadn't called by then, he would swallow his pride and call him. He was Miguel's only father, Miguel his only son, and he couldn't leave the realm of the living without speaking to his seed, his progeny, one last time. But he would not tell the boy — the man-child — about his plans for the evening. No, he would not.

Time had slowed to a crawl again. How could he kill it? He paced the living room floor, trying to collect his thoughts. Why did it have to be ten o'clock? Because the thing had to go precisely as planned, down to the smallest detail, or it wouldn't work. He was superstitious that way. Changes in a plan, last-minute changes especially, always triggered glitches, mistakes, fuckups, and other unexpected developments.

He stopped worrying about J. J. and Miguel and chose to worry about Argos again. The damned dog had still not eaten; even after watching his master and Meridel Baxter make love, as though it were a live sex show, Argos seemed lethargic. Maybe his master's performance had bored him and tired him out. Now the dog lay squarely in Bombazine's pacing path. Argos was depressed again.

Did he know?

Bombazine bent down and scratched his back. "Don't take it personally," he entreated. "Don't pout. Don't sulk. Daddy has to go away for a while. A long while. Mama will take care of you. You'll have a new home, a nicer one. You'll certainly eat better. Gourmet health food with ground milk-fed veal and paté de fois gras. Lots of fiber and protein. Your stepdad will treat you well."

Argos looked up, yawned, and farted. The smell of his broken wind was nauseating. His huge cerulean eyes glistened, as if he were about to cry. Bombazine patted his head and scratched behind his ear and told him he loved him. Why was it so much easier to say it to a dog than to a person? *You are not a loving person, George.* Hadn't someone told him that today? Hadn't everyone? It was too late to do anything about it now.

Bombazine's football knee was throbbing and his arthritic legs had stiffened up. His lumbars ached and so did his spine. Even his neck hurt; he rolled his head to relieve

239

its pain and began to feel guilty about Derek, his hapless brother-in-law with the chronic neck problem. He had not been sympathetic and Catherine had jumped on him for it. His stomach rumbled because he hadn't eaten. He felt the bridgework in his mouth and found it loose. Too late to fix that. "Understand, George," his dentist had told him, "that senior citizens outlive their teeth. At some point in time, you might consider dentures. We'll remove your choppers and make you some nice new ones."

Now that was something to look forward to. He had glowered at his dentist and narrowed his eyes and clenched his fists and frightened the man. False teeth? What better motive to kill himself could a codger need? Age meant a hundred ailments, most of them chronic but a new one every week. If he went on living, eventually he'd need someone to nurse and bathe and shave him, cook his meals, wash his dishes, administer his meds, wipe his ass, and put him to bed. Plato was right: the old are in a second childhood. We come full circle. We start out in diapers, totally helpless and dependent, and end up the same way. Actually worse, because babies are cute and the very old are hideous, loathsome, and repellent.

Dozing off, Argos groaned and twitched, as if having a bad dream. He had to leave Argos, Bombazine realized. Desert him. He had to desert J. J., too. Just as he'd had to desert Tencha and Miguel. He was nothing if not a deserter, and yet he loved them all. That J. J. and Meridel should speak of commiting suicide today of all days was a coincidence that gave credence to the telepathic ESP of "Twilight Zone"

240

reruns. Suicide, like the Asian flu virus, was contagious. Again he hoped that when J. J. learned of his suicide, he wouldn't blame himself but remember that his friend was writing a book about suicide. Or said he was.

Maybe he should leave J. J. a suicide note. Or one to Miguel. To how many friends and relatives and loved ones could one leave suicide notes? What was the current suicide-note etiquette? If one left too many, one might as well have written his obituary, mailed it to the newspapers, and posted it on Facebook. One suicide note was enough, dammit, and he was leaving his to Pru. Hemingway had not left a suicide note, nor had Hart Crane, Vincent van Gogh, Jerzy Kosinski, Adolf Hitler, or Judas Iscariot. One could leave a generic "To Whom It May Concern" suicide note, but that seemed too impersonal. One should not leave a suicide note that sounded like a legal notice.

He began to pace faster. Why didn't Miguel call? A watched pot never boiled. Time had stopped. How could one kill time that had stopped?

One could watch television, that's how. The tube. The telly, the idiot box. In the fifties Gore Vidal had called TV "chewing gum for the eyes." But there were nights when one was so anxious that chewing gum with one's eyes was better than pacing the floor with one's feet.

He trudged into the library, switched on the set, and turned on MSNBC. The Reverend Al Sharpton (whom he respected even though the tendentious little dandy was a peacock) was railing against Republican efforts to stifle the political voices of students and minorities and old folks by

making it harder for them to vote. Sharpton's rant, especially the part about old folks, tempted Bombazine to write
one last letter to the New York *Times*. Should he play the
angry crank, the political junkie, just once more?

The phone rang. He bounded up and grabbed it.

"It's me," said his son. "Hang up and call me back. I'm broke."

Heart thumping with excitement, Bombazine obeyed.
Miguel, of course, was going to ask for money: he always
did. He called when about to be evicted from his house in
Provincetown for delinquent mortgage payments or when
his floral shop there was about to close because he couldn't
pay the rent. Miguel also asked for money at Christmas,
Easter, on his birthday, on Pru's birthday (so he could buy
her a gift), and even on Bombazine's birthday. It took a lot of
chutzpah to ask a person for money on that person's birthday, but Miguel had a lot.

"*Hola*, Miguel!" Bombazine exclaimed with genuine en-
thusiasm. "*Buenas noches!* I'm so glad you called."

"Can the fatherly crap, George. I have things to say."

"Thank you for remembering my birthday. Your e-mail
could have been more affectionate, but I appreciate it."

"It was meant to hurt you, George," came the cold, hateful, androgynous voice. "But nothing can. You are... *como se
dice?* Hurt-proof. Desensitized. Numb."

Bombazine shut his eyes. More than anything else, he re-
sented Miguel's calling him George. Never once had Bombazine called his father Mirabeau. Miguel had called him

Dad until 1995; then, as an alcoholic and a heroin addict, he'd gone into rehab to stay out of jail; in rehab he'd been counseled to call his father by his first name. "It puts you on an equal footing," the counselor explained. "It fosters self-assertiveness and independence. It forces him to treat you like an adult."

"*Feliz cumpleaños*, Professor," Miguel was saying. "How are things up there in the ivory tower?"

"I have no idea. I'm retired from teaching."

"I heard you wrote a book they are making into a movie."

"Wrong on all counts, but no matter. Is your health okay?"

"If you ask am I using again, the answer is no. I have been clean and sober for months. Not even a beer. And how is your health, *borracho*? Still a closet alcoholic?"

Bombazine chuckled. "I didn't think I was closeted."

"You should try smack or some other opiod. But you do not understand the difference between physical dependency and addiction."

"Let's talk about you."

"I am in an LGBT rehab group, though I am not a transgender. I am not ready to transition. I am too masculine to be a woman and too feminine to be a man. I should have been an *hermafrodita*. Then I could fuck myself."

Unwilling to go there, Bombazine kept silent.

"I am seeing a Gestalt therapist. He keeps me broke, which I am now, but he is helping me get my shit together. You come up a lot in my sessions."

Bombazine was unwilling to go there, too. "How's Dimitri?" he inquired.

"You are changing the subject? You do not want to hear about my therapy? You spent a fortune sending me to shrinks when I was young. Though I think that money may have been mine. Insurance from my mother's death. Off the subject, did I tell you I write poetry now? It's part of my therapy. *Hickory dickory dock / I love to suck black cock.* Ha-ha, I am kidding. I hate licorice, and I am allergic to chocolate."

"Be serious, Miguel. I asked about Dimitri."

"Why should you care? Dimitri is sick. Some sort of pleurisy. It came from that pneumonia he had last winter. We want to get married before he dies. Isn't that romantic?"

"I'm sorry he's sick. Get married. Marriage is good."

"What would you know about marriage, *viejo*? Divorce is your specialty. How is *mi madrastra*? My stepmother?"

"Pru is fine. I saw her today. You should call her."

"I shall. How is Aunt Catherine? The last time I talked to her, she said Derek had broken his neck."

"Derek is always breaking his neck."

"Spoken like a liberal. Or do you prefer progressive? Your heart bleeds for strangers, but you care *nada* about family. You are a selfish man, George. What a father you were not! My therapist thinks you are why I am a *joto*."

"I can't believe he'd say that. Fire your therapist. Sexual orientation is determined by genes. Freud went out fifty years ago."

"*Muchas gracias.* To a man who knows everything and understands nothing. Maybe I should have a sex change. I deserve a *chocha*. I was raised by women. *Niñeras* and Mom and Pru. You had a father, I did not. You are straight, I am

244

queer. *¿Ya saben ustedes lo que quiero decir?* Do you understand what I am saying?"

"I reared you, Miguel. You had a father."

"When it was too late. All I had in my early years were Mom and my *niñeras*. I was just learning to talk when you left. You were a runaway father. *Desertor!* Never once did you fix my breakfast or lunch. Pru did."

He's regressing, Bombazine told himself. Stay calm. But his voice shook when he asked, "How many fathers make their kid's breakfast and lunch, Miguel? Is that how they do it in Mexico? Why do you blame me for everything?"

"Mom was in therapy when she got killed. She was doing est. Getting her shit together."

"I'm not sure doing est is getting your shit together."

"If you had been there, *zonzo*, she would not have killed herself."

"Right. She'd have killed me."

"Is that what you believe? *Cobarde!*"

"She threatened to. She'd bought a gun. I thought it best get away from her."

"Couples fight. I fight with Dimitri. I threw a lamp at him and he broke my nose. Domestic violence is part of everyday life. It happens in the best of families. To people who feel, *pendejo*."

Bombazine struggled to keep it together, but as usual Miguel was wearing him down. He was near the breaking point. "That's not how I wanted to live, Miguel! I'm not Rambo or Mike Tyson. My parents never fought. Your mother cut up one of my manuscripts and threw another into the fire. There were no computers then to save things. I had to leave."

"Then you should have taken me with you."

"For how long? No court will take a child from his mother unless the mother is an axe murderess. She wasn't an axe murderess yet."

"She wanted you back. She loved you. She missed you."

"That's why she bought a gun?"

"She never learned to use it. You deserted your family because your wife bought a gun to protect herself when you were away on tours. Even I have a gun. A Beretta nine-fifty Jetfire. I keep it in the shop, behind the pansies, ha ha."

"Great. Maybe you'll get to shoot someone. Stand your ground."

"I would love to shoot you, motherfucker."

Bombazine flinched and rolled his eyes into his head. The conversation had reached the point he'd dreaded. Had he and Miguel actually lived together for years as father and son? They were strangers, farther apart than he'd been from his own father. His heart was palpitating crazily. It was hard to breathe. He wanted the conversation to end.

Miguel didn't. "Speaking of Mom, are you sure I got the benefits I was due? I never saw her will."

"You were four. Now you're rehashing things that happened thirty years ago?'

"Is there a statute of limitations on it?"

"You got what you were entitled to." Bombazine's voice broke off. "I was executor. Pru and I used the money to send you to Rensselaer because you wanted to be an engineer like your *abuelo* Mirabeau. You were a mathematical genius. You earned an engineering degree. Why didn't you become an engineer?"

"I engineered the construction of my shop."

"And that was it? Why didn't you become an engineer?"

"Because instead I wanted to become an alcoholic junkie who likes a fist up his ass. I also wanted to become a poet. You would be proud of me—I'm obscure enough for you to write a book about. Want to hear a poem? *Little Boy Blue, come blow my horn / And we will film some kiddie porn.* Listen, *pinche*, I did not get all I should have from Mom's will. I want it now."

"There's nothing to get!" Bombazine cried. He felt his chest tightening and his face flushing as he struggled to breathe again. Probating Tencha's estate had been a nightmare that lasted eighteen months and involved two families, dual citizenship, translators, bilingual probate lawyers, and judges from two countries. "No, you didn't get everything," Bombazine sobbed. "Her mobster brothers got some of it." At Tencha's funeral at the Catedral Metropolitana in Mexico City, Raoul and Ramon and the Villa-Lobos *familia* would not speak to him.

"I need eight thousand dollars. Or I lose my shop."

Bombazine was silent.

Miguel added, "You owe me, *cabron*."

"Why do I owe you?"

"Because you are my father. You owe me something. You were never there for me. Even when it was me and you and Pru, it was just me and Pru because you were not there. You

247

were at some conference, reading some paper you'd written about some nobody. I am lucky I did not die from an O. D. or jacking up with an infected needle."

"Aren't we a little old to blame our parents for everything?"

"I don't. I just blame you. Mom told me you hated me because I was why you had to marry her. She wouldn't abort me the way you asked her to."

Bombazine felt that his head would explode. "She lied, Miguel! I loved your mother! I would have married her anyway! I loved you too. I never wanted you aborted —"

"She said you were not sure you were my father."

Bombazine ground his teeth again. This one he hadn't heard before. Tencha, you witch, he thought, you haunt me from the grave. "Another lie," he said. "Why would I not be sure I was your father? Why would I say that?"

"It sounds like something you would say."

"No. It sounds like something she would say."

"Go to hell. Go jump in the lake!"

"I may just do that."

"*Mentires*! Bullshit! You will eat and drink yourself to death. That is how you will die. I hear you weigh three hundred pounds and look like fat Orson Welles. You should join a support group. Fatass Fathers Anonymous." Miguel giggled like a little boy. He sang: "*Georgie, Georgie, two by four / Can't get through the bathroom door / So he shitted on the floor.*"

"I'm sick, Miguel. I can't send you money right now. I will die soon, I promise. You'll get most of what I have."

"*No te creo, viejo.* You will live to be a hundred. Why did I call you? You always say no."

248

"I haven't said no."

"Then help me. Put money where your mouth is. *Pajarito volando*. Why do you say you are going to die?"

He may as well know, Bombazine thought. "I have cancer, Miguel."

"I do not believe you."

"Prostate cancer."

"If it is true, forgive me for not giving a damn. *No me importa. Todo me chupa un huevo*. Find a quicker way to die, *viejo*."

"I'm working on it."

"Do you ever wonder why Pru left you? Why you are alone? Even I am not alone. Oh, wait—you have your dog. *Uno perro muy feo*."

"I have to go now. I love you, Miguel."

"Famous last words. Go die of cancer."

The line went dead. Bombazine sat motionless but inwardly trembling, unable to replace the receiver, unable to move. His mouth was parched, his face hot, his huge bulk immobile. Breathing heavily, he could not swallow. He wanted to cry but had no tears. He wanted to bellow curses but had no voice. "*Mom said you weren't sure you were my father.*" Where had that come from? Who could doubt that he was Miguel's father? There had been no other man in Tencha's life at the time; had there been, he'd have heard about it, since Tencha could not keep a secret. Miguel, like his mother, was a pathological liar. *Como la madre, como el hijo.*

That's all, folks, thought Bombazine. Talking to his son

had blown out the last candle. Turn out the lights, the party's over, Willie Nelson. Turn out the light and then turn out the light, Othello.

Bombazine turned out every light in the house. It was time to go.

Chapter Twenty-Five: 10:01 p. m.

DEAD MAN DRIVING

He hated driving after dark. His night vision was poor. But by now traffic would have thinned to almost none. He felt braver and calmer than he had all day, fully up to the task ahead. Bring 'em on, he thought. Now he was quoting George W. Bush? Laughter bubbled in his throat as he tried to smile. *It is a far, far better thing that I do, than I have ever done.* Dickens? Right. Sidney Carton. *Death be not proud though some have called thee mighty and dreadful.* John Donne? Yes, but where? One of his Holy Sonnets, circa 1618...

Before locking up to leave, he'd checked on Argos's dog bowl in the kitchen. The hunk of expensive cheese had remained untouched. Argos had fasted all day. A hunger strike? The dog had rejected half a T-bone steak, some dry Alpo, and two dollars worth of gourmet English Stilton. Exasperated, Bombazine had spent ten minutes (which threw him off schedule) composing a last-minute e-mail, asking Pru to drop by tomorrow morning and feed Argos. When she came, she would find his suicide note on the kitchen island. He hoped she would feed Argos before finding the note. Then take him home with her.

Eventually Pru would recover from her shock and grief,

but he feared that Argos was grieving already and this would finish him off. Dogs were prescient and known to starve themselves to death when their masters died or were at death's door. He'd whistled for Argos and hunted him down. He found him sitting on his haunches, sulking and listless, in the wing of the house where Pru used to play her cello and compose. The dog's behavior made him afraid. Dogs sensed everything. What if this ugly house in the middle of a mountainous desert, this surreal lopsided ranch-style eyesore that locals thought was haunted, really was haunted? People said a woman had died of foul play here. Had Argos picked up on the scent of death? His death?

No, that made no sense. And it was time to go. Bombazine squatted for a man-to-man talk with the dog. His tone was gentle but firm: "Argos, I know you understand what I'm saying. Please eat something. Don't look like that. Didn't I let you watch me make love to that blonde earlier? Okay, try to. I didn't do so well. But you did get to watch, so the least you could do is eat something. It's not often I ask anything of you, and normally you eat like a fucking horse. Last month I spent a hundred dollars on dry food alone. I also gave you half the red meat I cooked for myself. What's wrong, guy?"

Argos's marble-blue eyes widened in puzzlement. Guy! Why had he called Argos guy? He never called Argos guy. It was what his father had called him instead of using his name, which he disliked. Bombazine wondered if men turned into their fathers the way women turned into their mothers. The thought was disturbing. But no one could say he had turned out like his father. He had turned out worse. A suicide.

"Okay, dude," he said. "Old Odysseus is splitting. I love you, you fucking wolf." He held the dog's head in both his hands and kissed the top of his head and tried, without success, not to cry.

Nonplussed, Argos had stared at him; then his eyes widened with alarm, as if he'd realized something. He began to pant, his breath was an ill wind. Bombazine had risen to head out. Argos trailed close behind him. The dog whined as the front door closed in his face. He wanted to come along — he didn't know about the cold, deep lake water in which his master meant to drown himself. Could Argos swim? And how would he get home? He had to stay.

As he started up his Mercedes E-Class hybrid, Bombazine could hear Argos clawing the inside of the front door, barking in vociferous protest. Argos knew. He didn't know the details, but he knew his master did not intend to return. Through eyes blurred with tears, Bombazine took one last look at the split-level ranch-style eyesore Salvador Dali might have loved—a wackily designed house which, for all its creepiness and forlorn emptiness, he'd grown to love, or at least like, because it was home. With a terrible squeal of tires, spraying pebbles, he sped away from it for the last time.

His Mercedes—quiet, stealthy, powerful—seemed to glide through the cool September night. The air was sweetly redolent of honeysuckle and wisteria; that was strange, since neither grew in this area. He'd brought along a CD of the Mahler 2nd Symphony, the "Resurrection," which he planned to blast out sforzando on his state-of-the-art stereo system with its throbbing bass subwoofer as he gunned the Mercedes up the steep cliff at Mount Makeout that led to a breach in a dark stone wall through which he would fly the car, like a Kamikazi pilot, into the cold, deep, black water below. No music, not even Mozart's Requiem, could be more fitting than the Mahler as he zoomed through the air and nosedived to his death below. "Death by Water" T. S. Eliot had named a section of his poem "The Waste Land." One admired Eliot's poetry even though the dour pedant was a bank clerk from St. Louis, an expatriate who'd become more British than the Brits. Bombazine admired "The Waste Land" more than his "The Love Song of J. Alfred Prufrock," a poem with which he uncomfortably identified.

He had to drive past the campus and through The Village to get onto the interregional highway that led to Mount Makeout. That initial drive would call not for a symphony but a prelude, perhaps an overture. Or Country Western. Yes, a little Country in the plaintive mode. A "somebody done somebody wrong" song. He switched on the radio and touched the screen icon for the all-night classic Country station broadcast from Big Town.

Absently (he'd never cared for either number) he listened to Jim Reeves' "He'll Have to Go" and Faron Young's "Hello Walls," but the next classic fit so well that he sang along in a voice choked with tears. "Yesterday, When I Was Young," a late sixties hit by "Hee-Haw's" Roy Clark, was the confession of an aging, perhaps dying man defeated by life and humbled by regret. "Yesterday, when I was young, so many happy songs were waiting to be sung..." But he "played the game of love with arrogance and pride" and "ran so fast that time and youth ran out." He'd "never stopped to ask what life was all about," and only now, too late, does he see the error of his ways.

Bombazine wept; it was an appropriate night for tears and he was a weeper anyway. How was it, he wondered, that "Hee-Haw" music told us more about real life, and perhaps death, than Plato and Kant and Hegel had? More than Irving Berlin and Cole Porter, too. And certainly more than the writers and singers of today's pop and rock and rap and grunge and hip-hop. But why was he asking such a question now, with minutes to live? Why wasn't he asking about the final things, eschatological matters like heaven, hell, purgatory, judgment, reward, punishment, oblivion, reincarnation? And what about suicides? What happened to their souls in the hereafter? Was there a hereafter? He hoped not. He was hoping for total oblivion, a dreamless never-ending sleep. In death he would find peace, Poe's surcease of sorrow, the relief from pain promised by the television commercials.

Was he really going to suicide? Yes, he fucking was! The fact that he was so calm assured him that he could. For weeks he had wondered what this moment would feel like, and now he knew. With his life expectancy down to a few minutes, he felt celestially calm, as if he'd popped a Thorazine or a Valium. He cruised past the campus, where lights continued to burn in the ersatz cathedral-like edifices and along the boulevard that connected them. What infinite wisdom had been imparted in those buildings today? What lessons learned, eternal truths revealed, what Keatsian odes scanned for meter? Those buildings had been his workplace and he would never see them again. That wrenched his heart and he cried even more. It wasn't much of a campus, really — it looked like a studio set for some black-and-white thirties movie — and he no longer worked there. Yet he'd loved it. And still did.

When he reached The Village and eased up Main Street, he hoped for activity, a little night music, sounds of youthful mirth. But the street had rolled up its carpets and locked its doors. The Village was like a ghost town. He had never seen it so dead. Or was he dead? Not yet. He'd just never been here this late on a Wednesday night. The party animals were partying in private. Main Street in The Village wasn't Bourbon Street in the Big Easy. Main Street in the Village was Primrose Lane, and its merchants and residents turned in at a reasonable hour, early to bed and early to rise.

He would never see The Village again, never see its pastel hues melt together in rosy morning light the way he had this morning, driving in with J. J. Sighing with regret, he cruised on, pushing north, passing the dark closed-up shack of the restaurant Caramba! where they had breakfasted, though he had not eaten anything. Like Jesus's last supper, his last meal had been ruined by dread, portents of doom that killed his appetite. He wished the radio station in Big Town would

256

play that Roy Clark song again. Another of its lines went "The taste of life was sweet as rain upon my tongue." Nice. That might be a better epitaph for his tombstone than I TOLD YOU I WAS SICK, the waggish one he'd designated for himself. Edgar Lee Masters, a humorless poet, would have preferred the Roy Clark epitaph.

Main Street receded in his rearview mirror and now he was turning onto the Big Town highway. There was no traffic. Good. He didn't want company or human contact. He drove faster, exceeding the speed limit of sixty on this stretch at night, and soon he was doing seventy. In the glare of his brights, the highway took on a strange color, a shiny brownish sepia, tinged with red as if the pavement had been washed with blood and dried out. .

The landscape, what little of it he could make out in the dark, was a parched grassy flatland of saplings and juniper and bent-over trees festooned with Spanish moss, like those in the Gulf states of the Deep South. Further on, the country, with its fields of bluebonnets, was beautiful by day but spooky at night. Again he tasted fear, a metallic taste, as if a coin were in his mouth. Fear was called for at this moment. Fear and trembling were in order. Ask Kierkegaard. His fear contended with desire. Who wrote that? A. E. Houseman? How often in his life had fear contended with desire and won?

It would not win tonight.

What a merciless bitch of a day it had been. A day of epiphanies, dark realizations, bitter disappointment, dashed hopes, admissions of guilt, revelations coming too late to matter. How many character assassins had taken shots at him today with ad hominem attacks, personal stuff? He did not like the person they'd said he was, and it was too late to change that person. Better just to kill him.

Now he had reached the mountainous area; its rushing river, the Xanthus, or "River X," had been dammed into lakes to prevent flooding while it provided the area with hydroelectric power. In minutes he would be sinking to the bottom of a deep lake. His heart was in his mouth. It was Mahler time.

—–∿∿∿—–

He still had two or three miles to drive and needed the music to inspire him and keep him from turning back like the coward he'd always been and might yet be. His empty stomach churned and rumbled, as if to protest what lay ahead. Something craven in him wanted to live. But there was no turning back. Fumbling with his right hand, he slipped the compact disc into the player, found the last movement of the symphony, and maxed the volume, all without reducing speed. He was going close to eighty.

The Finale was long and he'd have to skip around to hear the part he wanted. He lowered the windows for the world to hear Gustav Mahler's heavenly music. Suddenly it filled the surrounding countryside. Were graveyards nearby, it would resurrect the dead. In the "March of the Dead" section he recognized the Dies Irae motif from the Catholic Mass. He heard drum rolls, ringing gongs, the clarion calls of hunter's horns played offstage. The trumpets of the Apocalypse rang out. A mezzo-soprano was intoning a sorrowful solo (about death) in German. The Last Judgment was at hand, the demons of the Day of Wrath unleashed. Graves were splitting open and moldy corpses, moaning and trembling, rose from their coffins to march in procession.

Abruptly he found himself behind two cars going too slowly, and two others, one a jeep, were cruising alongside him in the right lane. Horns were honking. He swore to himself. What was going on? There was also a vehicle, a pickup truck, right behind him, tailgating. For a moment, he came to a full stop. He looked around. He could not believe what he saw. Vehicles, vehicles going both ways.

He was caught in a traffic jam.

But why? At ten o'clock at night? It was worse than five o'clock rush hour. Where had it come from? What shit luck! God damn it! God DAMN it! He pounded the steering wheel with his right palm as hard as he could, hard enough to break it or break his hand. In the opposite lane, heading back toward the Village and campus, came a string of SUVs. There was a farm community nearby named Welfare, and apparently Welfare's hayseeds were either on their way home from Big Town or on their way there, the hour notwithstanding. Coming and going, the vehicles crept along single-file like hearses in a funeral procession. His funeral? Was this a time warp? A flash forward? Had he died already?

He swore again. Ignoring a sign that forbade passing, he veered between two pickups and passed a jeep and an SUV. The SUV gave a long angry honk. He honked back. Like the poet Alan Seeger, he had a rendezvous with death. He'd published a monograph on Seeger in *Partisan Review* and won an award for it.

In the Mahler Finale the whole chorus was singing now, its male half reaching the lowest vocal note in the classical repertoire, then rejoicing rapturously, joyously, victoriously with tolling church bells. *"Triumphieren! Wem in Leidenstagen! Herr ich habe miBehandelt"*! In the throes of musical ecstasy, he almost lost control of the wheel. He swerved in front of another pickup. Where were these asshole farmers going? Where had they been? Couldn't they hear the transformative music? Fifty meters ahead, the multi-pronged fork in the highway, with four traffic lights dangling from overhead wires, was visible.

That meant the turnoff was near. He'd been here often enough to find it blindfolded. His heart was in his mouth, yet he sang in fluent German along with Mahler's chorus, never missing a note, remembering every syllable from having heard the Finale so often. *"Hor auf zu beben!"* he sang at the top of his voice.*"Bereite dich zu leben!"* [Cease trembling! Prepare yourself to live!]

The light, his light, was red. He braked to a jarring halt and waited. Seconds dragged by like hours. What the hell was taking this long? Was the mechanism faulty? If the light was defective you could proceed with caution and go. You didn't have to wait all night. Did these stupid farmers know that?

There was more honking. Male shouting, a palpable fury in the air. He couldn't wait any longer. Heedlessly, recklessly, he ran the light and almost hit a black-leather-clad motorcyclist roaring through the intersection from the blind side. It was the first red light he'd ever run in his life. There was a cacophany of honking. A man was yelling, cursing at him. He honked back, uncaring. Fuck you, he thought, I am seconds from eternity. Mahler's celestial trumpets and moose hunter's French horns blared. Tympani boomed like thunder. The symphony was cracking his car speakers. The resurrection was at hand, his timing perfect. Crying out joyously, he steered the Mercedes onto the path that led up the steep narrow road to the crest of Mount Makeout.

He saw the dark breach in the granite wall. Galvanized with adrenaline, laughing like a lunatic, he had never felt so brave. Or free. Now it was happening exactly as he'd planned and hoped and dreamed. Ahead in his bright lights the road had a blood-red sheen.

Chapter Twenty-Six: 10:39 p.m.

OFFICER R. A. GABRIEL

Only yesterday he had timed it to the last second. The plan was fail-proof and foolproof. He was seconds away from the narrow opening in the wall on the left side of the road. He gunned the accelerator and realized he was wetting his pants — warm urine trickled down his right thigh — and that his bowels were loose. He slowed down enough to steer the Mercedes through the dark breach ahead. Eternity waited on the other side and below. The Mahler reached a thunderous climax. He felt an ecstatic terror, a supreme exhilaration, a release more pleasurable than any orgasm. His heart banged against his ribs, his soul flew out of his body, he whooped.

He had three seconds to live.

But something was wrong. There was no breach in the wall — just dark stone. Where was the opening? Gone! With a screeching lurch, he wrenched the steering wheel to the right. He managed to avoid a head-on crash as the whole left side of the Mercedes scraped and slid along the stone wall in a shower of sparks like a NASCAR racer. The car was out of control, its tires screaming in protest. It bounced over rocks and tree roots on the shoulder, banged back and forth off the wall, and threatened to capsize like a ship. For five seconds the car was moving on its right wheels only, at a forty-five degree angle, and Bombazine couldn't stop it or stop wetting his pants.

Then, with a jarring bounce, the Mercedes regained equilibrium. Bombazine's head thudded against the soft felt of the hard inner roof. It dazed him, but he recovered. Miraculously, he found himself on the road again and in his lane, gripping the steering wheel tight enough to bend it. A man was screaming. The man was himself.

Luckily, there had been no traffic — this was not the road less traveled but one never traveled. A few seconds ago a vehicle coming from the other direction would have crashed into the Mercedes or veered off the road and smashed into the wall. His heart was pumping so hard he couldn't breathe, but at least he'd stopped screaming. The Mahler kept climaxing and his ears were about to burst. Not crashing into that wall but sliding alongside it had been a death-defying stunt, worthy of a Hollywood car chase; he had survived it with the help of some primal instinct or supernatural force that had taken over the wheel.

Jesus fucking Christ, he whispered to himself. Part of him was relieved to be alive in once piece. But survival had not been his goal. Death had. He'd been thwarted, cheated — his fail-safe plan had failed. Why? A road crew had repaired the breach overnight or during the day; a section of wall, a slab, had been snugly inserted and cemented like an orthodontist's bridge in a row of teeth. Why was it so hard to die when he wanted to so desperately? He began to curse again and to pound the steering wheel until the pain was like a huge nail in his palm. If he didn't stop he would have a stroke.

Zooming along the frontage road, he had to decide what to do. The time was still right, there could be no slinking home in defeat. He couldn't drive into the lake from here, or anywhere nearby, but he could kill himself some other way. Half a mile ahead, just past a CAUTION SLOW TRAFFIC sign, the brick wall on the left would end but on the right he could smash through a white wooden guardrail, five feet high, reinforced with plastic and some flimsy lightweight metal that could not stop a Mercedes going this fast. He would crash onto the rocks far below the way those drunk teenagers had. He knew exactly where he would land. But he didn't want to die in a fiery explosion. They would call it an accident, denying his heroic suicide, and he didn't want to burn or bleed or suffer. He wanted to drown.

Then it came to him. He could drown without the car. He could still have his death by water if he jumped into the lake! He would turn around, drive back to the spot, climb out of the car, scale the four-foot stone wall, and dive into the water. He ground the Mercedes to a halt, took a deep breath, steered into a U-turn, and headed back to where the slab had been replaced. He would see the new stone for himself, touch it, feel it. Then he'd climb over the wall, loose a bloodcurdling cry, and take the plunge.

At last he'd reached his destination. He heard the clash of cymbals and a majestic chord from Mahler's brass section. He braked to a stop but did not shut off the ignition or his lights, or the music. He put the car in park. Go! he told himself. Just as he was clambering out, he saw the flashing, spinning red and blue lights of the patrol car approaching from the rear.

—⁓⁓— —⁓⁓—

Busted.

He was busted.

Not just beaten but busted. By a traffic cop on the prowl. Would he be arrested? This had to be the low point of his life. Now more than ever he wanted to die. It was too late to make a run for the wall and jump. For an instant he'd considered it, but now was too late. He slouched behind the wheel, slumped down in his seat, and wished he had never been born.

The past is with us always. His tenth birthday party had been canceled because his Aunt Marjorie — his father's ugly old sister in Gretna, Louisiana, whom Bombazine rarely saw and barely knew — had died. He'd cried all night, not out of grief for Aunt Marjorie but because he'd missed out on his party. He would cry all night tonight. But where?

Now it would have to be Plan B. Thanksgiving Eve. He would adhere to the schedule. Stick with the program. He'd have to go on living for two more months.

He shut off the ignition but not the music or his lights. He rolled down his window. He had stopped at a forty-five degree angle in the middle of the road. The white patrol car eased alongside him, facing the opposite way, leaving its lights on. No traffic could pass, but there was none.

265

A tall, gangly patrolman wearing a blue uniform and built like Ichabod Crane emerged from his car with a bright flashlight. He approached, cautiously, with a duck-footed shamble. As he drew closer, he bent his knees and slowed to a creep, as if about to confront a criminal armed and dangerous.

Bombazine drew a deep breath and clenched his fists until his fingernails dug into his palms. The cop's face came into view—a long thin face with an old-timey handlebar mustache like that of Rollie Fingers, the great relief pitcher for the Oakland A's. Crouching, he shone the flashlight directly into Bombazine's eyes, momentarily blinding him.

"Sir, you tryin' to kill yourself?" he said loud enough to be heard over the Mahler.

"You're amazing. How did you know?"

"Are you gettin' smart with me?"

Bombazine swallowed. "Not at all." He was scared of cops and feared he might grovel. Tonight he could not handle any more humiliation. "Sorry if I was speeding," he whimpered.

"If you was speeding? I clocked you at eighty in a Slow Traffic zone. You must have saw the sign. This is one of the most dangerous roads in the county. People have died up here. Turn off that racket."

Bombazine shut off the stereo. This can't be happening, he thought. O God, Higher Power, whatever you are, let this be a bad dream. What imbecile ever said suicide was the easy way out?

The cop barked, "You in some emergency situation?"

Blinking from the blinding flashlight, Bombazine said, "I had a bad day, Officer." He hoped the patrolman couldn't smell that he'd wet his pants; the odor of his urine was strong.

"You wasn't just speeding. You run a red light down at that six-point intersection that coulda caused an accident. I followed you up here."

"Well, thanks."

"License and registration, please. Let's see 'em."

With trembling fingers, Bombazine fumbled in his glove compartment and thumbed through his wallet, then handed them over.

"Step out of the car."

He complied with effort. His legs were so stiff he almost fell. He could barely stand. He braced himself against the fender.

"Are you drunk?"

"I am not."

"Are you injured?"

"No. I'm arthritic. A senior citizen."

"Did you get lost off the main highway?"

"Lost? No."

"Where was you going?"

"Nowhere. I don't know."

"You wasn't part of the event?"

"What event?"

"It was some nighttime evangelical religious ceremony. Seven Day Adventists. I was the police escort. It lasted hours. Just broke up."

"That explains the traffic."

"I'll ask you once more. Why'd you drive up here?"

"To check out the view."

A pause. "Mister, if you're trying to get my goat, you're succeedin'. Nobody drives up here at this hour. You musta had some reason."

"I'd like to go home now. Are you going to give me a ticket?"

The cop glared at him. Bombazine realized that he was only making things worse for himself. He'd never seen a cop with a waxy handlebar mustache before, and there was something faintly comic about this one. But scary, too. This bastard should be in a barbershop quartet, he thought. Probably lives in Welfare. A local yokel. The nameplate on his shirt read R. A. GABRIEL.

The cop shuffled around the hood and inspected the damage with his flashlight. "You had an accident."

"Just a scrape."

"It's more than a scrape. It was serious."

"No other vehicle was involved."

"Lucky for you. This ain't no way to treat a Mercedes."

"The car still runs fine."

"You think you own the road 'cause you drive a Mercedes?"

"Absolutely not."

"Why was you playing your music so loud?"

"Is there a law against it?"

"There oughta be. You was blasting it all over the countryside. They heard it in the next county. I could arrest you for disturbing the peace."

"I've lost some hearing," Bomazine said truthfully. "I'm seventy years old. It's my birthday."

"You coming from a birthday party?"

"No."

"Are you under the influence of a controlled substance?"

"I am not."

"You been drinking?"

"I had one drink two hours ago."

"It musta been a stiff one. Was it the whole bottle? You was drivin' like an inebriated drunk. You can't even stand up straight. You skidded along that wall and took a lot of paint off your vehicle. Your left fender is damaged. Only a drunk woulda done that."

"Or someone crazy."

"You saying you're crazy?"

"Not really. As I said, I'm old and I had a rough day."

"So did I. That won't cut it." The policeman shone his flashlight on the driver's license and looked up with interest. "George Gordon Bombazine? Ain't you a teacher at the college?"

"I was. I'm retired."

The cop smiled in amazement. "Doggone..." he said, handing back the identification. "My niece took a course from you. She made an A. Said you was the best teacher she ever had. Maybe you remember Mary Beth Gabriel?"

Bombazine's mind raced. The name did not ring a bell. "Of course," he said. "Outstanding student. Bright... eager to learn... She deserved her A."

"Doggone," Officer Gabriel repeated. "I won't tell her about this. It might ruin her picture of you."

"I'd appreciate that. Please don't tell her."

The cop motioned him back into the car. "Don't drive off," he said. "Stay here."

He trudged back to his vehicle. The crackle of radio static broke the still of the night. He probably has a computer, Bombazine thought, grateful for his perfect driving record. Absurdly, he crossed his fingers and shut his eyes. He was tired now, very tired.

Finally the policeman returned. "Okay, Prof," he said. "There's three ways we can handle this. One, I can haul you into Big Town for D. U. I. and erratical behavior that caused damage to your vehicle and recklessly endangered the lives of other motorists when you run that red light. You would spend the night in jail."

"D. U. I.? But I'm not drunk."

"You willing to take a breathalyzer test?"

Bombazine felt his sphincter muscles loosen. He must not soil his pants. He was terrified of going to jail. But this was his night to be brave.

"I am not willing," he said. Why he wasn't sure. "With due respect, Officer, I know my rights."

"Two, I could write you up a citation for speeding. You were doin' eighty. A judge would throw the book at you. With that plus a D. U. I., they'd throw you *under* the jail."

"What's the third option?"

"I could let you off with a warning and have you drive straight home. I'm off duty now and I'd escort you to make sure you don't kill nobody or have another accident or break any more traffic safety laws."

"I have a choice?"

"Only 'cause my niece thinks you hung the moon."

"I choose Option Three. I'd grateful to you and your niece, Officer."

"And what was her name?" It was a test.

Bombazine's memory failed him for one terrible second. "Mary Beth... Mary Beth Gabriel. Best student I ever had."

"You sure you're able to drive?"

"I'm sure. Really, I'm not drunk and the car is fine."

"All right, Prof. This is your lucky day. Or your lucky night."

Yeah, right, Bombazine thought. My lucky night.

"I'll be right behind you. Maintain the speed limit. Wait till the red lights turn green."

"I promise."

"Let's roll."

Chapter Twenty-Seven: 11:37 p. m.

RAISONS D'ETRE

The endless drive back to his house with a police car as his escort took forever. Bombazine didn't play the rest of the Mahler. If he had, he'd have heard a saintly chorus gently exhort mankind to resurrect and rejoice, for the Day of Reckoning was done and there were finally no sinners, no judgment, no reward or punishment, just serene forgiveness with a lambent glow softly illuminating the blessing of God's love.

It was a happy ending to the symphony, but it wouldn't have worked for Bombazine. It was wrong for his mood. He felt angry, frustrated, and thwarted, not unlike a zombie wishing to be back in his grave. He should be dead, he thought. He deserved to be. He'd wanted to be. Cowards clung to life, but he was no coward: life had clung to him. What had Bobby Burns said about making plans? *"The best-laid schemes o'mice an' men / Gang aft agley / An' leave us nought but grief an' pain."* In his original text Burns used the word schemes, not plans. Few English teachers knew that.

In a state of white-knuckled paralysis, he drove more carefully and deliberately than he had to, not unlike the "little old lady in tennis shoes" nobody mentioned anymore because the expression was politically incorrect. When they finally reached the house, Officer Gabriel waited until he was safely inside to drive off. "I guess you really was sober," he hollered from his patrol car. "You take care, hear? Don't go out again. Go to bed."

Bombazine managed a feeble smile and a halfhearted wave. Emotionally drained, he wasn't sure what he was feeling. Other than numb. Fumbling with his keys at the front door, he could hear Argos whimpering and jumping inside. Entering, he was attacked in a hero's welcome. Yelping, yapping, whining, barking, the dog pounced on him, knocked him down, and slobbered all over his face with a foot-long tongue. Argos needed a bath and his halitosis had gotten rank. When the real Odysseus had returned from Troy, his faithful hound could not contain his joy and relief. With a paw on each of his shoulders as Bombazine tried to rise, Argos licked his nose, his closed eyes, his compressed lips. Argos's nose was icy cold. Bombazine had never felt so loved.

Back on his feet, regaining his balance, he was able to laugh. Argos circled him, bounced up and down, panted with jubilation, howled with a joy so contagious that Bombazine was able to feel better about things. Not good but better. He rubbed Argos's back and scratched behind his ears. He noticed a little pile of wood shavings and splinters on the floor just inside the front door; how long had Argos, in rescue mode, clawed and chewed and gnawed at that door in his desperate attempt to follow his master, find him, save him?

273

"Good dog," he mumbled, petting Argos's head. "I guess."

Weaving as if drunk after all, Bombazine wobbled to the center of the room, stood tall, and took stock. He was back to Square One. He had failed again. He was still alive and had not gotten to see his life pass before his eyes. What he had gotten to see today, hour by hour, was a hideous portrait of himself forming like Oscar Wilde's picture of Dorian Gray. The day's voices echoed: *You are not a generous man, George. You are not a kind man, George. You are not a compassionate man, George. You are not a real man, La Bamba. You are not a real anything.* Today had not exactly been an ego booster or a pat on the back. What if Tencha and Catherine and Miguel were right about him? Then he deserved to die all the more.

But who could argue that he hadn't given, as football coaches said, a hundred and ten percent in the effort? No man had ever been more ready, eager, and willing to cash in his chips. He had wanted so much, maybe too much, for his plan to work and it hadn't worked at all. Adhering to every detail, he'd done everything right and everything had gone wrong. The traffic jam, the funereal procession of trucks and SUVs ("some nighttime evangelical Seven Day Adventist religious ceremony"), the interminable red light, the cop car pulling up... everything.

Sure, he would concede that he was fortunate not to be in some hospital, horribly mangled and disfigured, at the mercy of people who talked and thought like Dr. Billy Bob Fallopius. He had been lucky. Was it divine providence? Whose hand had steered the wheel as he'd skimmed and skidded in a shower of sparks along the granite wall? Even with an airbag, smashing into the wall head-on at that speed might have killed him. A miracle had saved him. What if the Mercedes had tipped over? It had wanted to. And then that Rollie Fingers policeman, that uncle of a former student (he'd already forgotten her name), that Ichabod Crane with a Gay Nineties handlebar moustache materializing like a deus-ex-machina! Officer R. A. Gabriel was just a traffic cop, but Bombazine would've cast him in a Greek comedy by Aristophanes.

Yet it had really happened. Life had imitated art. The Fates had saved him. He had not hallucinated, though things had seemed surreal at the time. He remembered the thrill, the exhilaration, the sheer ecstasy of being ten feet from the wall just before he realized there was no breach. It was like the instant before orgasm, only better, a high like none he'd ever gotten from a drug. A near-death experience. What else could you call it?

Eventually Argos settled down, and Bombazine staggered toward the master bathroom. He stripped, took a hot shower, and changed into clean shorts and fresh trousers. He did not need to urinate, having emptied his bladder in the car. He still couldn't believe he'd peed his pants. It hadn't been a squirt or a leak, either — his underwear had been soaked. He was lucky not to have soiled himself; the cop would have smelled it and whisked him off to jail. What unspeakable humiliations and depradations would he have endured in a night behind bars? He shuddered to imagine.

He was tired. Dead tired. He had never felt this kind of exhaustion. Yet he wasn't sleepy. What word could describe how he felt? Drained? Enervated? He lumbered to the kitchen, grabbed up the suicide note he'd left on the island, crumpled it in his fist, and tossed it into the waste-can. No one would ever read the worst crap he'd ever written. Corny, turgid, melodramatic, maudlin, self-pitying, verbose, it read like a cry for help. Not a suicide note but a suicide threat. He'd been too overwrought to write well or think straight. Not one sentence had the economical under-statement of the old philosopher Walter Savage Landor's note about the flame of his own candle going out: "It sinks and I am ready to depart."

Like a sleepwalker, Bombazine stumbled back to the living room and fell onto the couch. He could not decide whether to bemoan his future or exult in it. What wants to happen will — his father had used to say that, and for once Mirabeau had been right about something. Suicide had not been in the cards tonight. Not wanted to happen. The God in whom he did not believe had protected him. What if God really existed? The possibility was disturbing.

Argos stood guard — or sat guard — at the front door while his master stared into space thinking about God. What right had He to interfere? Finally Bombazine gave a yawn, closed his eyes, and lay back. No use to try to sleep — he was too wired, discombobulated, agitated. Nevertheless, he did fall into a half sleep. In it he was drowning. Like Eliot's Phle-bas the Phoenecian, he heard the cry of sea gulls, the deep sea swell, the seductive song of sirens. I must've made it into the lake after all, he congratulated himself, victorious at last. But he was not drowning, he was swimming, and the green water, cool and clear, was bracing. He felt an upward surge that powered him to the surface, and when his head emerged and he'd stopped gasping for air he was back on the couch again.

Something was different now. He felt energized and re-freshed and renewed. He sat up and looked all around the living room, which now had an air of comfort and welcome. Home sweet home. It offered refuge — not from the outside world but from himself, his demons, his suicidal psyche. With acute microscopic vision he was made aware of details in the room that had escaped his notice until now: a thin crack in the slanted white ceiling above his head, a chip in the stone step that led from one split level to another, a warp like a gentle billowing in the uncarpeted floor. He had never been so aware of — what? Everything. Though for several moments he was no longer aware of his body and its great bulk. Outside it, he could not feel his own flesh; he had become vaporous, ethereal, lighter than air. A pure spirit. He felt enveloped in a serene calm, a total relaxation such as he had never known. Argos climbed up on the couch and lay his head in his lap. Petting the dog, Bombazine heard a noise from one of the other rooms, but for once it didn't frighten him. He was fine with it. He felt safe. The worst an intruder could do would be to kill him, and that was fine too.

Then, with a jolt, a light flashed in his mind's eye and he returned to reality. Argos was gone, lying across the room by the door, where he'd been before. Bombazine won-dered what had happened. Had he been dreaming again?

Dreamed a dream within a dream? Gone into a trance? Some weird out-of-body experience? It was as if time had called time-out. For a few seconds he had been perfectly, absolutely centered in the universe rather than lost in it.

He would not question what had happened. Not right now anyway. He would analyze it tomorrow. Maybe it had something to do with his supernatural close shave at Mount Makeout an hour ago. Or maybe it had been a mystical experience — if J. J. merited one, he deserved one too. This was a night for such craziness. Or maybe it was physical exhaustion, though now he felt refreshed and renewed, as if he'd just wakened from a deep sleep.

He gazed around the room again. He really ought to buy some furnishings, he thought. Some paintings or prints or statues. A dinner table, a set of chairs. A rug or two. He'd be living here at least till Thanksgiving. He lay back and propped his feet up on the coffee table, where Meridel had forgotten her mentholated Marlboro Lights 100s and sparkly sterling silver Zippo. He picked up the lighter and kissed it. Ah, Meridel. You naughty girl. Smoking in my house. It's not even my house, it's Pru's. And Pru thinks second-hand smoke causes lung cancer and emphysema. Can I get lung cancer if I already have prostate cancer? Bombazine chuckled. Pru warned me about you, Meridel. *"Watch out for that woman, she's a man eater."* But you're not. You're just a forty-four-year-old flack with a cheerleader's body and a face like Scarlett Johansson's and a bountiful heart. What sweet gifts you gave an old fool for his seventieth birthday. You kissed him on the mouth. You opened your thighs to him. You kissed his limp dick. Only a fuck could have made things perfect, and it wasn't your fault that one never materialized.

He closed his eyes and shook his head. He should put Meridel out of his mind. Pretend it hadn't happened. All this time, she'd wanted to go to bed with him, and now that she had, she didn't want to again. She'd said so. Of course, other women who'd gone to bed with him had said the same thing afterward but gone to bed with him again anyway. But Meridel was different. Tougher, stronger, more resolute. This afternoon had been enough for her. He had certainly gotten her off. Only his old mentor Irenka Wozniak could have done it better—Irenka who'd appeared uninvited and summarily disappeared. But Meridel had still gone off like a howitzer. And then explained to him why she would not be back. Her reasoning had made sense.

But what if he were to say Yes to radiation, forget about Thanksgiving, and choose to go on living? Would he ask Meridel for a second chance? (Hadn't she said, "Want to go again? I know tricks we could try.") No, he would not. Dr. Fallopius said the radiation would make him impotent if the cancer didn't, and today it appeared that the cancer had. One did not wish for a love affair with no fucking. He would not resort to Viagra or Cialis or Yohimbe, and certainly not to those creepy vacuum pumps or battery-operated plastic dildoes advertised in the back pages of the stroker magazines.

Wisely, Meridel had ruled out a rematch for professional reasons. She wanted to be his agent as well as his publicist but not his lover. An affair would be logistically impossible

279

anyway. It wasn't as if she lived across the campus or in the Village or Big Town. She lived 2500 miles away. Meridel would not be a factor in his deciding what to do as Thanksgiving approached.

And what would he decide? Should he tell the doctor he'd changed his mind about IMRT and chosen life? Or wait until Thanksgiving Eve and drown himself some other way? Had he subconsciously chosen an unreliable method of drowning, dependent for success on a hole in a roadside wall remaining unrepaired for three days because he didn't really want to suicide? If the answer was yes, he should forget about killing himself and stop kidding himself.

But he hadn't been kidding. He remembered the exaltation he'd felt on reaching the wall. He would never forget it. So Thanksgiving Eve, Plan B, would remain an option. He'd have two months to think about it. We are free to do what we choose, Arthur Schopenhauer wrote in his "Essay on the Freedom of the Will," but are we free to choose what we choose? Tonight he had chosen death and come so close to dying he'd heard angel wings flap overhead. But could he make that choice again? Or want to? By Thanksgiving he would know.

This much he did know. Some force had intervened to save his life. What? A police force. A traffic cop. A man in blue. A total stranger. "I've always depended on the kindness of strangers." Thank you, Blanche DuBois. But had something else intervened too? Invisibly carved on the newly inserted slab in the wall might be a message from One Step Beyond: *It's not your time yet. Wait your turn.*

Now I'm really out in the Twilight Zone, he thought now. Far out, as they said in the sixties. Indulging himself further, he let his imagination run wild, like a child's. Maybe that gangly cop with the handlebar mustache was not really a cop but an angel. His guardian angel. Or his spirit guide. Bombazine thought of phoning the highway patrol tomorrow to ask if an Officer R. A. Gabriel was active on its roster. He could also call the campus registrar's office and ask if a Mary Beth Gabriel had ever attended Mount Olympus College.

He laughed out loud. And what if both answers were no? Would that indicate a divine intervention? Or simply that he'd imagined everything? Stop! he told himself. You did not imagine anything. You did not hallucinate. That policeman was no apparition. You will never be certain what happened tonight or why. Bombazine was sure the hand of fate had intervened but equally sure there was some perfectly logical explanation. Reason can only take us so far, poets and existentialists agreed. Reason could be unreasonable. Martin Luther wrote, "Reason is the devil's bride." W. H. Auden wrote, "We are lived by powers we only pretend to understand." Shakespeare wrote and Hamlet said, "There are more things in heaven and earth, Horatio, than are dreamt of in your philosophy."

All the same, just for the hell of it, he would telephone the campus registrar and highway patrol tomorrow.

———

"So what do you think, Argos?" he called from the couch.

"Has Odysseus lost it? I guess it's too late for me to get metaphysical on you, right?" Still guarding the front door, the dog looked up, grinned, panted, and farted.

The phone rang, giving Bombazine a start. Who'd be calling so late? It was close to midnight. If this was that damned J. J. ...

But it wasn't. It was Miguel.

"Miguel? Miguel! I'm so glad you called --"

"*Callate la boca, viejo*. Cut the crap. I called to say I am sorry you have cancer and I guess I hope you beat it."

"Seriously?"

"Yes, you old *zonzo*. Unfortunately, you are the only father I have. I know you are my father. Forget what Mom said."

"I love you, Miguel."

"Now things are getting too rich. *Es demasiado dulce y empalaga*. Happy Birthday, George. Remember — I could use some dinero. *Vaya con Dios*, Papa." The line went dead.

Bombazine felt like whooping. Grace filled his soul. Hope freshened his heart. Thank God he had been spared tonight. Had he killed himself, he'd have missed that call. As he returned to the couch, his base of operations, he heard the grandfather clock in the master bedroom chime twelve times. The day of reckoning, his *dies irae,* was over. How had he survived it? He hadn't intended to. But this was a new day, and who knew what a new day might bring?

Later this morning, on his way to the auto body shop in Big Town, he would stop by the Western Union office in the Village and wire $10,000 to his sister and the same amount to his son even though Miguel only asked for $8000. They needed the bread and he had it. *"Bread for myself is a material question. Bread for my neighbor is a spiritual one."* That was Nicolai Berdyaev. Catherine and Miguel were more than just neighbors; Catherine had come from the same womb he had and Miguel was his seed. Might both be reasons to go on living?

And what about John Jacob Auchincloss? J. J. was another reason to. The old popinjay could not survive without him. Tonight had proved that. J. J. too had considered suicide. And Bombazine had treated him badly. The man had been in pain—his tears had been real whether he'd actually stared into Sartre's nothingness or not—and the friend to whom he'd come running in panic and terror, George Gordon Bombazine, had been impatient, annoyed, and hostile, having more important matters to deal with.

And what about Pru? As usual, he was forgetting about Pru. That had been why their marriage failed. What if (having realized the mistake she'd made by marrying a goose like Trevor T. Merriman) she wanted her first husband and split-level ranch-style house back? For sure he wanted her back. It was too lonely here without her. Loneliness killed even more slowly than prostate cancer. He was certain her marriage to Trevor would not last. He would ask her to remarry him. He'd promise to be a better husband the second time around. Or the third time—there had been that first marriage. Sex would be a problem now, but Pru had never cared much about sex anyway. He hoped Trevor had not changed her in that respect.

And finally there was his best friend. Man's best friend. Argos had little time left, but it had been wrong to go off

283

and leave him. Only now did Bombazine realize this. Only now did he realize that he had many raisons d'etre. Miguel and Catherine and Pru and J. J. and Argos were five, and there was a sixth: work.

Maybe he couldn't teach anymore, having sat inactive for so long, but he could still write. He had a new book, *Return to Spoon River*, on the way and he'd need to push it. And what of that book about suicide he'd lied to J. J that he was writing? It might interest Grove/Atlantic. Meridel could sell it to Motherwell for him. She wanted to be his agent, and he had done the research. But it would not be a book about suicide in literature. It would be a true story, heavily researched and annotated, about the attempted suicide of an English professor emeritus. A tell-all about himself. It would chronicle what had happened today. It would be his magnum opus, his masterpiece.

To be or not to be. For Camus the only serious philosophical question. "In the absence of hope," Camus wrote, "we must still struggle to survive, and so we do—by the skin of our teeth." Actually, his late pen pal William Styron, not Camus, had written that, paraphrasing Camus in *The Myth of Sisyphus*. But it was true. Maybe, Bombazine thought now, toying with Meridel's pack of cigarettes, maybe even the miseries of old age—the aching joints and hobbling around, the wheelchairs and walkers, the false teeth, the adult diapers and memory loss, the sleepless nights and weeping—had a purpose in the grand scheme. Hurdles to be confronted, challenges to be met, rites of passage to the next life. That was a consoling thought.

Yes, he had all sorts of reasons to live, and the best of them was the fact that his heart was still beating. Abruptly he felt young again. Or at least not so old. Propelled by a burst of energy, he bounded from the couch. With bold, headlong strides, he marched to the kitchen. Ravenously hungry, he whistled for Argos, who came running; the dog was his old self again, panting, eager for food. Bombazine had a hunch that Argos would break his fast and go for some USDA prime.

He poured a drink—a full tumbler of the Scotch he and J. J. had tapped into earlier—and pulled a thick Porterhouse steak out of the freezer. Then he took a heavy black cast-iron skillet from the cabinet. He and Argos would enjoy a midnight snack. A man's meal. A guy thing. Hot damn! he rejoiced as the Porterhouse sizzled in the skillet. It was good to be alive and safe at home rather than in a morgue or hospital or jail. Thank you, God, if you exist, and thank you even if you don't. In a moment he would put on some music. Not Mahler but something light, maybe Country Western. And not that Roy Clark tearjerker but a happy, carefree Willie or Waylon. He might even dance—not the Texas Two Step but the Texas One Step.

He pulled out his iPhone 5S and chose on his Pandora device Waylon Jennings' "Luckenbach, Texas" (Willie came in at the end), a country song he'd liked in the seventies. The music came on and he danced a jig. He felt like a death row inmate who's gotten an eleventh-hour reprieve from the governor. Never mind that he hadn't wanted a reprieve— he was grateful for one now. He was not the same man he'd been when he woke up yesterday morning. Not even the man he'd been an hour ago. Today he'd tell Dr. Fallopius that he'd submit to those damned radiation treatments. He didn't look forward to it, but he would take the plunge. At least that's how he felt right now. Should he feel differently later, he could start marking off on his calendar those sixty-five days until Thanksgiving.

And there it was. Like Hamlet, a man had the right to change his mind about whether to be or not to be. And the next time George Noel Gordon Bombazine decided not to be, he would choose a better, more reliable way not to. But for now, as he skillet-fried that Porterhouse and sipped his Scotch and listened with Argos to Willie and Waylon while he danced around the vast kitchen, he wanted to live.

Fomite

A fomite is a medium capable of transmitting infectious organisms from one individual to another.

"The activity of art is based on the capacity of people to be infected by the feelings of others." Tolstoy, What Is Art?

Writing a review on Amazon, Good Reads, Shelfari, Library Thing or other social media sites for readers will help the progress of independent publishing. To submit a review, go to the book page on any of the sites and follow the links for reviews. Books from independent presses rely on reader to reader communications.

For more information or to order any of our books, visit
http://www.fomitepress.com/FOMITE/Our_Books.html

Nothing Beside Remains
Jaysinh Birjépatil

*The Way None
of This Happened*
Mike Breiner

*Summer on the
Cold War Planet*
Paula Closson Buck

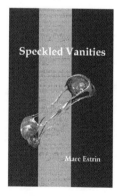

*Foreign Tales of
Exemplum and Woe*
J. C. Ellefson

Free Fall/Caída libre
Tina Escaja

Speckled Vanities
Marc Estrin

Fomite

Off to the Next Wherever
John Michael Flynn

Derail This Train Wreck
Daniel Forbes

Semitones
Derek Furr

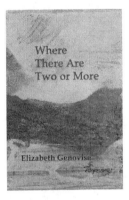

Where There Are Two or More
Elizabeth Genovise

The Three Lives of Jonathan Force
Richard Hawley

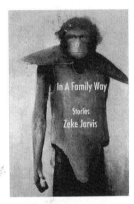

In A Family Way
Zeke Jarvis

A Rising Tide of People Swept Away
Scott Archer Jones

A Free, Unsullied Land
Maggie Kast

Shadowboxing With Bukowski
Darrell Kastin

Fomite

Feminist on Fire
Coleen Kearon

Thicker Than Blood
Jan English Leary

A Guide
to the Western Slopes
Roger Lebovitz

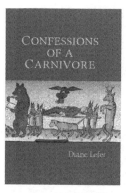

Confessions of a Carnivore
Diane Lefer

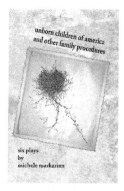

Unborn Children of
America
Michele Markarian

Shirtwaist Story
Delia Bell Robinson

Isles of the Blind
Robert Rosenberg

What We Do For Love
Ron Savage

Bread & Sentences
Peter Schumann

Fomite

*Planet Kasper
Voume 2*
Peter Schumann

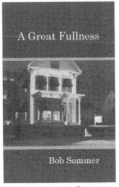

A Great Fullness
Bob Sommer

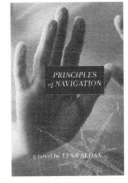

Principles of Navigation
Lynn Sloan

Industrial Oz
Scott T. Starbuck

Among Angelic Orders
Susan Thoma

*The Inconveniece
of the Wings*
Silas Dent Zobal

Fomite

More Titles from Fomite...

Fomite

Fomite

Tony Whedon—The Falkland Quartet
Peter M. Wheelwright—As It Is On Earth
Suzie Wizowaty —The Return of Jason Green

Made in the USA
Charleston, SC
18 August 2016